Convergence
of
Time

by
Layne Walker

Wild Mustangs Publishing, LLC

Convergence of Time

This is a work of fiction.
All characters and incidents are a product
of the author's imagination.
Any relationship to persons living or dead
is purely coincidental.

ISBN-13: 978-0-9883534-2-8

Cover design by
Layne Walker
All rights reserved

Published by
Wild Mustangs Publishing, LLC
Lake Havasu City, AZ

Visit Layne's website at
www.laynewalkerbooks.com

Printing history
First edition published in April 2013

To Anne Cote,
I could not have done it without you.
Thanks for all the late nights, early mornings,
and everything in between.

Chapter 1

A slight breeze, blowing across my skin, cooled the sheen of sweat I'd worked up as I climbed out of the wash. I took a minute to catch my breath as I stood on the bleak, barren Arizona desert I'd come to love in the past ten years. The only creatures I could see were two dark specks in the sky. *More than likely ravens*, I thought as I took off my battered straw cowboy hat and wiped the sweat out of my eyes with the back of my hand.

All the other residents of this hard, brutal land remained safely tucked away in their burrows and holes, waiting out the heat of the afternoon. If I were to stick around for a few hours until dusk, I would see a marked increase of animal activity, but I wasn't planning on being out here that long. I wouldn't be out here at all except for the fact it had been a hard week at work, and to make matters worse, my in-laws had popped in for a surprise visit on Wednesday afternoon. It was now Sunday and they were still at the house.

Don't get me wrong, I love them dearly, but since they'd "found God," they'd become a little hard to be around. Now, they were always preaching to me about being a better person, or telling me I'd better change my ways or I'd go to Hell. The worst part comes from the little digs they'd make, like, "What would Jesus do?" or "Choose the right." Apparently my three girls, aged five, seven, and nine, were bound to become minions of the devil unless they were saved immediately by my unrelenting and, by my thinking, slightly demented in-laws.

They had planned on taking all of us—the whole Clark family—to church with them today, but at the last minute, I told them I had business to take care of. I strapped my .40 Glock pistol and two extra magazines to my waist, threw a little bit of food into a small backpack, added a water bottle, and drove out on the desert. I knew there would be hell to pay when I got home, but I just couldn't bear sitting in a stuffy building for two hours with forty or fifty other people singing songs and listening to someone preach.

I'm thirty-four years old. I figure that's old enough to decide for myself if I want to go to an organized church or not. Personally, I'd rather go out on the desert or into the mountains. I feel closer to God in the outdoors than I do in any building.

Taking a deep breath, I let my eyes rove across the landscape laid out before me. I stood on the southwestern foothills of the Mojave Mountains with the town of Lake Havasu City, two miles to the northwest, between the lake and me. My house sat right on the southern edge of town, just two blocks from the BLM (Bureau of Land Management) ground that surrounds the area.

The late-March sun burned hot, but at least we weren't experiencing record-breaking temps this year like we had last year. Eighty, ninety degrees...I could handle that for a while. Once it got over one hundred, my body became lethargic and I had a hard time functioning. Last year at this time, our highs had ranged from a hundred-ten to a hundred-fifteen.

Everybody always says, "It's a dry heat, so it isn't that bad." Yeah, right. Once it gets over a hundred, it's just plain hot, no matter how "dry" it is. True, high humidity would make it worse, but not by much by my reckoning.

Adjusting my glasses on my nose, I saw an interesting outcropping of greenish rock on a hillside about a hundred yards away. An impulse to check out the rock came over me. I decided to look at it more closely. My watch said I had a few hours until dark. I knew I should be getting home, but I was stalling.

Walking on the hard-packed dirt went easier than the soft sand of the wash I'd just come up. I recalled how five years back, I'd gotten curious about rocks, gems, and geology. I had joined the local gem-and-mineral club to learn more about the area from the people who knew all about it. One of the first club members to make an impression on me was an old gold miner from Alaska named Mike. "A change in the color of dirt on a hillside," he'd said, "means a change in the mineral content of the ground. It's often a good place to find gems or minerals." Mike turned out to be a good friend. Unfortunately, he'd died three years ago. I still missed him.

As I strode toward the outcropping, suddenly, out of nowhere, I walked into what felt like a large spider web. All around me, unseen silky threads tickled my exposed skin. I jerked side to side, wiping desperately at my face and skin. I couldn't see anything visible. I felt silly dancing in a circle, trying to swipe away the prickly sensation.

I stumbled forward, hoping the feeling would stop. Instead, it grew worse. I began to sweat. My gut wrenched in fear that I'd gotten myself into some kind of harrowing trap. I continued struggling to brush off the invisible strands, which seemed to cling tighter and grow thicker. With each step, I felt like I was walking into a huge pile of cotton balls. I still couldn't see anything, other than the desert terrain.

The stuff clinging to me seemed light in weight. It piled up thicker around me and pushed against me. I grunted with the effort to move my legs forward. Soon, I realized the stupidity of continuing forward, only getting myself more entangled. I turned back the way I'd come, but a force more substantial than what I'd been fighting stopped me completely.

I still couldn't see a web or netting or matter of any kind, just the vista of desert and mountains around me. For a moment, I wondered if I could be imagining this, but the sensation felt all too real against my skin.

My fear began to turn to anger. I used both my arms to thrash at the invisible barrier surrounding me. My hands started bouncing off an unseen wall in front of me, as if the wall were made of rubber. Obviously unable to return the way I'd come, I spun around.

Instantly, the going got easier. Within ten feet of the invisible webbing, the area completely cleared.

My legs shook from the struggle. My hands trembled. I staggered a few feet and knelt down in the dirt, still not quite believing what had just happened. I looked back to where I'd been. I could see nothing but desert. No web, no strings, nothing. I exhaled my breath with a deep sigh.

I slipped off my backpack and opened the pocket holding my water bottle. I broke the seal and guzzled half the bottle before lowering it from my still-dry mouth. "What the hell just happened, Gavin?" I asked myself, comforted to hear the sound of my own voice.

It was so bizarre, I couldn't even begin to comprehend it. Was this some previously unknown type of spider web? Some kind of invisible barrier being tested by the government? A time warp? A message from God? I chuckled. "Now, I'm getting ridiculous."

My heart rate slowed. My hands stopped shaking. I stared back at the location for a long time. I couldn't distinguish any difference between the desert sand beneath me and the continuous vista of landscape that stretched beyond and through the invisible barrier...if it was still there.

Now that I was seemingly out of danger, I considered checking to see if the *thing* remained. I decided to find out before I lost my nerve. Still on my knees, I put the water bottle back into the pack and threw the pack on my back. I wanted my food with me, just in case I couldn't get back to this spot to retrieve it.

I stood up. Holding my hands out in front of me, I slowly walked toward the *thing.* I moved my hands from side to side, hoping I'd feel the beginnings of it before I got trapped inside it again.

My right hand suddenly slammed into a hard rubbery surface and bounced off. I jumped back and stood completely still. No small spider-web-type strings tickled my skin. No force pushed against my body. I gulped. Tentatively, I reached forward with my right hand until my fingers came into contact with the *thing* again. It gave the sensation of my hand rubbing against a cotton ball, a very warm cotton ball. I shoved my hand a little harder against the barrier.

This time, the *thing* pushed back.

I gasped, jerked my hand away, and stumbled backward ten feet. I tripped and fell, landing on my butt. I quickly scurried backward a few more feet and hoped the distance between the *thing* and me would be far enough to keep me from being sucked into it. *It moves like it's alive. Like it has a will of its own. How can that be? What can it be? This is too weird.* Although fascinated and curious as hell, I wasn't about to touch it again.

To tell the truth, I'd never been more frightened in my life. A deep gut feeling told me to get away from this *thing* as fast and as far as possible, but right now, the barrier seemed to stand between me and getting back to my truck and my home.

Once my legs stopped trembling and were strong enough to support my weight, I rose to my feet. I'd been walking east when I had first run into the web. I looked around and decided to walk north for five or more minutes to make sure I moved around the invisible barrier. Then, I'd cut back to the west and head toward my truck. Since I couldn't see the *thing*, I couldn't be sure where it stood or how much space it consumed. But one thing certain, the thought of getting stuck in it again sent shivers down my spine. I kept my hands out in front of me like a blind man. I was sure anyone watching me would have thought I was crazy, but at that point, I would have welcomed anyone else's presence, even a person who might have thought I'd lost it.

After a few of minutes of hiking north, I turned and walked westward. Immediately, I ran into the *thing* again. Discouraged and frightened, I stepped back and continued walking further north.

* * *

An hour later, and ten failed attempts to find a break in the rubber-like barrier, I grew scared out of my wits. *What the hell is this thing? How did it get here? Will it ever end?* For all I knew, it could go on for miles. It could take me days or weeks to get home, and I'd only brought with me enough food and water for the day.

Normally, I didn't panic in troubling situations. I had a pretty level head and a practical bent, but my encounter with this *thing* had me on edge.

I pulled out my cell phone and pushed the button to call home. Nothing happened. There seemed to be no reception. I'd been in this area on other occasions and had always gotten a signal. I tried again. No response. No service.

I scanned the area. The mountain just north of me topped out at four thousand feet. *Maybe I'm in a dead spot. I'll try again in a few minutes.* If by tomorrow, I hadn't checked in with my wife Erica, she would surely send out the search-and-rescue teams to find me. I hated the thought of not being able to let her know where I was.

As the sun continued to lower on the horizon, hunger pangs rumbled in my stomach. I sat down and ate a few potato chips and half the one sandwich I'd brought. I thought I'd better conserve the food in case I'd be out here another day. *Worst case scenario*, I told myself, *I'll have to spend the night with the coyotes and the weeds.* I hadn't thought to bring any survival gear in my backpack for an emergency situation like this. It had never dawned on me I might be stranded. I checked all the pockets of my pack. I found a book of matches. Well, I could build a fire to keep myself warm and to help ward off any unwanted animals. I wouldn't be all that comfortable during the night, but I'd survive. Still, I hoped it wouldn't come to that.

I looked around with a hard decision to make. Should I continue north? Should I go south? From my starting point, I figured I'd only traveled a mile, maybe less. I had nearly reached the base of the mountain. If I pushed north, the grade would grow steeper and steeper from this point forward. It would be a tough climb. On the other hand, maybe this *thing* would end at the mountain.

The availability of firewood made for the deciding factor to continue north. If I were going to be out here all night, I wanted plenty of firewood. The narrow washes coming off the flanks of the mountain trapped lots of deadfall, which lay in the many bends where the water had flowed downhill during rainstorms. This being a desert where no large trees grew, I would have to make do with smaller branches and brush, which I could gather from the washes as I climbed the mountain. Not ready to concede defeat yet, I reminded myself to remain optimistic that I would be home in a few hours.

Continuing to work my way north, I began to climb the increasingly rough terrain. Each time I attempted to turn west, I ran into the *thing*, that unseen rubber wall. Forced to climb higher, I grew more and more discouraged. I wanted to get high enough to see some of the lake and the town in the last of the evening light, but a ridge blocked my view. I pulled out my cell phone again and pushed the button to call home. Still no signal. I looked at my watch. I estimated the sun would be going behind the western mountains in about twenty minutes. It would be difficult to cross the desert in the darkness.

I blew out a frustrated sigh. It was time to start looking for a place to spend the night. I turned southeastward and hiked until I found a wash with a sandy bottom. A large rock sat alone in the middle of the wash, a perfect place to bed down. Next to the rock, I piled sticks and brush, every piece of wood I could find in the area.

Just as the sun moved below the horizon, I got out my matches. Shortly, a small fire roared to life and helped to take the chill off the quickly cooling air. Luckily, I had worn a long-sleeved western shirt, jeans, cowboy boots, and a cowboy hat, rather than my usual shorts, tank-top, and ball cap for warmer days. I wished I'd brought my lined jacket from the truck and that I'd packed a blanket.

Starving, I had to eat the other half of my sandwich and the rest of the chips. I washed it all down with a few swallows of water. By this time, I was willing to take my chances that I would get back in the morning and feast on a full-sized breakfast. My cell phone still would not pick up a signal. I put my cell, my keys, and my wallet into the backpack beside me. I leaned against the rock and, aiming my feet toward the fire, I could only hope the incomprehensible *thing* would be gone in the morning.

I couldn't help but think about Erica and the kids. Surely, they all wondered why I'd not come home for the evening meal. I could picture the worry on Erica's face as she picked up the phone to call me and couldn't get a response. She probably had ten messages waiting for me on my voicemail right now. The first messages would be angry and full of accusations because I'd copped out of the church ordeal and wasn't home to buffer the interactions between her parents and the girls. Her parents had probably told her to pray for me, but I didn't think that would offer her much comfort. Her last phone messages, more than likely, would be colored with worry and doubt. I wished to hell I had a way to contact her and tell her I was okay.

Meanwhile, I thought about my home-inspection business, which I ran from a small office downtown. I didn't have any inspections scheduled for this week, so Erica could handle the phone calls and set up the new appointments until I got back. Should something come up, I hoped she would be wise enough to call Brian Daily, a friend of mine in the same business. Sometimes, when Brian or I had to be out of town, went on vacation, or got too much business to handle, the other would help cover the work.

It wouldn't surprise me if Erica had contacted Brian already. Between the two of them, they would, no doubt, get a rescue operation going in the morning and keep my business running.

Why am I thinking I might not get back for a while? I shook off the idea and closed my eyes as I tried to think positively. *In the morning, the thing will be gone. If not, I will either find a way to get through it or the rescue party will find me and help me get past it. Tomorrow, I'll be back with my family and my normal routines.*

I crossed my arms to keep warm as the temperature dropped and, eventually, I drifted into a soundless sleep.

Chapter 2

In the morning, I came awake with a start, immediately regretting the move. A sharp pain shot up through my stiff neck from having spent the night leaning up against the hard rock. To work out the kinks, I sat forward and rolled my head from side to side with my eyes closed.

"Howdy," said a voice much too close.

My head jerked up and my eyes flew open. My right hand moved down to grip the butt of my gun in my holster. I tried to focus on the blurry form sitting on the other side of the fire pit.

"Whoa. Down there, pardner." The blur held out both hands, palms down, moving them gently in a calming motion. "I don't mean ya no harm."

"Who-" I stopped to clear the night mucus out of my throat. I finally got out, "Who are you?" I blinked my eyes until they cleared and his form took shape.

"Sorry 'bout that." Dressed head to toe in buckskins, he stood up and took off his tan cowboy hat, with its shabby wide brim, which had seen better days. "M'name be Maxston Vanguard." Tipping his bearded head slightly, he bowed with his hat against his chest, like they did a hundred years ago. Strands of silver ran through his long dark hair, mustache, and full beard, all thick and greasy-looking. On one side of his hair, he had attached a string of bird feathers. A bright-blue-and-black beaded Indian design stretched across the front of his buckskin top. He appeared pretty weathered. I guessed him to be in his late fifties. He might have been a lot older than he looked...or maybe younger.

Sensing he might not be alone, I glanced around, checking to see if he had buddies waiting in the bushes, ready to pounce on me.

"Be by myself, if that's what yer a wonderin'."

The twinkle in his cobalt-blue eyes bothered me. *Should I be worried or shouldn't I?* My right hand still held the butt of my gun, just in case. Noticing my backpack, which held my wallet and keys, a little distance from my side, I reached out with my left hand and pulled it toward me. "Why are you dressed in buckskins?" I asked.

The grizzled old man looked down at himself as if he hadn't noticed what he was wearing. "Don't know. Always wore 'em. Don't like store-bought. Wear out too fast." His eyes flicked to my backpack.

I pulled it closer, intending to put it on my lap.

"Wouldn't do that if I were you," he said brusquely, shooting another look at my backpack. Before I could speak, he took two quick strides over the fire pit and slapped the backpack so hard it flew out of my hands and landed in the sand five feet away.

I fell to my right side to avoid him. "What the hell are you doing?" I sputtered. "Are you crazy, or what?" I tried to draw my pistol but, now, lying on my side, I couldn't get the gun out of my holster.

"That," he said with a big grin, pointing to a spot in the sand about ten feet away, "was about ta crawl up yer arm and sting ya."

My eyes followed his finger to a four-inch-long scorpion, scurrying away in the sand. Swallowing hard, I managed to say, "Oh...okay. Couldn't you have just *said* something, rather than scare the hell out of me."

He chuckled. "Could'a. But it wouldn'ta been as much fun." He slapped his hat on his leg. "Whoowee, Boy, ya should'a seen the look on yer face. Ya looked like ya was gonna shat in them fancy pants of yers."

Growing annoyed at his impudence, my confidence began to return. "What the hell are you doing here anyway?" I stood up to retrieve my tossed backpack from the dirt. I studied it cautiously and shook it to make sure no other critters had made a home of it.

"Was passin' by an seen yer tracks. Didn't know somebody be out here but me. Thought ya might need some help, so I followed yer trail."

"How long have you been watching me?"

"Half-hour or so."

A horse whinnied to my right.

I about jumped out my skin as I turned toward the bend in the wash. *Who else is here?* I wondered. I couldn't see the horse.

"Yer sure a jumpy sort, ain't ya?" the old man said as he knelt down and stirred the ashes in the fire pit. "That be my horses. Left' em down there so's they don't wake ya."

I sighed, relieved I wouldn't have to deal with any renegades or other strangers for the time being.

I needed to relieve my bladder. I looked around for a private place to go as I made conversation. "Can you blame me for being jumpy? After my encounter with that strange *thing* yester-" I stopped abruptly, about to tell the man something that might make him think I was mad.

"What *thing*?" he asked. His blue eyes, now serious, bore into me.

"I need to go to the bathroom."

He pondered me a moment then shrugged his shoulder. "Take yer time. I ain't goin' nowhere."

I picked up my backpack and hauled it with me. I walked up the wash until I found a bunch of thick shrubs around a hill that gave me some privacy. While I did my business, I thought about this old gizzard who called himself Maxston Vanguard. Why was he out here? Why did he dress like a mountain man from the 1820's? In the ten years I'd lived in Lake Havasu City, I'd never seen nor heard about a crazy old man hanging around the area. I'm sure someone would have said something. In a small community like Havasu, word got around fast.

I had no intention of going back and talking to the man. Instead, my thoughts turned toward home. Erica had to be frantic by now. I pulled out my cell phone. Still no reception. I put it in my shirt pocket so I could check it every now and then as I walked.

I climbed out of the wash and headed northwest, following the tracks I'd made the night before. When I reached the area where I was sure the *thing* had stood in my way, I stopped and studied the ground. My footprints, along with numerous scuffmarks, indicated where I'd stumbled around, trying to get away from the *thing*. My footprints ended at the place I had last touched the invisible rubber barrier. Beyond there, the desert sand and brush seemed untouched. *Is the barrier still there?* I wondered. My heart raced at the thought.

I swallowed hard. No matter what, I had to get to my truck. I had to get home. My family would be worried to death about me.

My palms perspired as I lifted my arms to feel my way. I took a tentative step forward. Slowly, I took another step. My feet now rested in the last set of footprints closest to the *thing*. I couldn't feel anything but air. Taking a deep breath, I moved forward a short step. Nothing. Another step. No spider web. No cotton ball. No rubber wall. Gathering my courage, I took another short step, then another. I found myself moving freely and easily forward.

Joy flooded through me. I was certain the *thing* was gone. I had walked well past the barrier. After several more steps, I picked up speed and ran as fast as I could toward the site where I had left my truck.

With intermittent walking and running, it took me only a half-hour to get to the last hill that stood between me and the sight of the truck that would take me home. As I started climbing the hill, a strange feeling came over me. Something seemed different. With each step, a sense of dread began to creep into my mind.

I crested the hill. There, I saw no truck, no tracks in the sand, no indication a vehicle had ever been in the wash below me. I stopped and stared out over the valley stretched out before me. Something was definitely wrong. Where was the lake? Where was the town? I couldn't even see the river that normally divided the land between Arizona and California. All the familiar landmarks had disappeared...and so had civilization.

I glanced up at the blue sky, usually full of contrails, left by jets traveling from L.A. or San Diego to all points east. Not one contrail. This hadn't happened since September 11,

2001, when the FAA had grounded all planes after the New York disaster. An eerie silence had filled the air back then, but now, it seemed even more ominous.

The dread welled up in me as I dropped to my knees. I could hardly breathe. *My God, what happened to the town? Where's Erica and the girls? Where am I?*

I took off my glasses and rubbed my eyes to make sure I wasn't dreaming or having hallucinations. After putting my glasses back on I kept scanning the desert panorama and eyeing the mountains on the horizon. The view seemed different, like the mountains were closer. I couldn't put my finger on the bizarre sensations I was picking up from the visual images that surrounded me and the disappearance of all I had known.

I stared numbly at the empty land. One thing was certain, my world was gone. *How do I get back? Where do I go? What do I do?*

I thought about Max, the only human being I'd met since yesterday afternoon. *Is he part of this phenomenon?*

Feeling desperate, I glanced back toward the mountain where I had spent the night. It seemed I had only one choice: to go back and find the old man. Maybe he knew what was going on. Maybe he could help me figure out how to get home. I just hoped he would still be there. The idea of being one of the last humans on earth scared the hell out of me.

I dragged myself to my feet. Stumbling through the brush, I started hiking into the hills again.

* * *

As I trudged up the wash, I saw Max sitting alone at the campsite with his back to me. He had a fire going. Despite the weirdness of his buckskin outfit and his odd mannerisms, I felt a sense of relief to have the company of another human being. His presence, alone, helped to quiet my jumbled nerves.

I seriously debated about whether or not to tell him what was happening to me. I kept hoping I might wake up any minute from a bad dream and find myself in my truck, bouncing across the desert toward my customary life. But the stark reality of the missing town and missing lake hovered over me like a hammer of doom. I feared I might not see my normal life for awhile. Did I really want to get Max involved in my dilemma? It all seemed just too crazy to explain to someone. I decided to wait to get to know Max a little better before I shared my story.

As I walked to the fire and sat down, Max said not a word about me being gone for almost two hours. He took a bite of some kind of cooked meat-like food that had nuts or berries pressed into it.

My stomach growled loudly at the sight and smell of the food. It'd been a long time since I'd finished off my sandwich the night before. I opened my backpack and took a swig of water from my water bottle. I then rummaged around the bottom of the pack and in the pockets to find a piece of hard candy or snack I might have missed the day before. Coming up empty, I sighed and put the pack down next to me.

The old man handed me a piece of his food. "Here."

"What is it?"

"Pemmican."

It sounded like some backwoods soul food. Skeptical about what it might contain, I asked, "What's in it?"

He shook his head and smiled. "Fer a man who be hungry, ya sure'n be picky."

Going on the defensive, I blurted, "I just don't want to eat something I might be allergic to." It was a lie. As far as I knew, I wasn't allergic to anything, but I didn't want to eat lizard or snake or scorpions.

"It be venison. Mixed with bear fat n' blueberries." His beefy hand held out the food again.

I took it and bit off a tentative nibble. I chewed it slowly. *Mmmm. Not bad.* I bit off a larger chunk and savored the flavor. While I chewed, I studied Max more closely.

I would guess him to be about five-foot-eight, with a sturdy, powerful build. He wore his hair loose, falling well past his shoulders. His unkempt silver-streaked beard hung to mid-chest. The rough, dark, leather-like skin of his hands and face told me he'd been exposed to the elements more often than not. On closer inspection, his buckskin outfit showed patches and stains in numerous spots. I couldn't figure out why the front of his buckskin pants looked completely black and slightly shiny. He solved that riddle when he used them to wipe the grease and soot from his hands. Knee-high moccasins covered his feet.

A bone-handled knife and tomahawk stuck out of the wide leather belt at his waist, along with the butt of a black-powder pistol. An assortment of bags, potentially containing anything from tobacco to tinder to magic dust, for all I knew, hung from his belt. I noted the rifle held casually in the crook of his left arm. All of his weapons looked well-used and well-cared for. He could have easily killed me in my sleep if he'd wanted to. Hell, anyone could have attacked and killed me as soundly as I'd slept.

The more I studied the man, the more intrigued I became. He seemed like an enigma. However, before I dared put my trust in him about my problem with the *thing* and the missing town, I wanted to learned more about him. "So, Max, where do you live?"

He shot a stop-dead glare at me that would have made a grizzly bear cower in fear.

My eyes grew wide and I almost choked on the venison going down my throat.

"Name be *Maxston*. I'd 'preciate it if ya'd use it."

"Uh...sure...no problem." Wow, he seemed mighty fussy for being a mountain man. Hell, I would have thought with an uncharacteristic name like Maxston, he'd prefer Max. I shrugged. *To each their own.* After I bit into another piece of the venison, I dared to ask my question again. "Okay, Maxston, where do you live?"

"North Town. 'Bout twenty miles from here. That way. Other side a the mountain." He pointed northeast.

North Town? Never heard of it, I mused to myself. *He must be wrong. Maybe he's talking about Kingman, the town northeast of Lake Havasu City.*

At this point, I decided not to correct the man, not after his deadly look when I'd misused his name. Although I was taller at six-foot-one, Maxston carried a lot more muscle on his bones. His feisty nature would be formidable in a fight. He looked to be a little crazy, too. If I were going to correct him, it would have to be by tripping him up. I decided to do just that. "And just how long have you lived there?" I asked, trying to hide the sarcasm in my voice.

He smiled. "Too long." He stood up abruptly. "Time ta go." He kicked sand into the fire pit until he had completely covered all the burning embers. Without a word, he turned and walked down the wash.

I didn't move a muscle as I watched him, yet something in me grew anxious at the thought of him leaving me behind. I still wasn't sure I could trust him with the *thing*, nor did I want to leave the area for fear everything would return to normal and I could go home. *Maybe I should try returning to my truck again.* The thought made me shudder. I couldn't bear to see the missing town again. Something deep inside me told me it wasn't going to be there, and I wasn't going to get home by going back that way.

Maxston called over his shoulder, "Ya comin'?"

"I...I'm going to go back to my truck," I yelled after him in a maneuver to stall a decision. I sensed I really had no other choice but to go with him. I certainly didn't like the idea of being completely isolated out here on the desert while strange things were happening around me. I didn't have any food or shelter. My water would run out before the day was over. It only made sense to stick with Maxston until I could figure things out. I really needed some answers.

The old man stopped in his tracks and turned around. "Let me guess. Yesterday, ya went for a walk. Got yerself caught up in some kinda invisible spider web....Right?"

I nodded hesitantly. *Did he read my mind? How does he know about that?*

"Then, ya wasn't able ta get back home, so ya had to spend the night out here....Right?"

I reluctantly nodded again.

"Then, this mornin', ya went ta try'n get back home. But ya cain't....Right?"

I nodded again, feeling embarrassed, like he'd somehow caught me doing something wrong.

"What year it be?" he asked.

I squinted at him, wondering if he was serious. "2015. Why? Don't you know what year it is?"

He grunted. "Trust me. Yer better off comin' with me. I can explain on the way." He turned and took off again, this time with a long loping gait.

His words about the spider web started to sink in. I jumped up and grabbed my backpack. Hurrying to catch up with him, I spewed forth my questions in a jumbled haste. "You know about the web? How do you know about it? What is it? Where did it come from? How come I can't see it?"

"Hold on, Son. Everybody knows 'bout the web. How ya think we all got here?"

Before I could get out another question, we rounded the bend of the wash. I got distracted, seeing four horses. Two carried loaded packs, one had what looked like a saddle on it, and one wore only a halter. It quickly dawned on me that I'd be the one riding bareback, not a comfortable way to travel for someone not used to it. Oh, I'd ridden plenty of horses in the past, but it'd been a long time since my last ride.

Maxston rummaged through one of the packs and pulled out a red-and-white-striped blanket. He threw it over the back of the horse without a saddle and tied the blanket down, front and rear, with a strip of leather. "Not the best," he said as he handed me the halter rope, "but's all I can do for ya. You can ride, cain't ya?"

Having no other option, I put my backpack on my back and, holding to the leather strip on the horse's back, jumped up, belly first. I wiggled, pushed, and pulled with my long lanky body until I sat upright on the blanket. "It's been a while," I said, "but as long as we take it easy for the first part of the trip, I should be okay."

As I watched Maxston gather the lead ropes of the packhorses, I kept telling myself that the only reason I was going along with him was so that I could get more information about the spider-web *thing*. The sooner I could get the information, the sooner I could find a way to get back home.

I had to admit I didn't really want to be left out on the desert alone for another night with no food and water, nor did I want to take a chance that I would never see another human being again.

Maxston climbed into his saddle, which I noticed to be nothing more than a plain wooden frame, held together with strips of dried rawhide. A leather pad, attached to the saddle, formed the strips for two stirrups, one on each side. Someone, probably Maxston, had whittled the stirrups out of wood and wrapped them with leather. For some reason, I'd expected the saddle to be decorated with beads or feathers or some other fancy ornamentation, like Maxston had tied a string of feathers to his hair and wore beads on his buckskin top. I found the plainness of the saddle somewhat disappointing for this colorful character out of the 1800's.

With his rifle in the crook of one arm, Maxston turned the horses and we started down the wash in single file. I brought up the rear. All the while, my mind flipped through the eerie events I had experienced the previous day and all morning. I just couldn't get my mind around anything.

I pulled my cell phone out of my shirt pocket to check for a signal. Still none.

Chapter 3

After about a quarter-mile of riding, the grizzled old man rode out of the wash and stopped.

Going up the side of the wash, my horse lurched. I grabbed onto the horse's mane, saving myself from falling off the blanket.

"Need ta go downhill fer a while. 'Til we can cut 'round the end of them hills." He pointed to the mountains behind us. "Then head northeast, 'til we come ta North Town."

As he started his horse forward, I rode next to him so we could talk. "How far is it to this *North Town* again?"

Instead of answering me, he opened one of the pouches hanging off his belt and dug his thumb and forefinger into a leafy brown substance. He pulled out a pinch of tobacco and stuck it between his front teeth and lower lip. "You ain't soundin' too convinced it be a real place." He nudged his horse with a heel and moved it ahead of me into a trot.

I pressed my horse to keep up with him. "No, I'm not convinced," I replied with annoyance, trying to talk to him and stay on my horse as we jogged down the sandy desert hill. "I've lived in Lake Havasu City for ten years and I know the surrounding area pretty well. I've never heard of any place called North Town."

He eyed me with a funny look. "Where'd ya say yer from? Lake Hav…"

"Havasu. Lake Havasu City. You know, the town that sits next to the big lake on the Colorado River, just below Needles, Laughlin, and Bullhead City."

He shook his head and continued forward. "Don't know any'a them places. You sure ya didn't fall'n hit yer head?"

"Positive," I barked, growing more and more impatient with his evasive attitude. "So," I said hotly, "tell me everything you know about this web thing I ran into yesterday. I want some answers. What do you know about it?"

He slowed up a little. "Why don'tcha tell me what happened to ya first?"

I began with my initial encounter with the *thing*, the rubber wall, and the missing town. It didn't take long to tell the whole story.

When I finished, Maxston grunted and nodded his head as if everything I'd said made perfect sense.

When he didn't offer to say anything, I asked, "Well? What can you tell me? Where's my town? Where's my family? What happened to them? What happened to me?"

Riding along nonchalantly, he chewed his tobacco and kept his horse moving at a steady gait forward. "Sounds ta me just about like everybody else's story…includin' mine."

"What do you mean? Did the same thing happen to you?"

He stared off into the distance, making no effort to look at me or answer my questions.

Growing increasingly frustrated, I couldn't hold back my anger. "So, what is it? What is this damn web?"

He shrugged. "Don't know. Fer as I can tell, nobody knows."

I halted my horse and shouted, "You told me you could explain everything to me on the way to this North Town you claim exists. I'm stopping right here. I'm not going anywhere with you until you start talking."

The old man yanked hard on his reins, causing his horse to stop so fast the two packhorses ran into each other. He turned in his saddle and glared at me with his blazing blue eyes. "I did explain it to ya. You 'n me n' everybody else in this here world got caught in the web. None of us can go home again…ever."

A chill ran down my spine at the definitive tone of his voice when he'd said the word *ever*. He had to be wrong. But I wasn't about to tussle with the guy over it with his short-tempered streak.

"'Bout three ta four hours. You be seein' North Town fer yerself. N' fer hell's sake, relax. Yer stiffer than a week-old piece a meat." He clamped his mouth shut behind the thick mustache and beard, kicked his horse in the ribs, and rode off at a brisk trot.

"Fine, you ornery old fart," I hollered at his receding back. "Go ahead. I'll bring up the rear." If I'd had someone else—anyone else—to count on, I would've just turned around and headed out on my own. But no such luck...at least not yet.

Okay, so I'd go to this so-called North Town with him and find out what was going on. If the old man wouldn't give me any answers, I'd find someone else who would.

Maxston stayed well ahead of me for the next part of the ride. That suited me fine.

* * *

As I rode along, I must have dozed in the saddle, so to speak, since I wasn't in a saddle. When I woke up, something bothered me. The country around us didn't look familiar. I'd been all over this part of the country, exploring the desert for years. I knew the terrain well and had visited many of the popular spots for rock hunting with the gem-and-mineral club. Now, I noticed we'd moved from the cacti and mesquite bushes of the low desert to the cedars and sagebrush of the high desert. *How did we travel so far in such a short time? I couldn't have dosed off for that long a period without falling off my horse. Did Maxston do something to change our location?*

I looked at my cell phone. Still no reception. The battery was starting to go dead. My watch said only two hours had passed since we'd left the camp. If the changes in the terrain kept up like this, we'd be among quakies and pine trees before long. That eerie feeling that I'd gotten this morning when I'd looked out over the desert and saw Lake Havasu missing, started creeping up in me again.

An hour later, sure enough, we passed a stand of pines. The temperature changed, too, cooling off by at least ten to fifteen degrees.

A while later Maxston stopped on top of a hill.

I continued climbing toward him as he waited for me. Not sure of the reception I was going to get from him after our hours of silence, I hesitantly approached.

"There she be," he announced as I pulled to a stop next to him. "North Town." He acted like we'd never had our little spat.

I looked out across the valley floor, now laid out directly in front of me. My eyes bugged out at the sight of the collection of ramshackle huts, log cabins, and sod shanties. In the center part of town, it looked like someone had built a wooden rampart, a fort of some kind. From what I could tell, North Town stretched two to three miles across, with cultivated fields of flowers and plants surrounding the town for miles. A wide, lazy river flowed north of town, running from east to west. This was certainly no town I'd ever seen or heard of.

A cool wind blew through the trees toward town. The chill on my back made me shiver.

I had to admit that, as bad as the place looked, I couldn't wait to get there so I could get off my horse. My inner thighs, not used to the constant motion a horse makes as it moves, burned from blisters. I was pretty sure I had blisters on other parts of my body, too…parts that should never get blisters.

Maxston urged his horse over the edge of the hill. "Come on. We be almost home."

Not me, I thought defiantly as I followed him down the hill. *I'm not home. This ain't gonna be my home, Mister.*

For some reason, Maxston's earlier words rang through my head. *None of us can go home again…ever.*

Well, if what he'd said was true, that might be good enough for Maxston and these people, but it wasn't going to be good enough for me.

As my horse made its way down the hill, trudging through a field of cotton, that ominous, wary gut feeling about everything around me being wrong came tumbling over me again. I looked at the shabby town ahead, something akin to the slums of L.A., or maybe a gathering place for homeless refugees. It just didn't look right.

Convergence of Time

Oh, God, what have I gotten myself into now?

* * *

Up close, North Town looked shabbier than my impression from the hill. The houses on the outside of town, mainly built from rough lumber, seemed to have been added, one by one, to each other by attaching to its neighbor to form one side wall. Most appeared flimsy, as though the walls would collapse if someone leaned against them. The houses furthest from the main part of town seemed to be the most dilapidated.

The majority of the people walked barefoot in the dirty, unpaved streets. Some wore home-made moccasins. The children ran around in grimy pants with no shirts or tops. The tattered, patched clothing, worn by all the townspeople, seemed to come in three colors only: white, blue, and red. They all looked like a ragged, dirty lot.

The backyards, as well as the spaces that happened to be empty between some of the houses, contained gardens, chicken coops, and, sometimes, a corral with a horse, a cow, or pigs. Several self-standing buildings, just off the road, smelled like community latrines. As I passed by, I pinched my nose and breathed through my mouth to avoid the stench. The combination of the unwashed bodies, stink from the latrines, and odor from the animals made me nauseated as we rode up the street.

With a quick glance at me, Maxston said, "Gits better further on up. People live out here cain't come ta terms with what's happened to 'em. They get by…just barely."

"What do you mean, 'can't come to terms'? Are you talking about this poverty?"

"More'n that." He pursed his lips behind his beard and pondered for a moment. "They ain't believin' what happened to 'em really happened to 'em. Think they be wakin' up one mornin' and all be back ta normal. They ain't willin' to do more'n get by. Big drain on the resta us…ones who gotta support 'em."

I scanned the faces of the desolate-looking men and women. They seemed lost with their hollow eyes and shallow stares. I'd say they were in the lowest class of poverty I'd ever seen. Turning my attention away from the sordid lives of these poor people and getting back to my own disconcerting situation, I said, "You still haven't answered my questions about the web."

"Get yer answers soon enough. Let's get on inta town. Settle ya in a room first. Then, we be seein' Master Benjamin. He be the mayor, the one ya need ta talk to."

"Fine," I shot back, irritated with another evasion of my questions, "but let's get on with seeing this Master Benjamin first. I don't need a room. I need to find a way to back to Erica and my kids. I'm sure they're worried sick about me."

"Don't get yer dander up, Young Fella. If he still be in his office, Master Benjamin'll see ya. If not, ya have ta wait 'til tomorrow." He looked at me and shook his head. "An' quit bein' a pansy. You already been gone from yer family one night. One more ain't gonna kill ya."

I could see that arguing with Maxston was a waste of time. I shut my mouth and silently rode on.

The further we moved along the street, the cleaner and better-dressed the people became. The homes looked more cared for and more stable in structure. Two-story houses started to crop up along the side streets. Many of the front yards were decorated with flowerbeds, homemade pots, and inventive hand-woven mats. Maxston had been right about the town getting better as we moved closer to the central area.

The smell of the latrines and animals still hung heavily in the air. I supposed it was something the people got used to if they lived here all the time. What struck me most were the strange clothes the people wore, almost like costumes. One man had on a western outfit from the 1800's. His lady friend wore a long gingham skirt, like something you'd see on *Little House on the Prairie*. A pair of young women walked along the street in long, plain-white cotton dresses that looked like nightgowns. They'd woven flowers into their long, dark tresses, looking like a couple of maidens you'd imagine seeing in King Arthur's castle.

Past the better-constructed wooden houses, larger buildings began to appear with businesses of every kind. One quaint-looking store sold clocks. Another claimed to sell "100% cotton clothing." Next door to the clothing store stood a bakery. Now, there was a smell that made me hungry. I hadn't eaten since the meat Maxston had shared with me in the morning. My mouth watered at the thought of a piece of homemade bread, slathered with fresh-melted butter and strawberry jam. I looked at Maxston pleadingly, but he ignored me and rode right on past the bakery without a hint of interest.

We passed another building where whiffs of delicious cooked meat hung in the air. The sign out front read: *We serve the freshest deer and elk in town.* Judging by the crowds at the door, I figured they served good food.

I was about to ask Maxston to stop when he pulled up in front of the largest building I'd seen so far. Made from squared-off logs that stood on end, it seemed like a strange building. As I studied it closer, I realized it wasn't a building at all, but a long wall. Visions of an Old-West fortress popped into my mind. This had to be the fort I'd seen from above town.

When a door opened in the wall, I could see just enough inside to have my images of a fort confirmed.

Out stepped a young man wearing a red shirt, black pants, and a black hat similar to a derby. In the crook of one arm, he cradled a Winchester rifle. "What can I do for ya today, Boys?" he asked as he checked us over carefully. His eyes narrowed slightly when he saw Maxston's rifle and my pistol, which I'd left openly strapped to my side.

"Wan'ta see Master Benjamin," Maxston said in a firm tone. "If'n he be in."

"And who are the two of you?" the guard asked in an uppity manner. "What's your business with Master Benjamin?" His eyes flicked daringly from Maxston to me and back.

Abruptly, Maxston urged his horse forward and forced the guard back against the wall.

I held my breath.

"I be someone who knows yer not s'posed ta be givin' strangers a bad time. Yer posted here ta help 'em."

The guard's face had gone pale. Obviously, he'd intended to take advantage of us when he'd seen we were strangers and thought we didn't know how things worked around here. "Sure," he gulped, "no problem...Sir. I think Master Benjamin is still in." He sheepishly scooted away from the horse, turned to the wall, and knocked loudly three times. A gate, large enough to admit a wagon, opened outwardly. "It's the third-"

"I know where ta go," Maxston barked as he rode past the guard. "Won't mention yer treatment of us," he said, turning in his saddle and glaring at the man, "...this time."

"Thank you, Sir," the guard responded politely, giving an appreciative bow of his head. "I promise it won't happen again." He shut his mouth, seeming smart enough to figure out he'd screwed up plenty for one day.

Maxston shook his head. "These new guys," he mumbled. "Think they run the place."

I glanced around at the log cabins and buildings inside the fort: a small town within a town. Women and men went about their business. A number of soldiers, wearing dirty, worn uniforms from the Civil War era, bustled from building to building like they were on some kind of official business. I felt like I was on a movie set for a feature film about the Old West, a stalwart fortress built by soldiers to protect themselves from the Indians. I looked around, expecting to see a director, movie stars, and cameras.

"This fort be the original town," Maxston stated. "Town keeps government offices here. Makes it easier to protect officials and important records...be there an attack."

I nearly laughed out loud at his seriousness. I thought I'd play along. "An attack? Who would attack such a fort? It wouldn't be *Indians*, would it?"

"Injuns mostly," he said somberly. "Young Sioux bucks still try ta raid us now 'n again. Lookin' ta get 'em a slave or two. Signed a treaty with 'em years back. Now, they be pretty quiet."

I looked at Maxston, his eyes unblinking, no hint of a smile on his lips. *He has to be kidding.* "Sioux Indians? Slaves? Are you serious?"

"Big village of 'em 'bout fifty miles ta the east a here." He nonchalantly rode his horse to a hitching post and came to a stop. "Okay, here we be." He swung his leg over his saddle and dropped to the ground as if he'd only been riding for ten minutes.

I, on the other hand, had to lay forward across the blanket and half-slide, half-fall to get off my horse. With my feet on the ground, I dared not take a step for fear my legs would buckle and I'd fall flat on my face, embarrassing myself in front of Maxston and all the people moving about the fort. My butt stung from the blisters.

Maxston's blue eyes glittered as he tied his horse to the hitching post. "Little stiff, are ya?" His tightly pursed lips turned almost white under his thick mustache.

I sensed he was trying hard not to laugh at my condition. "Go ahead, laugh," I said bitterly as I took a painful step forward.

He chuckled. "Ya look like a youngun takin' yer first steps." Suddenly, the delight in his eyes disappeared and his brow formed a frown as he stared at me.

The sudden change in his manner made me nervous. "What is it?"

"Nothin'," he replied gruffly. He wiped at his nose. "Come on. Let's introduce ya ta Master Benjamin." He turned and strode toward one of the doors along an interior wall of the fort. Without knocking, he walked inside and disappeared into a dark room.

I hobbled along as best I could, trying to keep my balance and avoid falling over. I still had my pack on my back. I intended to keep my personal possessions close.

Despite my physical pain and the all the weird things going on around me, the thought that I might finally get some answers from the mayor brought on a new wave of hope.

Chapter 4

After I stepped into the room behind Maxston, I closed the door behind me, effectively shutting out the sunlight. I blinked several times as my eyes slowly adjusted to the dark, gloomy atmosphere in the room.

Maxston took off his hat and announced, "Here ta see Master Benjamin."

A woman's voice from the back of the room responded. "If you'll follow me, Sir, I'll take you to his office." A vague form stood up from behind a desk. A small candle sat on the desk, giving off the only light in the room. Maxston followed the lady through an open door.

I took off my hat and stayed close behind the man, doing my best to keep up, what with the pains smarting in my legs.

We passed through another dingy office before entering a hallway. The thickness of the walls surprised me as we walked along the long corridor that must have run the entire length of the fort. Candles, burning in holders about every twenty feet along the walls, barely gave sufficient light to see where we were going.

I stumbled over on unseen object on the dirt floor. *Ouch.* New pain shot up my legs as I caught myself. After tripping a second time, I learned to lift my feet high enough to clear any objects beneath me. This made the cloth of my pants rub more roughly against my blisters.

Curious about what was making me stumble, I pulled a candle out of a holder and held it close to the floor. The upper tips of large rocks penetrated up through the dirt, probably due to the heavy foot traffic that had packed the dirt down. No wonder I kept tripping.

"Ahemmm!"

I looked up.

The lady, standing over me in some kind of long, loose dress, held her hand on her hip as she waited to get my attention. In the candlelight, her sharp nose, protruding from her pinched face, reminded me of a mean librarian who once yelled at me for bringing my books back late.

"Oh, sorry," I said. I rose and hurriedly set the candle back in the holder.

She shook her head as if I were out of my mind to be inspecting the dirt floor. Spinning around, she continued to lead us down the long hallway. When she came to a stop in front of a plain wooden door, she knocked, waited a slight pause, then opened the door to a more brightly lit room. She stepped aside for us to enter.

As I got my bearings inside the room, the woman shut the door behind us and left us alone. Candles, strategically placed around the room on holders, flickered at the light breeze created from the movement of the door. Shelves with dusty ancient books lined three of the walls.

A small man, maybe five-foot-one, stood up from a plank table and rushed toward Maxston like he'd found his long-lost friend. "Maxston, My Good Man. How fare thee?"

"Good ta see ya, Master Benjamin," Maxston said, leaning his rifle against the wall and wrapping the much shorter man in a big bear hug.

I suppressed a laugh at the sight of the two of them. Maxston towered over Benjamin by a head. His brawny body seemed to crush the small figure in his grasp.

When they separated, I noticed Benjamin's hilarious Halloween costume. He wore a black shirt with a white collar—the collar so large it covered his shoulders and part of his chest. The sleeves ended with six-inch cuffs of stiff white material. His black baggy pants stopped just below his knees. They made me think of breeches or knickers. Black stockings led down to his shiny black shoes, ornamented with big silver buckles. He looked like one of those pilgrims who had arrived in America on the Mayflower. I had to bite my lower lip to keep from laughing. This town seemed more and more like some kind of movie set, something out of

Universal Studios, where all kinds of movies were underway.

Master Benjamin suddenly turned his attention toward me. "And who doth thou haveth with thee, My Good Friend?" This little oddity of a man not only looked like a pilgrim, he talked like one.

As he studied me closer, his eyes strayed over my thick brown hair. He wistfully ran a hand over his own head, appearing self-conscious about his partial baldness.

Maxston nodded to me. "Master Benjamin, this be..." He stopped and looked at me with surprise. "Don't think I ever got yer name."

I thought back over our conversations and realized I'd never taken the opportunity to introduce myself. Neither did the old man ever ask. To make it official, I held out my hand to Maxston as though meeting him for the first time. "Gavin. It's Gavin Clark."

"Well, Gavin," he said with a hearty handshake, "good ta finally know yer name."

Benjamin stepped forward in his funny outfit and said formally, "Goodman Clark, what cheer thoust bring. Pray tell, any friend of Goodman Maxston's shallst forever be a friend of mine."

"Gavin," I said, emphasizing my wish for less formality. "Gavin is fine."

"Fine, fine," Master Benjamin repeated offhandedly as he returned to his chair at the table. He pointed to two high-back wooden chairs sitting against the wall. "Recline with me, if thou willst."

Maxston grabbed the two offered chairs and began facing them toward the table.

Benjamin sat erect in his own wooden chair and placed his hands, palms down, flat on the table. It didn't look like he was reclining to me.

Maxston sat down.

I remained standing, not willing to suffer the pain of sitting down for a while.

The amused glint in Maxston's eyes told me he understood my choice to refuse the seat. In explanation,

Maxston said to Benjamin, "Boy had a rough day on the horse. Excuse him fer stayin' on his feet."

Benjamin nodded, not seeming to understand at all. To Maxston, he spoke slowly, enunciating every word with some kind of Old English inflection. "Now, Goodman Maxston, what, praise God, brings thee back to town so soon? Was it not thy plan to be absent for another fortnight or two."

"Woulda been gone longer," Maxston stated as he stretched his legs out in front of him, "but ran inta Gavin here. He be havin' himself some questions ta ask ya,"

"Is this so?" Master Benjamin now leaned back in his chair and intertwined his fingers. He placed his pointer fingers against his lips. His beady black eyes focused on me. "Am I not correct in that thou haveth come newly to our world?" He bounced his fingers off his lips while he talked.

I still couldn't get over Benjamin's costume and language. Did everybody in this town, even the mayor, take roles in movies? I intended to ask *Goodman Maxston* when we finished the meeting. I had other things of more importance to discuss right now.

"Yeah, I guess I'm new," I said hesitantly. "At least, that's what Max here says."

Maxston gruffly cleared his throat and gave me a dirty look.

"Sorry, I meant *Maxston*."

Benjamin smiled politely. "Yay. Goodman Maxston renders his name to be as his parents had wished at his birth." He turned back to me. "Now, pray tell, Goodman Gavin, why haveth thou comest before me?"

Benjamin's annoying mannerism with his fingers popping against his mouth made me nervous. "I don't know what's going on. I just want to get back to my family. My wife's got to be going out of her mind trying to get hold of me or find me. The longer I hang around here, the more I fear she will be looking for me where I had left my truck. I need to get back there."

"'Tis needful, first, for thee to tell all that cometh before," Benjamin said in his convoluted way, still playing his fingers against his lips. "Bear forth thy whole story."

"Tell him what you told me," Maxston said, giving me a nudge.

I leaned forward against the back of the chair and repeated the version I had given to Maxston earlier.

In the middle of my story, the woman who reminded me of the mean librarian delivered a blown-glass pitcher of water and three wooden goblets.

Not more than fifteen minutes later, I finished up. "So, that's my story." I reached for my goblet, which was sitting on my chair, and took a drink of water to wet my dry tongue. As I set the goblet down, I found myself growing miffed. I glared at Benjamin, wanting some straight answers for a change. "Now, why don't you tell me, how can I get home?"

The small-eyed man continued bouncing his fingers off his lips a few more seconds. He finally separated his hands and put them down, palms flat against the table. He sat erect and glanced at the two of us, settling on me. "Thou must knoweth the truth," he said softly. "Pray tell, we knoweth not how any man may returnth home."

I stood stiffly at the chair. *He's got to be kidding. He's still saying I can't go home?*

"Thou needest to know that we…all of us," he swept his hands in an arc meant to encompass the whole of North Town, "would'st have traveled home long, long ago." Even with his stiff posture, his shoulders seemed to droop a little with his sad tone. "To thee, Goodman Gavin, I extend my truest sorrow."

I stared at him. My throat tightened. No matter what these men had been telling me, my mind wouldn't let go of the belief that I could get back. It was impossible for me to think I would never see Erica or my girls again. This wasn't how life worked. You got up in the morning, went to your job, worked hard to make a living, went home to your family at night, had a few days off, and the whole thing started over again. Just as I counted on the sun coming up every day, I counted on my life moving along a continuous, logical path.

Only in movies did things like this happen, that someone suddenly found himself in another place and time.

These guys had to be wrong. Why the hell should I believe some scrawny little man in a pilgrim costume or a crazy old mountain man in buckskins? I wondered if I should just head back to the spot where Maxston had found me and try getting home again. Maybe this nightmare would simply go away. Somehow, I didn't think that was going to happen. I shook my head. "There's got to be a way."

Maxston reached out his rough hand and put it on my arm. "Like I told ya," he said sympathetically, "people tried everything they could think. Even them scientists in South Town cain't figure the problem out."

"Scientists?" I said, looking at him with skepticism, not wanting to get my hopes up that maybe there would be reasonable, logical, well-educated people in this mixed-up world. "You're saying you have scientists."

"In South Town."

Is this another runaround? I wondered. "And where, pray tell, is this town?" *Oops, I didn't mean to mimic Benjamin, but it just came out.*

"Many scores to the south," Benjamin answered.

"He means South Town sits hundreds a miles ta the south," Maxston explained.

"To travel to South Town," Benjamin went on, "thou must journey through dangerous territories. Wagon trains only, moving supplies betwixt the two settlements, be allowed to make the journey."

Great. Now wagon trains. Add that to the Indians who attack the fort and government authorities wearing costumes. Everything seems to be getting crazier and crazier. Hell, all I want to do is go home.

I debated about what to do. My gut feeling told me a trip back to the desert would be useless. I needed to keep moving forward, looking for the right people who knew what was going on. The more I thought about it, the more I wanted to go to South Town. "Okay," I said, resigning myself to the situation, "I want to talk to the scientists. Maybe one of them will give me a straight answer. Scientists have the world figured out, don't they? I'll take the next wagon train out, if that's the only way I can go."

Master Benjamin lifted a piece of paper off the top of a stack of files. "Now," he said officially, as though he hadn't heard me, "to the matter of where to put thee. What skills hath thee to offer this town, and for which we can make use?"

Tired of beating around the bush with these guys, I stepped around the chair and shot back angrily, "Driving a wagon."

Benjamin's small eyes widened briefly in alarm. He set his jaw. "Praise God, Goodman Gavin, but I fear such action will not be possible-"

I slammed my fist down on the table and knocked over his water goblet. I leaned into the man's face. "I'm not *asking* you. I'm *telling* you. I'm going to South Town. If you won't let me go on the next wagon train, I'll find another way to get there. I *intend* to go home. I'll do whatever it takes to get there. And you'd better not try to stop me." I straightened and glared at both of them. "Now, if you'll excuse me, I have to go." I turned on my heels, ignored my sore legs, and stomped to the door. I slammed it shut behind me.

Standing alone in the dim hallway, my shoulders slumped and an overwhelming fear gripped me. I didn't have anywhere to go. And if I did, I sure didn't know how to get there.

* * *

I sat on a bench inside the fort walls and waited for Maxston to appear. When I saw him exit the outer door to what I now understood were the government offices, I looked at my watch. A full ten minutes had passed.

At this point, I felt so frustrated with my situation that the soreness of the blisters on my butt, rubbing against the rough wood on the bench, no longer seemed important. Nothing felt as painful as my desire to get back to my family and the thought that I wouldn't be able to find a way to do it.

Maxston seemed a little shy as he said, "Master Benjamin wants ya ta come back in fer a minute. Has some things ta explain." He casually leaned against the fort wall and hooked his thumbs into his leather belt. He stood silently, patiently waiting for me to decide what I was going to do. His eyes roamed across the way at the groups of soldiers in worn uniforms and women in long dresses who milled around the area.

Hell, I didn't want to go back inside. I didn't think I could take any more of this runaround. But despite Benjamin's odd dress and manners, I sensed he was the top authority in town. I knew he might be the only person with enough information and authority to help me get to the next leg in my quest. Still, I resented the fact that he wouldn't tell me more and ignored me when it suited his purposes.

"Why do they call him Master Benjamin, anyway?" I asked Maxston. "Why don't they call him Mayor Benjamin?"

"Just the way his people speak, so we oblige 'em."

I sighed. I really couldn't afford to miss out on some new information that might help me get home, nor miss out on a chance to catch the wagon train south, if that's what this next meeting would come to. Having nowhere else to turn, I stood up, my stiff legs protesting under me. "Fine," I stated, hobbling toward the building, "but he'd better tell me what's going on. No more of this stuff about me being stuck here forever."

Maxston said nothing. He strode ahead of me and opened the door to the dark reception room. He motioned for me to enter first.

The woman at the desk didn't even bother to get up this time. She shot me a disgusting look as I passed by, like I wasn't worth her effort.

I hoped Benjamin wouldn't be offering me the same sentiment.

Chapter 5

When we entered Benjamin's office, the little man didn't get up from his chair. He didn't even look at us.

Oh, oh, bad news.

Maxston sat down in one of the chairs.

I sat next to him, setting my butt down gingerly on the hard seat. Someone had moved my drink from the chair to the table.

Benjamin's dark eyes looked into mine. An uneasy silence passed between us before he finally said in a polite, humble tone. "Goodman Gavin, hath we not gotten off to a wretched start this day? I ask thy pardon. Allow me to explain to thee more fully about our world and how we work things here."

It's about time, I thought. Still, a part of me felt guilty for blowing up in his face and treating him so rudely, now that he had apologized. "It's okay. I shouldn't have gotten mad, but this whole thing has me a little freaked out."

"'Freaked out'?" Maxston said, shooting me a look of puzzlement. "What ya mean by 'freaked out'?"

"You know...upset...worried."

Benjamin shook his head, like a father who feels hopelessly frustrated with a child. "Thy language, I understand not."

Same here, I thought. As I studied them, I could see they were serious about the term *freaked out*. It shocked me they'd never heard it before. After all, *freaked out* was a common, widely-used phrase. If they were kidding me that they'd never heard it, they managed a great job hiding it. "I thought everybody knew what 'freaked out' means. It's been around a long time."

Maxston said dryly, "Someone from yer time might know of it. Master Benjamin here and I come from earlier times."

I glanced at their strange garbs and began to get an inkling that some important revelation stood before me. "What do you mean? Are you saying you're time-travelers from the past or something?"

"Not so much time-travelers," Maxston responded. "More like trapped in time."

Before I could digest the idea and formulate my next question, Benjamin sat forward in his chair. "Permit this humble servant of the Lord to explain it to thee. This world—our world as we knowest it now—containeth folk from every century since the earliest form of mankind: Cro-Magnon man, or what some folk call 'cave men.' I, myself, came forth from the womb in the Year of Our Lord, 1593. To this world, my transport came in 1625."

I stared at him as the numbers started hitting my brain. "Whoa, wait a minute," I said, holding up my hands. "That would make you over three hundred years old. That's not possible."

"In this world, it be possible," Maxston stated, "but not what ya think. Master Benjamin be in this here world just fifty years."

"That doesn't make sense," I blurted. "It's 2015. That makes Benjamin three hundred and ninety years old."

"This ain't 2015 fer me nor fer Master Benjamin. That be on yer timeline. We be in our own timelines. I be here fer almost forty-four years now. Born in 1758. Came to this world in 1814 when I be fifty-six.."

This was getting almost silly now. "Well, that can't be. How come you still look like you're fifty-six?"

"Knowest we not how this can be," Master Benjamin answered. "Folk age but slowly in this thy new world. Thou willst remain nearly the same from year to year."

I had reached the end of this foolishness. I said sarcastically, "So, if people age that slowly, you're telling me they could live for thousands of years? Is this whole thing some kind of joke. Am I on *Candid Camera*?" I looked around the room for hidden cameras.

The two serious men watched me with a hint of sadness in their eyes, like they pitied me.

Layne Walker

My mind traveled back to the web, to the missing town, to the changed terrain that surrounded Lake Havasu City. Could I have really stepped into a different world? Could it really be possible that others had stepped into it, too, all from different centuries and different cultures? It started to hit me that maybe what Benjamin and Maxston were trying to tell me wasn't all that foolish, that these people were really stuck here in some kind of weird, contorted time structure. From what I'd seen of the town, so far, it could be a merger of people from different times and different places.

If these other people are stuck here as I've been told, then maybe I am stuck here, too. The thought made my knees weak. My head began to spin. I tried to calm my nerves and breathe normally. "Okay, if we are stuck here and it takes forever to age, do people eventually die of old age?"

"We die if we be shot or stabbed," Maxston said forlornly, "or fall down and break our fool necks. From what we seen, nobody dies fer agin'. Like Master Benjamin told ya, we age real slow-like."

The melancholy in Maxston's voice caught me off-guard. I wondered why not dying would be a problem. "If that's true, why do you sound so sad? Everyone is always looking for eternal life. No one wants to die. I would think you would be happy."

"Just longer ta live with yer regrets and yer wishes fer somethin' you ain't got."

I thought about the children I'd seen running around in the streets. "What about the kids who are born here? Certainly, they grow up." I paused to consider the implications. "Or do they stay babies forever?"

"Of great pain to all is such as thou sayest," Benjamin said softly. "No births there be in this world. No new childers come forth from the womb to carry on a man's family name."

Maxston added. "Kids be aging real slow-like, too. Many years pass 'n we see 'em grow up just a might. That be how we know we be growin' older, too. Nobody knows how that can be."

In the midst of all the confusing information, I started seeing these two men in a different way. One wore a pilgrim's garb and the other looked like a mountain man. They weren't play-acting. They had come through the web from their own time periods.

A memory flitted into my mind, something Maxston had said about me looking like a kid, taking my first steps. The old man's face had dramatically changed from a happy taunt to a deep sadness. I wondered now if he wanted children and could never have them, not if this world did not allow children to be born.

"I don't get it," I said, mostly to myself. I sat back in my chair, completely ignoring the pain from the blisters. My perceptions were starting to change, no longer seeing these events as just obstacles to getting home, but something much more, something much bigger. It was no longer just an idea, but I was starting to believe that maybe I did get caught in some kind of web and that other people had gotten caught, too.

My mind tried to grapple with this information and what it ultimately meant. Was it true that I might never get home? No, I just wasn't going to believe that. If I could get into this world, I could get out of it. I just had to find a way to do it.

I thought of Erica. *No, I will not accept the fact I will never see my wife's beautiful face again, that I will never see my children again. I'll put up with my in-laws every day, if I have to, but I won't lose my family. No matter what, I'm going to find a way out.*

Refocusing my attention back into the candle-lit room, I felt grateful that the two men had allowed me silent time to gather my wits and try to put all this into place. Earlier, I had thought all of this was a joke, that there was a simple explanation. Now, I was beginning to feel that my gut feelings had been right from the beginning, from the moment I'd stepped into the web. Something had changed...and changed severely.

As I pulled together the facts that people aged slowly and children weren't born, questions started popping into my mind about other issues in this world. "Okay, so what about

Layne Walker

the animals? I saw cows, pigs, and chickens in town as we were riding in? How do you keep yourselves in meat if they don't reproduce and age?"

Maxston smiled wanly. "Here things get a little tricky."

Benjamin took up the explanation. "Animals seem not to be under the same laws in this world as humankind. In normal cycles, they come forth from the womb, age, and die."

"Somethin' ta do with natural selection," Maxston broke in. "Animals make fer predator or prey. Predators keep the population in balance, so the resta the animals cain't breed and get outta hand."

"Tis smaller this world than thou hath known," Benjamin added.

Maxston sat forward and looked at me directly. "I know it be hard fer ya ta believe, but this here world measures a might five hundred miles by five hundred miles."

All the convincing evidence I'd been gathering in my mind about a different world being real seemed to float away. How could I believe anything they were telling me with this kind of ridiculous information? "Oh, come on," I said disgustedly. "Only five hundred miles across each way. No world could be that small."

"It be true," Maxston said, his blue eyes full of conviction. "Been ta all four edges many a time. Been with the scientists along the coastline. Mapped it out."

"Edges," I guffawed, doubting even the validity of my own growing questions in the middle of all this absurdity, like I was playing along with some kind of unwritten script. "You make it sound like this world is flat."

"It be flat," Maxston stated, giving me a blunt nod of his head to confirm his position. "All four edges. Straight as a ruler. Like someone cut it off with a knife."

"Yeah, right, and if you fall over the edge, do you end up in outer space?"

Benjamin interjected, "Tis the landmass he speaketh of being square. The distance of the ocean, we know not how far it reaches."

40

"Well, then," I said, settling in my seat and feeling justified, "if you don't know what is beyond the oceans, how do you know how big this world really is."

A knock on the door interrupted the meeting. The stoic woman in the long dress opened the door and stuck her head inside. "Master Benjamin, if it's okay with you, I'm going home now."

Benjamin reached under his white collar into a pocket on his shirt. He pulled out a fancy pocket watch on a golden chain. "Oh, God be praised, time hath passeth the mark. Mistress Martha shall be wondering wherefore hath I been." As he put his watch back into his pocket, he said, "Go ahead, Goodwife Gloria. Be it morning that shall I see thee again. Fare thee well, My Good Woman."

Gloria shut the door.

Benjamin stood up. "Pray pardon me, this discussion we must complete tomorrow. Goodman Maxston, shall thou not see to it that Goodman Gavin gets settled into Maria's boardinghouse for the eve? Relay to her that she shall render unto the town's expense account her charge."

I frowned. "Do we have to stop now? Can't we finish-"

"Oh, Gracious Lord, no," Benjamin said brusquely. "Never do we work past five. The Lord askest that we rest and not over-work ourselves in any manner."

Maxston clamped me on the shoulder. "Come. I'm hungry. Let's get ya settled into Maria's place. Then we go eat. I know a place. Best grub in town. My treat." Maxston picked up his rifle, opened the door, and waited for me to get out of my chair.

Frustrated that nothing had been resolved as to how I was to get to South Town, I wanted to stay and argue, but seeing the-meeting-is-over looks on their faces, I knew I had to go along with them.

My hopes to be back home by now, back with Erica and my girls, had been dashed. But what could I do? I let out an aggravated breath and resigned myself to having to spend another night away from my family. I sluggishly stood up and followed them out the door.

I planned to pump Maxston over dinner for more information. New questions kept popping into my mind, and the old ones kept cropping up, too.

How in the hell did I get here? How in the hell did these other people get here if they really did come from different places and different time periods? What is this all about? Is God playing a joke on us?

* * *

Before we left the fort, we led Maxston's horses to a nearby stable.

"Why do they have a stable in the middle of the whole town like this?" I asked. "I would think they'd put it on the outskirts of town, or at least outside the fort, where the smell wouldn't bother anyone."

"It be a government stable. Always kept horses here. Always will."

Sounds like the same idiotic reasoning for everything else happening around here. They just always do it.

Maxston paid two coins to a ragged boy of about twelve years of age to carry his personal effects to the boarding house.

"May I carry yours, too, Sir?" the boy asked me as he hefted Maxston's things on his back.

Politely, I told him, "Thanks, but I would rather keep my pack with me." No way was I going to let anyone touch the last of my personal belongings. I had to keep them with me, too, just in case I popped back into my own world as quickly as I had come into this one. I'd wanted everything I'd come with when I returned home.

As we walked out of the fort gate and into the town, I asked Maxston, "If Benjamin has been here for fifty years, how come he still wears that silly outfit? Wouldn't he want to update himself? Get closer to the times?"

"Funny 'bout people who come to this world. They be staunch about keepin' the customs they brought in."

"How does he keep his clothes so well cared for after all these years? It seems like those pants and shirt would wear out and get ragged. You know, like the clothing of that boy there and a lot of the other people we see around here."

"Not the puritan community. They be neat and clean. Women make new clothin'. Weave the cotton. Live off to 'emsleves in a little place up the hill. Them people keep real clean."

It hadn't occurred to me that people of the same bent would gather together in communities, like ghettos. It made sense that this would be the way to preserve their customs, their language, and the integrity of their beliefs. When I started to ask about other communities in the town, Maxston waved me off, as though he had other things on his mind.

I looked at my cell phone. The battery was dead. So much for that connection. Even if I had my charger, I don't know where I would find an electrical plug to plug it in. I saw no electrical wiring or towers in the area.

As we walked, I watched the boy carry Maxston's load down the street just ahead of us. I couldn't tell what era he might have come from. His ragged clothes made him look like an urchin from the slums of England or maybe New York. I wondered how many years he'd been here and how old he really was. What would it be like to be pre-pubescent for years and years, no longer a child, but taking forever to be a man? As his body aged slowly, would he grow wiser with the years, or stay in the same teenage mindset until he became a man? He didn't seem to be particularly wise. Just an ordinary kid.

I still couldn't get a grip on the idea that all these people were aging so slowly. Nor could I buy the bill of goods that this landmass was only five hundred miles across and had straight edges at the boundaries. I looked at the horizon. With low mountain peaks on all sides of the valley, I couldn't see the curve of the earth. Five hundred miles square meant this world covered about 250,000-square miles. It sounded like a lot until I considered my home state of Arizona covered only 114,000-square miles. That meant this world was about twice the size of Arizona. Not very big, if I were to believe these people.

Maxston called to the boy and waved him on to the boarding house, then grabbed my shoulder and pulled me toward a rinky-dink building. It turned out to be the shabbiest restaurant I'd ever dined in. The walls, made from medium-sized logs, formed crooked angles. The cool evening breeze blew through the cracks and chilled my back as I sat on a bench against one wall. Again, I wished I'd had my lined jacket, now sitting in my truck *somewhere* in another world. Strange, but I was starting to think about this world as a completely different place than my own Earth. The solid ground beneath me seemed the same, but the displacement of what I had known all my life seemed frighteningly different.

For a torturous moment, a deep emotional pain ran though me at the thought of my truck. It made me think of Erica, which made me think of being lost to her. My heart plummeted to the pits. I couldn't function with that thought, so I quickly shook off the grief and turned my attention back to the shoddy dining room with three roughly hewn tables and wooden benches.

The smell of cooked meat and baked bread wafted into the room from the small corner kitchen, which consisted of a large fireplace made of stone, a small sink, and a long serving table. My mouth watered at the smells. I couldn't wait to be served. I was happy to see a fork and a knife sitting next to my plate. I hadn't thought about what to expect about the culture of these strangers.

The cook, an older woman with her hair tied up in a bun and a long apron over her dress, worked industriously to cook the meals and serve the guests. A small boy and girl ran the plates to and from the guest tables. The place looked like a family home that had been converted into a restaurant as a means to make a living.

During the meal, Maxston remained preoccupied and ignored all my questions. I might as well have been eating alone. I finally gave up and concentrated on savoring my food, which consisted of an elk steak, fresh corn, and homemade muffins. Wow, it turned out to be one of the best meals I'd ever eaten. That surprised me no end.

After the meal, Maxston silently led me to the boarding house, a sturdy-looking building with two floors. He purchased a room for each of us.

Before I started upstairs, the old man stammered for the first time since I'd met him. "Um...listen, Gavin...I got someone I need ta go see. You gonna be okay if I leave ya on yer own fer a bit?"

I shrugged. *What the hell? My life is a lousy mess. I could use some time to myself.* "Sure, no problem. I'll find something to do. I might walk around, talk to people, see the town."

He smiled broadly through his thick beard. It seemed like a huge weight had been lifted off his shoulders. "If'n ya get lost, ask anybody how ya get back ta Maria's. Everybody knows Maria's." He shot toward the front door at a good clip, saying, "See ya in the mornin', Son." With that, he disappeared out the door.

I glanced upstairs. Before going to my room and settling down for the night, I decided to take a walk while it was still light. In a way, I liked the idea of being on my own, looking around, seeing what other kinds of strange things this town had to offer. Also, I wanted to test what Maxston and Benjamin had said about people coming into this world from other times and places, and find out what they could tell me that might give me a clue to finding my own way back.

I adjusted my backpack on my back and straightened my glasses. With my gun snug-tight in my holster at my hip, I was ready to face the next challenge.

Chapter 6

I stepped out onto the street and looked around. It felt like I'd stepped back in time two hundred years or more. Most of the women wore home-spun cotton dresses of various soft colors, which probably came from natural plant and mineral dyes. The men, for the most part, wore what looked like simple home-sewn loose pants. A few others wore buckskins, but not as fancy as Maxston's outfit. I noticed many of the men wore guns at their hips or carried rifles. That told me a lot about the neighborhood.

As I walked along the dirt road and peeked into some of the stores, I saw none of the modern conveniences I was used to, like plumbing and electricity. The shops were lit by the natural light coming through windows. On the streets, I saw no automobiles, no telephone poles, no electrical wiring, and certainly no signs of technology like iPods or cell phones.

If Maxston and Benjamin are right, unless I am lucky enough to get killed, I'll be spending not just the rest of my life here, I'll be spending hundreds, maybe thousands of years here. The idea turned my stomach. No, it just wasn't going to happen. Not to me.

I drew curious looks from people as I passed along the road. I suppose my presence was as much an oddity to them as their presence was to me. Plus, I stood quite a bit taller than most of these people.

One couple looked up at me in alarm as I came down their side of the street. They quickly crossed to the other side and avoided me altogether. To those who were friendly, I tipped my hat.

"Hey, pawdner," someone said behind me.

I turned around to see a young cowboy with a big grin on his face. About five-foot-six, he wore a long-sleeved shirt on his back, spurs on his boots, and chaps over his jeans. Wisps of dark stuck out from underneath his dusty cowboy hat. He carried a rope in one hand and a bridle in the other. He looked like he was on his way to a rodeo.

"Y'all must be new 'round here," he said in a strong Texan accent.

I looked down at my modern, factory-sewn clothes. A little dusty, but no patches, no tears. "Is it that obvious?" I said jokingly.

He laughed. "No matter what ya wear, most of us can spot a newbie a mile away. Not that we get many. When we do, ever'body sure knows 'em on sight."

I liked his friendly attitude and the fact he looked more like me with his western clothing, although his were more outdated than mine. The rough whiskers on his face and stocky build made him seem like a rough-and-tumble guy who could meet any challenge. Taking advantage of the opportunity to get some information, I asked, "How long have you been here?"

His hazel eyes beamed. "I was born in the great state a Texas in 1859 and was brought here in 1880 when I was twenty-one. Let me see. I been here...what?...'bout thirty-five years now, I guess." He cocked his head to the side. "Hmmm...don't seem like that long, really."

He didn't look more than twenty-two, twenty-three. "How does that timeline thing work? I don't get it."

"After a while, ya just don't think about it no more. Ain't no one ta explain it."

"Did you come through some kind of web-like thing?"

"Sure did."

"What happened after you got here? Didn't you try to get back home?"

"Hey, yeah, sure. We yall do. But eventually, a man learns he ain't gittin' back, so he settles on in and makes the most of it."

"I don't know if I can do that. I have a wife and three girls back home. I can't just up and forget about them."

His shoulders dropped in response. "Yeah. Know what y'all goin' through. Believe me, I do. I left behind the sweetest woman in all a Texas and the best lookin' newborn baby boy ya ever seen. After all these years, I still remember what they looked like." His voice cracked slightly. He cleared his throat, stood a little straighter, and put on the big grin again. "But, ya cain't dwell on the past. Ya have'ta live in the here-and-now or ya end up like the poor fools livin' on the outskirts a town, goin' ta bed at night and hopin' in the mornin' ya'll can go home agin. Instead, ya wake up to find nothin's changed. Me, I cain't see how a person can live like that ever' day. I know I cain't."

"I don't know," I said, feeling somewhat discouraged by the cowboy's words, which reiterated what I'd already been told. "I'm not ready to admit defeat yet. I heard there's some scientists down in South Town. You know anything about them?"

"Yeah, word gits 'round fast, but ain't nothing ever come of the work of those guys. Not that I know of."

"Well," I said, shifting my feet, "I'm going to South Town in the morning to talk to the scientists down there."

He laughed, then gave me a skeptical look. "How y'all gittin' there? Don'tcha know there ain't no wagon train leavin' fer a bit. Takes time ta get 'em together, ya know." He shook his head. "Nope, won't be one in the mornin', fo' sure."

Well, if the wagon train wasn't available for a few days, I'd find another way. My mind started spinning with possibilities. "Hey, if that's the case," I said, lowering my voice so as not to be overheard by the wary townspeople, "then I could use your help. You know where I could get a couple of good horses and some supplies?"

His hazel eyes seemed amused. "You thinkin' a goin' on yer own, eh? Ya ain't been 'round these here parts long enough to know the territory. Mighty dangerous territory between here'n South Town."

A feeling of defiance rose up in me. No one was going to tell me what I could or couldn't do. "I'll get around it. Now, where do I get horses?"

He put the bridle in his left hand with the rope and used his free hand to rub his chin as he studied the ground. He acted as if I'd asked him to tell me the meaning of life, rather than just answer a simple question about finding horses. When he looked up, he said, "Even if I could help ya get a horse and supplies, I don't think y'all want ta travel ta South Town alone. Far as I know, nobody's ever done it and lived ta tell of it. Come to think of it, nobody's ever been crazy enough to try since I been here."

"All right, then," I said quietly, "why don't you come with me? Then I won't be doing it alone."

His pupils shrank as he eyes widened and stared up at me. He shook his head vigorously. "No, Sir, not me. No way, no how. Nobody ever goin' to get me out there, 'less'n I'm with a wagon train. And only if it be a *big* train with lots a people and lots a purtection."

This tough-looking cowboy didn't seem like the type who'd be scared to travel outside the city by himself. I wondered what he wasn't telling me. "So, what's out there?" I asked. "What's got everybody so scared?"

His eyes softened a little. He rubbed his chin again. "I see. Nobody told y'all what's out there."

"Not really. I get the idea it's dangerous, but that's all."

"Well, let me be the one ta tell ya. It ain't purty roses you be seein'."

Several people came down the street and were stepping around us.

After they passed, the cowboy leaned closer to me and said, "Thar's all kinds a beasts out there: mammoths, saber-tooth tigers, dire wolfs-"

"Whoa, hold on," I said, wondering if he expected me to laugh at his fairytale. "Mammoths and saber-tooth tigers? Those animals lived thousands of years ago. They're extinct."

"We even got us some dinosaurs," he added soberly, watching for my reaction.

I didn't know whether or not to believe the man. I'd been seeing and hearing a lot of weird things, but *dinosaurs*?

I studied the cowboy again. Was he keeping back the true reason why he and everyone else didn't want me to go to South Town? No matter what, there had to be a way to get to the town. I wasn't going to let any tall tales scare me and keep me from getting back to my family. I certainly wasn't going to stay in North Town the rest of my life. "I don't care what's out there," I said intently. "I need a couple of horses and enough supplies to get me to South Town. Are you going to tell me where to get them or not?"

He slowly, purposely shook his head. "No, Sir, I ain't. I cain't. I won't be responsible for sendin' y'all ta certain death."

Aggravated, I looked around. The townspeople had started thinning out. The sun would be setting in a little bit.

I felt exhausted. The stiffness in my legs and the blisters on my butt became all too apparent again. I didn't want any more trouble. I just wanted to get a good night's sleep and get on my way. I turned back to the cowboy. "Do me a favor, would you? I don't want anyone to know what I'm up to. People around here don't seem to understand what I need to do. Could you keep this quiet?"

He held his lips tightly together and said nothing. He turned and walked away, shaking his head as if I were the crazy one.

I watched him saunter down the street. I hoped he could keep his mouth shut. If word got back to Master Benjamin that I was inquiring about horses for a trip southward, I'm sure he would come down hard on me and try to stop me. And who knew what kind of laws or punishments these people had for those who stepped out of line. Would they burn me at the stake like the puritans did with their own people who were convicted of being witches? The thought gave me the chills. One thing was sure, if nothing else, the last thing I needed to do was get thrown in jail.

I looked down at myself, dusty with grime. It was time for a hot shower and a soft bed. It seemed like days had passed since my last shower. I was pretty sure I was starting to stink, just like the other people around here.

Then it hit me. *These people probably don't have showers. Heck, they probably don't even have indoor toilets.* The thought made me realize I hadn't brought any personal toilet articles with me. I wondered if I could buy such luxuries as a toothbrush, toothpaste, or deodorant in one of these shops.

Spinning sharply on my heels to check out some shops, I ran smack into a blond-haired woman, one of the most beautiful women I'd ever seen. I grabbed her shoulders to help her keep her balance. Seeing her embarrassment at my touch, I quickly let go.

Shockingly, this young woman looked like the spitting image of Erica when I'd first met her in college: blond hair, big baby-blue eyes, skin the color of ivory. The young woman before me wore a small red scarf over her hair to hold back her long wavy tresses. A treat to the eyes, this girl even smelled pleasant, like she'd been baking pies or something. She smelled...well...*homey*.

"Excuse me, Kind Sir," she said with her eyes down as she backed up a little and blushed. She seemed to be purposely avoiding direct eye-contact with me.

"No, pardon me, Miss," I said, tipping my hat like a gentlemanly cowboy. "I should've been watching where I was going."

My eyes ran down her body, not to check out her figure or anything like that, but just to see what she was wearing. Her homemade white blouse, gathered slightly at the low neckline, exposed her bare shoulders. Long, flowing sleeves draped gracefully down her slender arms. The gathered red material of her skirt fell neatly to the ground. Around her middle, she wore a black bodice with a cross-corded, lace-up front that nicely emphasized her youthful breasts. She reminded me of the costumed waitresses Erica and I had seen during the Oktoberfest celebration the previous year in Lake Havasu City. This girl's clothing, however, looked more authentic, like the real deal. If I had to guess, I'd say she'd come from a period around 1700. She reminded me of what I pictured a German milkmaid might look like.

Her uncanny likeness to Erica stirred a desire in me I hadn't felt since I'd met my wife twelve years earlier. I took a deep breath and tried to push those thoughts aside. "Allow me to introduce myself," I said, fumbling to tip my hat again and hoping to keep her from running off. It was starting to get dark, and I imagined she would be on her way home. "I'm Gavin-"

Still not looking me in the eye, she erupted with, "Vhat you are, Sir, is *rude*." She walked around me, her back now stiff with anger as she continued down the street.

I ran to place myself in front of her to make her stop. "I'm sorry, Miss. I'm not from around here. I don't know the rules...at least not yet. Please," I pleaded, "forgive me?" I didn't know why the hell I felt the need to please her, but I did.

A tall, big-boned woman in a long green skirt and gathered white top rushed to the young girl's side. She took the girl's shoulders and marched her a few feet away from me. She turned and bellowed at me, "Agggh! Vhy do you talk to my daughter zeez vay? Haff you no manners?"

"I was just trying to be friendly," I said, taking off my hat to show respect to the red-faced, angry mother. Clearly, the daughter resembled the woman's fine skin, light-colored hair, and blue eyes. The girl, however, stood a few inches shorter than her mother and had a much more delicate frame.

"If you vish to talk to my daughter, you must haff present her papa or me. And only if she vishes to talk to you."

"I see," I said, considering that the opportunity to get to know this girl had presented itself at the moment, and I had better hurry up and take it. "So, may I talk to her now, since you're here with us?"

The mother leaned over to her daughter and whispered something in the daughter's ear, probably asking the girl if she wanted to talk to me.

I waited pensively, my fingers fidgeting with my hat in my hands.

Finally, the girl nodded to her mother and looked directly into my eyes. She gave me a shy smile.

I thought my knees would buckle. I'm not sure I'd ever felt as attracted to Erica as I was now to this girl. She mesmerized me with her perfectly sculpted face and big blue eyes. She had to be what? Twenty, twenty-one years old? I told myself my reaction stemmed from missing Erica and wanting to go back home to her.

The mother crossed her arms over her considerable bosom and glared at me. "You may speak. One minute only. Eez dark and vee must go home soon."

I was pretty sure if I touched her daughter, the mother would tear me from limb to limb and feed me to the dogs.

The mother continued. "I am Gretchen Jorgensen. Zeez my daughter, Hannah. Now, you haff been properly introduced. You may speak to her." She tightened her lips as she glared at me and waited for me to make my statement.

I turned to Hannah, took a step forward so I wasn't so far from her, and cleared my throat. "As I started to say earlier, I'm Gavin Clark. It's a pleasure to meet you." Feeling like an idiot, I bowed from the waist as though that was expected of me.

Hannah added a little curtsy of her own. "I'm pleased to make your acquaintance, Mr. Clark." She seemed to have less of an accent than her mother. A hint of mischief sparkled in her eyes. Something told me she was up to something.

Now that I had permission to talk to her, I found myself at a loss for words. I wondered it if was because she looked so much like Erica, or because her robust mother, still glaring at me, stood next to her. Of course, I understood I was a stranger in this world and her mother would be wary of someone talking to her daughter. Because I didn't know the rules of this society, I didn't know what would be proper to ask or say. I feared being too forward or making her angry. Instead, I stood towering over her like a dummy.

Hannah came to my rescue. "You are new here?"

I nodded. "Yes, I am. I just got here today."

"And from vhere do you come?"

I pondered this a moment. I wasn't exactly sure what she wanted to know: my city, my state, my country, my planet?

Seeming to intuitively sense my confusion, she asked another question. "From vhat time period do you come?"

"Oh...um...2015."

Her face lit up like a kid on Christmas morning. She clapped her hands together. "Tell me. Oh, please, tell me about your vorld."

Her mother huffed in exasperation. She grabbed Hannah's arm. "If that eez all you haff to speak about, you do it later. Eez getting dark. Vee must go home." She started pulling Hannah away from me.

Hannah stomped her foot in the dirt. "Mama, I just want to know a little about his vorld. I vahnt to know if he is *the one*."

"Vizzout knowing about his vorld," Gretchen said, "you vill know if he *zee one.*"

Puzzled by their words, I looked from one to the other and continued fiddling with my hat.

"May he come to the house tomorrow night for a visit, Mama?" Hannah asked with a pleading look. She gripped her hands together and held them at her chest in a prayerful manner. "Please, please, please."

It gave me pleasure that Hannah wanted to see me so badly. I decided to keep my mouth shut to see where the conversation would go.

Gretchen glanced from Hannah to me, her mind appearing to race a hundred miles an hour. "Vee must haff Papa's permission. And you know Papa hates people from zee future times."

Hannah continued in her pleading tone. "I know, Mama, but I feel positive he's *the one*. Papa can meet him tomorrow and talk to him. He can find out for sure."

Although I had no idea what they meant by *the one*, I picked up a bad vibe that they were referring to me. I began to fear I was getting into something that might not be all that easy to extract myself from.

A team of men moved down the street along the front of the buildings and lit lamps that I assumed were burning kerosene or some similar oil. The streets were clearing out. Shop owners started closing up their doors. It was getting dark.

Gretchen nodded her agreement to Hannah, who squealed in joy and turned to face me. "Tomorrow. Go out of town to the north. Two miles out of town you vill find a large building standing by itself. This is vhere Papa works. Go in and ask his permission to come to dinner tomorrow night and to visit vith me." Her excitement bubbled over into a little dance in the street.

I couldn't help but smile. "Okay," I said. "I'll go talk to your father, but only because I need a *friend*, not because I want to date you or anything like that." I had no idea why I was agreeing to see her father. Maybe because she seemed so happy about me visiting her home, and I didn't want to see her hurt or disappointed.

She giggled. Tipping her head to the side, she looked at me from the corner of her eyes. "If Papa approves of you, vee can speak more about that tomorrow night." She cheerfully turned and took Gretchen's arm in hers. Together they hurried away.

A shiver came over me. What had just happened? Did I get myself caught up in something that would have dire consequences later?

Even though Hannah looked amazingly like Erica when I'd first met Erica years ago, I knew this wonderful girl that had just stood before me wasn't my wife and never would be. I had to admit I was attracted to her charm and her beauty, but I had always been true to Erica and I intended to do everything in my power to stay that way. Were I to stay in North Town—which wasn't going to happen—I liked the idea of building a friendship with Hannah. She seemed like a wholesome person who would be a good friend.

As I stood watching mother and daughter disappear out of sight, I wondered how Hannah would react tomorrow when I didn't show up to talk to her father. I did feel a little guilty, lying to her like I did, but she'd get over it in time. It wasn't like I'd promised to marry her or anything. Besides, after meeting with Master Benjamin and Maxston in the morning, I planned to leave for South Town. I'd probably never see her again.

I put on my hat and headed down the dusty street to the boarding house for a good night's sleep and anticipation of getting out of town soon.

Chapter 7

The next morning, a few hours after sunrise, I sat on the bench outside the building of Master Benjamin's office. With my backpack safely next to me, I crossed my arms over my chest to keep warm. My long-sleeved shirt wasn't enough to keep off the chill. My butt was still sore this morning, but my legs worked fine. The stubble on my chin itched. I needed a shave.

I'd slept restlessly, what little sleep I could get in the tiny, stark room of the boarding house. The thin floor creaked when I'd roll over on the narrow straw mat lying directly on the floor. Between the folds of a thick woolen blanket, I'd managed to barely keep warm enough. Other than a small bench to sit on, the room contained only a candle and smelly chamber pot. It was like rooming in a monk's cell.

As Master Benjamin approached in a black top hat with a big buckle in the middle that matched the buckles on his shoes, I stood up and grabbed my backpack.

Maxston hadn't yet made an appearance. I figured he'd had a late night. It didn't take a stretch of imagination to know he'd gone to see a lady friend last night. For all I knew, he'd never come back to his room at the boarding house. I'd just bet that he hadn't come in.

As I entered the building behind Benjamin, I was dying for a cup of coffee. The place we'd eaten dinner the night before hadn't opened yet. Neither had any stores or shops along my path. Although I had a few twenties in my wallet, I didn't know what kind of currency these people used. I wasn't sure if I were allowed to charge everything to the town's account. I should have thought to ask Maxston before he'd run off the night before, but it hadn't crossed my mind.

Benjamin led me to his back office in silence. Fresh candles burned in the hallway. Someone must have gotten up early to light them. I didn't see anyone else around, not even the grouchy receptionist.

Inside the office, Benjamin motioned for me to sit across from him at the table. I sat down gingerly, still babying the blisters. While Benjamin had seemed so confident and steady the day before, this morning he fidgeted with papers and files on his desk. Something was on his mind, and I wasn't sure I wanted to hear it.

Finally, he said, " Goodman Gavin, I hear tell of thy inquiry to gather horses and supplies for a trip to South Town." With his words out on the table, he now frowned at me with a disapproving look.

Oh, hell, what do I say now? No use denying it. "Yeah," I said, starting to grow annoyed at the man's implication that I couldn't do as I pleased. "I told you yesterday, I was going to go, no matter what I had to do to get there." I folded my arms across my chest in a defiant stance. I decided he wasn't going to bully me today. Despite the restless night, a little distance from the disturbing events of the previous day gave me more confidence.

He glared at me with his little black eyes.

A knock came at the door. Maxston stepped into the room and nodded a greeting to Master Benjamin. *Goodwife Gloria* followed him into the room with an old-fashioned percolating metal coffee pot, three tin cups, and wooden containers of cream and sugar, all sitting on a metal tray. The smell of freshly perked coffee filled the room and made my mouth water. The woman set down the tray and poured coffee into all three cups.

Not shy about being the first one to grab a steaming cup, I quickly fixed it with sugar and cream, then I sat back and took the first sip. *Ah...heaven.*

Maxston leaned his ever-present rifle against the wall next to the door. He didn't say a word. Just stood against the wall and watched us.

I had a strong feeling he'd also heard about what I'd been up to. That made me angry, too, but I didn't care. I was a free citizen, wasn't I? After just one night, I'd already grown tired of being in this decrepit town. What did I have going for me here, anyway? This wasn't my home. I could do whatever I pleased. And certainly, I was going to do whatever it took to get back to my home, even if people got pissed off. I took another sip of coffee and set my cup firmly down on the table. "Okay, here's the deal."

I stood up to make myself more imposing. With the hasty move, I winced slightly at the sting from my popped blisters. "Like I told you last night, I want to go to South Town to see these scientists. Now, I can go on this wagon train you told me about, or I'll find some other way to get there, but whether or not you like it, I'm going. One way or another." I looked from Benjamin to Maxston. "So what's it going to be? Are you going to help me get there or not?"

They glanced at each other for a long moment, seeming to make some kind of silent communication. Maxston's blue eyes remained non-committal from what I could see.

Benjamin looked up at me and stated, "As Mayor of North Town, tis my responsibility for the welfare of all townsfolk. Nay, would I not be guilty of negligence before the Lord should I allow thee, a newly arrived citizen, who knows not of what he speaks, to partake in such an activity that endangers his welfare?"

My hands tightened into fist as my anger rose. I narrowed my eyes on the scrawny little man. "I'm not sure, but if I'm understanding you correctly, you're saying you won't let me go to South Town. Is that right?" I clenched my teeth, forcing myself to stay calm for fear I'd lose it again. Still, I could feel the explosive tension growing in my gut.

"Thou be correct, Goodman Gavin," Master Benjamin said firmly, his eyes hard. He placed his hands flat on the table and stood up. Ignoring the fact that I towered over him by a foot, he leaned forward on the table as though daring me to disobey him.

From the side of the room, Maxston guffawed. "That be a bunch a malarkey if ever I heard any. Yer just bein' pig-headed and stubborn, and ya know it."

Shocked by the force in Maxston's voice and words, I broke eye contact with Benjamin and looked at the old man.

He stepped forward, glaring down at Benjamin. "If'n ya wanted to, ya could get him on the next wagon train. Yer just afeared the town council gonna give ya a hard time about lettin' him go."

I swallowed silently, pleased to see Maxston come to my defense. I decided it would be wise to keep my mouth shut and wait to see how far he'd go for me.

Benjamin now stared hard at Maxston and looked, for all I could tell, like he was going to argue with the stocky man. Finally, Benjamin's body relaxed. His face loosened. He sat down at the table and conceded with his words. "Right thoust be, My Good Man."

Even though the tension in the air quickly dissipated, I decided to remain standing to protect my sore butt. Maxston remained on his feet next to me.

Benjamin spoke to Maxston in a softened voice. "Alloweth him on the next train? Yay, such falls within my authority. I fear the town council, however, maketh plans for him. Thou must know, every healthful man carrieth value in North Town. Goodman Gavin tis of sturdy body. He hath talents that shall be of great service to the welfare of our townsfolk. Thou must know, too, we lose well too many strong men to the village of South Town. Must we lose another?" He stared at Maxston and waited for an answer.

Confused by this information, I, too, looked to Maxston and waited for an explanation. It sounded like everyone wanted to go to South Town.

"South Town be ten times as large as North Town," he said to me. "Much more advanced. Indoor plumbing. A phone system, too. Limited mind you, from what I hear of yer times. And, if a man can afford it, they got electricity."

"Yay," Benjamin said in a sad, wishful tone, "South Town renders a man more quality and diverse opportunities."

I wondered if Benjamin preferred to live in South Town, too, but somehow got stuck in this town. Or, maybe he preferred this place with his own community, but resented the fact all the good help went south. I didn't think this was the time to bring up such a question. I made a mental note to ask Maxston about it later. Right now, I was more concerned with getting Benjamin to agree to let me go on the next wagon trip. I could only hope the cowboy I'd talked to last night was wrong about how long it took to get the wagon train together.

Maxston spoke again. "I be buyin' passage fer him, if that's what it takes."

Benjamin jerked his head toward the older man as if he'd been slapped. "Wouldst thou go so far? Pray tell, thou knoweth the cost of coin for such passage?"

"Of course, I know the cost," Maxston bellowed. "I even be willin' ta pay double." He lowered his voice to a more soothing tone. "Unlike you, Master Benjamin, I can see how much it means ta my friend Gavin ta go. Cain't you see he's goin' one way or another? I'd rather help him make the journey than have him go on his own. Plus," he added timidly, "I kinda feel responsible for him. I'm the one brought him here in the first place."

Benjamin pursed his lips, his fingers tightly intertwined in a hold on the table in front of him. As though lost in his own thoughts, he stared into space and shook his head slowly, back and forth. "Pray tell, no matter what decision I declare, tis a problem for me still." He chewed on his lower lip.

I squirmed in anticipation of his decision, fearing that I would continue to be given a hard time, maybe even be thrown into jail without Benjamin's approval that I could leave.

Maxston chuckled.

Both Benjamin and I shot a look at him.

The old man grinned. "By the way, I signed up last night ta be the wagon master of the upcomin' train. Asked the Minister of Trade ta take along an extra man of my choosin'. A man ta help with camp chores 'n all. He be agreein' with me."

For a long moment, Benjamin stared at Maxston as though digesting the information. I got the idea that the Minister of Trade had more power than the mayor.

Finally, Benjamin let out a big sigh and glanced back at me with defeat in his eyes and his voice. "So be it," he said dryly. "As a worker on the wagon train, Goodman Gavin may go. Tis up to thee, Goodman Maxston, that I pronounce the duty for procuring this gentleman a job on the wagon train. Praise the Lord, thou willst find him a *real* job, as say the newcomers from his world. Let not his duties be merely an easy task, completed in but a short time each day. And I pronounce to thee, too, that he shall work in North Town to the very day the wagon train leaves."

"So be it," Maxston said with a slight bow to the little man. He turned to me with an amused grin playing on his lips. "Come, Gavin. Don't know 'bout you, but I'm hungrier than a newborn colt."

To show my gratitude, I held out my hand to Benjamin. "I want to thank you for allowing me to go to South Town with the next wagon train. I get a feeling you're going to take a lot of crap over it."

Master Benjamin laughed for the first time, his beady eyes twinkling. "Strange sayings hath thou." He stood up and took my hand. "Worry not about my responsibilities. As thou sayeth, 'taking crap' tis much of my duty. Now, off with thee. Official tasks I haveth at hand." He waved us off with his bony little hand. "Fare thee well."

* * *

As I stepped outside with Maxston, it felt as though the weight of the world had been lifted off my shoulders about getting out of town.

I wondered about the political structure of South Town. "Who's in charge of South Town?" I asked Maxston. "Is it the mayor or the Minister of Trade?"

"They be puppet heads," he said dryly. "Scientists run South Town. Nobody bucks 'em. They be telling everybody what ta do. Make the rules."

"How is that?"

"Got the brains fer it. Know how to fool the rest a us. They be runnin' North Town here, too. Appoint the mayor and Minister of Trade. We be lucky our leaders be more amenable, if ya know what I mean."

I studied him. "You sound pretty bitter."

"It be the way it is." He headed toward the fort exit. As an afterthought, he added. "Man in South Town ya want to see be Howard Blackman. Head scientist. He be runnin' the show. Don't like the guy."

"Why not?"

"Just the way it be." His tone told me that was the end of that topic.

Well, if the head scientist was in charge of the towns, it seemed all the more reason for him to know what was going on. Thus, it was all the more reason for me to talk to him. As I moved quickly to stay up with Maxston, I asked, "So, when does this wagon train leave?"

He stopped. "Hmmm. This day's the fourteenth. Just over three weeks, I'm thinkin'."

"Three weeks?" I roared. "I can't wait three weeks. My wife's got to be out of her mind over my disappearance. They'll think I'm dead if I don't show up for weeks or months. Isn't there any way to leave sooner? Can we talk to the Minister of Trade or something?"

"Wagon train won't be ready 'til it be ready."

I could just imagine that long wagon trains had to be well-organized ordeals and, of course, dependent on someone being in control. My mind went back to toying with other possibilities about getting to South Town more quickly.

"'Sides," Maxston said, slapping me on the back in a jollier mood, "from what I hear, yer gonna be mighty busy keepin' Miss Hannah company fer the next couple a weeks." He wiggled his eyebrows and grinned at me.

Annoyed with his presumption, I jumped on the defensive. "I was just looking for a friend. I've got this feeling I'm going to need all the friends I can get in this world." I dared not tell him, if it came down to it, I'd abandon him in a heartbeat, just as quickly as Hannah, should I find a way to get myself to South Town faster than the upcoming wagon train.

"Whatever ya say," he said, giving me a wink. "I used ta be *just friends* with a couple a women myself, but that be a long time ago."

Preferring not to get into the topic of his love life, I remained quiet until we reached the diner where we'd eaten dinner the previous night. During the meal, it seemed neither one of us had much to say, other than make a few comments on the delicious food.

As we left the place, Maxston said, "I got me some things I need ta do. You be okay on yer own now?"

It surprised me how this old man wearing buckskins and hanging bird feathers from his hair seemed to really care about me and take seriously his responsibility for my presence in town. I couldn't be sure if he wanted to reassure himself that I wasn't a totally lost soul, or if he were just concerned I would cause problems with my inexperience in this new world. "I appreciate you getting me off the hook with Master Benjamin," I said. "I'm fine on my own. I'll try to keep out of trouble."

He gave me a wan smile.

I looked around the streets, busy with people walking alone or together in groups, going in and out of the shops. The smell of cooking meat from the diner helped to cover some of the stink in the air. Or, maybe I was just getting used to it. "Since it looks like I'm going to be here for a few days, I think I just might head out of town and talk to Hannah's father."

The humor went out of Maxston's blue eyes. He leaned toward me and whispered. "I know the man. You watch yerself. He can be a might touchy when it comes to talkin' 'bout his daughter."

I laughed. "Don't worry. I can take care of myself."

"Ya want me ta arrange a horse for ya?"

"No thanks, I think I'd rather walk. My backside isn't ready to sit on a horse so soon."

"Here, ya might need ta buy somethin', like a shave." He winked and handed me a few coins. "That should tide ya over fer a couple a days."

"Thanks, Maxston, I appreciate it," I said feeling moved that this man whom I'd only known for one day was being so generous towards me.

After he gave me detailed instructions on how to find Hannah's father, we parted ways.

While a part of me grew excited about seeing beautiful Hannah again, I hoped I wasn't getting myself into something I might later wish I'd left alone. I intended for us to simply be friends. And I intended to find a way to get to South Town as soon as possible.

Well, I have nothing else to do right now. I might as well meet Hannah's father and see what he has to say. Maybe I can get answers from him about how to get back home.

Chapter 8

It amazed me how fast I learned to navigate my way around the winding streets. Within a half-hour, I passed the stinking outlaying shanties and headed down a two-wheeled dirt track. According to Maxston, I had two miles more to go. Being in no hurry, I took my time. My hiking shoes would have been more comfortable for the walk than my boots, but my good hiking shoes sat in a closet in another world.

Just like my backpack with my keys, wallet, and cell phone, I kept my gun with me at all times. In this strange land, I never knew when I might need it to protect myself. Right now, I wore my shirt out to cover the gun. That way, it was out of sight, not threatening anyone. Plus, I wasn't sure how Hannah's father would take it if he saw me packing a gun.

The sun warmed my skin and shirt as I sauntered down the empty path. I'd gotten lucky as far as the weather getting warm in the daytime. The temperature had to have moved into the mid-seventies. A slight breeze blew out of the west. Perfect weather for a walk.

The country surrounding North Town consisted mostly of gently rolling hills covered with cultivated gardens and long rows of vegetables. I recognized lettuce and corn and cabbage. A number of fields contained cotton, probably to keep the townspeople in clothing. A number of people worked in the fields. I crossed a wooden bridge spanning the river where it narrowed to make a turn. The river flowed slowly, and I had the feeling it was fairly deep.

The further I got from town, the more I began to see randomly scattered clumps of trees, appearing like islands rising out of a sea of waving grass. I recognized pines and quaking aspens. Others might have been birch trees. I saw no animals, large or small. The people living on the outskirts of town had probably hunted most of the nearby fauna for food.

It'd been over twenty-four hours since I'd last brushed my teeth. My mouth felt like I had moss growing in it. Finding the feeling increasingly annoying, I stopped to break a small twig off a tree. I pounded the broken end with a rock to make a frayed edge. I rubbed the make-shift brush over my teeth and tongue. It didn't do the job of a toothbrush, but my mouth felt fresher.

Before I knew it, I'd come up over a hill and saw a large square-cut-log building in the valley below me. A small creek ran next to the building and along one corner of a pole corral, which held a single horse. This had to be the barn where I would meet Hannah's father.

As I made my way closer, I studied the building in more detail. It stood maybe thirty feet wide and roughly fifty or sixty feet long. Wood shingles covered the roof. The building had no windows that I could see, but large doors on the front and back stood open, allowing light to enter and fresh air to circulate.

When I came within a few hundred feet of the building, the wind changed direction. A sickening, putrid smell assaulted my nose. Something had died and was rotting. I covered my nose and tried breathing through my mouth, but I could still smell the stench. If I could pick it up this far away from the barn, I couldn't imagine how bad it would be inside the place.

Nobody had mentioned what Hannah's father did for a living, and I hadn't thought to ask. Hopefully, I wasn't going to be here long, just long enough to ask him if I could be friends with his daughter.

I almost gagged as I reached the open door. I had to force myself to step inside and look around. I kept my hand over my nose and mouth.

Six huge round wooden tubs, each four feet high, sat in the middle of the floor. Some contained water. Hung along the log-formed walls were round frames holding animal hides. It didn't take long for me to realize this was a tannery.

With the horrendous odor, it made sense to me that such a place would have to sit so far out of town.

In the middle of the barn, a man knelt on the ground with his back to me. Not wanting to scare him by walking up behind him with no warning, I reached out and knocked loudly against the door.

He glanced up at me and yelled, "Yah! Vhat you vahnt?"

I kept my hand over my nose as I walked toward him. "I was wondering if I could talk to you for a minute."

The knot in his thick dark brow seemed to overshadow his whole face, like he was a busy man in the middle of something important.

"I want to talk to you about your daughter, Hannah."

With those words, he stood up and his puny body stormed toward me with his fists tight at his sides. His eyes filled with rage. I swore I could see steam coming out of his ears. "Agggh! Yore the scoundrel bozzering my dear, sweet Hannah yesterday." He stopped barely two feet from me and placed his fists on his hips. Sticking out his chest, he stood as tall as he could manage and looked up at me with his demanding brown eyes. He couldn't have been more than five-foot-two or three, skinny as a rail. He wore dark britches with suspenders. He reminded me of an adolescent kid. I didn't know why Maxston had seemed so worried about me meeting this man. With no trouble at all, I could beat this guy up.

His brave show of prowess almost made me laugh out loud. I bit my tongue and tried to be polite. "I apologize if that's what you think, but I was merely trying to be friendly. I'm new to this world, you must know. I'm still trying to adjust. I'm sorry if I offended you or her in any way."

He kept his glower on me and shifted from foot to foot. He seemed to be full of nervous energy. "Vhy you haff to pick her out of all vimmen in town?"

The stench of the place made me want to vomit. "Could we, by chance, step outside to talk about this?" I asked, trying to bear the smell without pinching my nose.

Still holding his fists on his hips, he turned and stomped toward the open back door, where the breeze would help the smell blow away from us. I could see his feisty body easing up a little, like the change of subject took the fire out of his act.

Outside the barn, the odor became more bearable, barely. At least, we could get on with the conversation.

He kept his glare on me. "Now, vhat you gotta say for yoreself?"

I shrugged. "Well, meeting your daughter was an accident, really. I turned around after talking to a cowboy and bumped into her. I didn't know anyone was standing so close to me." It suddenly dawned on me that no one else on the street would come that close to me, but Hannah had suddenly stood in my space, as though on purpose. The idea that the meeting might not have been such an accident suddenly crossed my mind.

"Yah," the little man said, still trying to act tough, "so my Hannah and her mama claim."

"I assure you, sir, my intentions are completely honorable." I found it bizarre that I was standing outside a stinking tannery, in a world that wasn't mine, and talking like an English nobleman to a German father about my intentions toward his daughter. *What the hell am I doing?* I had to close my eyes for a moment, reminding myself I would be leaving for South Town as soon as possible and would never see Hannah or her father again.

"Vhat your intentions?"

"I would like to be her friend...nothing more," I responded. "I'm going to South Town in a few weeks to talk to the head scientist. I'm hoping he will help me get back home to my own world where I have a family. I love and miss them very much."

He harrumphed and shook his head, relaxing a little and giving up his show of trying to intimidate me. "You new here, yah?" He chuckled and looked at the ground. He quietly talked to himself as he rubbed his thin head of hair. "Silly fool. Zinks he can go home. Vouldn't that be nice? As eef nobody else has tried to go home." He jerked his head back up toward me. "Bet you zink you special, yah? Zink we stupid. Haffn't tried every-zing to get back home?"

I didn't like where the conversation was going, nor did I like stalling here outside the meat-rotting barn. "Getting back to your daughter?"

His eyes blinked. "Yah, yah." The scowl returned to his face as he said bitterly, "Supposed to invite you to house for supper tonight...at six." Obviously, he'd been *ordered* to make the invitation, maybe by his wife, or maybe by Hannah, or maybe by both.

I wondered how this skinny little man fared with his tall, husky wife and his clever, determined daughter. "By the way," I said, holding out my hand, "I'm Gavin Clark."

"Sven Jorgensen. Can't say eez my pleasure to meet you, due to zee circumstances."

I just smiled. What could I say? If I had been in his position, I'd probably feel the same way.

As the breeze changed again, the smell became more unbearable. It was making me sick to my stomach and I didn't want to lose my breakfast. "I'll be at your house at six," I said, then turned away and quickly fled to find some fresh air.

On the way back to town, the stink of the tannery clung to my clothing. I definitely needed a bath and a way to wash my clothes before I showed up for dinner at Hannah's house, which Maxston had told me was in the German section of town, only two blocks from the boarding house. I couldn't very well show up for my first friendship date smelling like week-old road-kill.

* * *

Promptly at six, I arrived at Hannah's house. The modest one-story home, built of heavy logs, stood by itself. The front yard overflowed with fragrant flowers. Around the side of the house, I could see signs of a vegetable garden.

I'd managed to take a good sponge bath in my room while airing out my shirt and jeans. Thanks to the barber, who splashed a little aftershave on my cheeks after he'd scraped off the two-day growth of whiskers on my face, I was smelling good, about as spit-and-polished as I would ever be under these conditions.

I found myself taking off my hat when I entered the house. In my world, men wore hats indoors and outdoors, but something told me that courtesy required the removal of a man's hat in someone else's house here, so I obliged my gut feelings and carried my hat in my hands until I saw a hook on the wall with other hats. There, I stuck my hat for the time being.

At dinner, Sven and Gretchen remained cordial in their attitudes toward me, but nothing more than that. For the most part, they seemed to pretend like I wasn't there, but I caught their discreetly watchful eyes on occasion.

Hannah sat next to me at the table. Her blue eyes danced. She smiled when she passed me the food.

On the other side of me sat her older sister, a homely-looking girl who took after her mother in build and temperament. She sat hunched over her food, never looking at me.

Across the table sat Hannah's two younger towheaded brothers. The youngest boy had talked to me briefly before dinner. Now that we had been seated, nobody said a word through the whole meal, unless someone asked for something to be passed.

Coming from a society that communicated verbally almost continuously, I found the silence during dinner difficult. At first, I wondered if the silence had something to do with me, but when I'd opened my mouth to ask a question, Hannah had quickly put a hand on my arm and lightly shook her head, telling me not to speak.

I also found it hard to eat slowly. The whole family seemed to take their time at eating, starting with the long German prayer over the food, the slow process of selecting the food and putting it on the plates, the waiting for everyone to be served before eating, and the slow movement of the food going from plate to mouth. It took me a few moments to catch on to each of these phases and fall into line. I could have completed the whole meal in ten minutes if it had not been for the scathing looks of Sven when I picked up my fork at the wrong time, or when I started gobbling down the tender lamb and potatoes that I had placed on my plate. Doing my best, I still finished before everyone else by at least five minutes.

After everyone finished the main meal, Hannah's mother served us each a slice of pumpkin pie with a creamy sauce on top. I savored the delicious flavors. I had to admit the food in this world put the food in my world to shame. These people had no preservatives, chemicals, or man-made substances to add to the food. Everything came directly from nature.

Once dinner was done, Sven and Gretchen directed the other children to clean up, then retired to the front porch with Hannah and me in tow.

Great, I thought nervously, plucking my cowboy hat off the hook as I walked out the door. *Are they going to sit right next to us and listen to everything we say to each other?*

As it turned out, they sat on a couple of handmade chairs at one end of the wooden porch, while Hannah took my hand and led me to the other end. We were still being supervised, but we had some privacy to speak to each other.

Our end of the porch held a cozy-looking wooden swing that someone had attached with strips of leather to a bar in the overhead roof. Next to the swing sat two chairs made of small diameter logs about two inches around. Strips of leather bound the logs together. Old flour sacks, filled with hay or straw, made pads on the seating areas.

Not wanting to be too forward, I sat on one of the wooden chairs with my hat in my hand.

Hannah sat on the swing. "Vhy are you sitting clear over there?" she said coyly, patting the seat next to her. "Come over here vhere ve can get to know each other better." She batted her long eyelashes at me.

Her blatant flirting and assertive manner gave me the willies. I could see that I'd made a big mistake coming here. Obviously, she wanted to be more than a friend. She was looking for a husband.

I'm sure I'd sensed that from the beginning, which was why I'd distinctly told her the previous night that I didn't want to date her, that I just wanted to be friends. I could see that she hadn't taken me seriously, and maybe I hadn't taken it seriously enough either. Not only did I intend to get back to my own world as soon as possible, but I intended to be faithful to my own wife. *So, what*, I asked myself, *am I doing here? Why the hell did I agree to talk to her father and then come over here for dinner?*

"I'm fine over here," I said, still holding my hat in my hand like a gentleman and kicking myself for getting involved, for showing up, and for agreeing to sit here with her in the dusk of a cool, romantic evening.

Her face fell a little in disappointment, but she accepted the situation with more style than I'd seen other women handle. "So, tell me about yourself," she said, leaning forward and clasping her hands in her lap. "How old are you?"

I hadn't considered these kinds of questions would be part of our conversation. I wanted to talk about her life, her family, her world. Suddenly, I realized I wasn't sure what I'd say if she asked me about being married, or if I had kids. The thought surprised me. *Why wouldn't I tell her I'm married? It would help me in this situation. If I'm married to someone else, she can't marry me.* I began to wonder if, deep down, I really was thinking of getting involved with her. Did her resemblance to young Erica stir up a new longing in me? I felt more confused about my own feelings than anything else going on.

Hannah eagerly awaited an answer, studying me with her big blue eyes.

Rather than openly lie, I decided it would be easier to play along and just stay away from any subject that got too personal on my end. I smiled. "I'm thirty-two. How old are you?"

"I came into this world at seventeen."

Oh, great. I thought she was at least twenty. I'm really robbing the cradle. No wonder Sven and Gretchen were being so protective. With Hannah's unusual beauty, they'd probably had to fend off a lot of young men.

"Don't vorry about the age difference," she said as though reading my mind. "In this vorld, age doesn't matter. Only love matters."

At the mention of the word *love,* I almost jumped up and ran back to the boarding house. I squirmed in my chair. It was time to find a way to gently let her know that nothing was going to happen between us. We weren't going to fall in love.

I looked toward the other end of the porch. No doubt, her parents had overheard our entire conversation.

Gretchen held a knowing little smile on her lips. Sven glared at me as he held a piece of wood in one hand and a whittling knife in the other. I had the feeling the little guy was just waiting for me to break his little girl's heart. Then, he'd jump up and stab me with his knife and beat me to death with the stick.

I lowered my voice to a whisper. "Listen, Hannah, I think you should know, I'm leaving in a few weeks. I'm going to South Town to try to find a way back to my world."

She didn't bat an eyelid. "I know. You're going to try to get home to your vife and three children."

Damn, how did she know about them?

"That's okay," she continued in a soft, understanding tone. "Go try. I'll vait for you. I'll vait as long as it takes."

I now suspected she knew a lot more about me than just my wife and children. The only person who could've told her these details had to be Maxston. The next time I saw him, I was going to kill him for messing in my affairs.

Hannah continued to look at me, her lovely long golden tresses falling softly over her bare shoulders. I hadn't noticed until now that she had pushed the gathered neck of her blouse a little lower across her chest.

"I might be gone a long time," I insisted, not wanting her to be disappointed if I never returned.

"I've been vaiting for you for seventy-one years. Another few months von't make a difference."

I did a double-take as my eyes came back to her face. "I'm sorry. Did you say you've been waiting seventy-"

"Seventy-one years," Sven said from his perch at the other end of the porch. "Eez how long vee been stuck in zeez miserable world."

Gretchen gave him a dirty look. "Hasn't been so bad. But I haff to admit I grow tired. Sometimes, it vould be a relief to die."

"Mama, don't talk that vay," Hannah said sharply. "I vorry you'll go for a valk one day and never come back."

"Whoa, wait a minute," I said, looking from the parents to Hannah. "You're trying to tell me you've all been in this world for seventy-one years? And, you, Hannah, have been waiting for someone all this time? How can that be? There must have been hundreds of men who came through this town and would want such a beautiful lady."

"Vhen I vas fourteen," Hannah said, reaching out and taking my hat into her hands, "a fortuneteller came through our village in the Oregon Territory. She said I vould meet my true love, but not for many, many years. She said I vould know him because he vould be older and have a striped shirt, blue pants, and a vhite hat made of straw. Isn't this a snakeskin band around your hat? She told me about a snakeskin band. That's how I knew it vas you yesterday."

I winced, finding all this hard to believe. Everyone in this world seemed to be crazy. "Ooookaaay, I see," I said, making a point of looking at my watch and taking my hat back from Hannah. "I hate to say it, but it's getting late. I have to be up early in the morning to find a job. I really should be going." I stood up and walked toward Hannah's parents. "Sven, Gretchen, thank you for a wonderful meal. It truly was delicious."

"Don't zank me," Gretchen said. "Zank Hannah. She cooked every-zing vee eat."

Hannah now stood next to me. "I vanted to show you how good a cook I can be. A man needs a voman to cook hearty meals." She took my arm and turned me toward the steps. Over her shoulder, she said, "I'll just valk Gavin to the end of the street, Mama."

"Only zee end of street," puny Sven commanded, putting in his two-cents worth, along with a stern glare at his daughter.

At the end of the street, we stood under a street lantern to say our goodbyes.

"Vill you come to dinner again?" she asked.

What could I say? I didn't want to hurt her feelings. "Yes," I lied. I just couldn't tell her I would never see her again.

She smiled and gave me a quick peck on the cheek before she turned and skipped back home, her long red skirt flowing behind her.

Wow, she looked and acted way too much like Erica. With her belief that we were destined to be together, I just plain didn't trust myself not to fall in love with her. No, it wasn't going to happen. I had enough other complications going on in my life right now.

I put on my hat and headed to the boarding house.

Chapter 9

The next morning I met Maxston at the restaurant. Well, technically, it wasn't a restaurant, just a family's house, but the woman who lived there made a pretty good living feeding whoever stopped by.

I was still a little shaken over the events at Hannah's house, so I wasn't really hungry.

"Better eat a hot meal while ya can," Maxston said around a mouthful of eggs. "Ain't gonna have nothin' but a cold sandwich 'til dinner tonight."

"Why do you say that? What do you have planned for me today?"

He took a gulp of coffee, then set the mug down hard. "Work. Master Benjamin wants ya ta start today."

"Fine," I said, sitting back in my chair. "What am I going to be doing?"

"You be seein' soon enough."

At the mention of work, I couldn't help but wonder how my business was holding up without me. Erica knew the business well and I had Brian to count on for doing any inspections that might crop up. I expected them to do whatever they could to hold things together until I got back. Of course, they didn't know that I was still alive, but I was sure they'd be doing everything they could to find me and to keep the business going for the time being.

* * *

A half-hour later, I stopped with Maxston in front of an old barn on the outskirts of town. The building had been made with wooden slats, all warped and turned to patina. An offensive odor wafted from the openings between the slats.

"Here we be," Maxston said, setting the butt of his rifle on the ground for a moment.

I looked at the dilapidated building with disappointment. The place smelled badly. "This is it? I'm supposed to work in here?"

"Yupper. Good hard work, too. Make ya a better man." He picked up his rifle, opened the door on the side of the barn, and walked in.

Inside the damp room, the smell increased, but luckily, it didn't smell as unpleasantly as Sven's tannery. *I guess I should at least be grateful I won't be working for Sven.* I noticed a line of ten-foot-tall stall doors on each side of the barn. Some were painted green, some red. Most of the doors had a thick board running across them as a lock to keep them shut. A small portion of each door, about two foot square and at chest height, could be opened like a window to look into the stalls. Light came in from the back of the barn where the big doors lay open. I could hear animals rustle around in the stalls. They made an occasional grunt or groan.

"Already talked ta the owner," Maxston said. "Said ta go ahead and walk ya through what he needs ya ta do." He pointed upward. "Hay be stacked up on them there rafters. Use the pitchfork ta put hay in every stall. Every stall that's got a animal in it, that is. When yer done with that job, fill them water buckets and muck out the stalls." He pointed toward the open doors at the back of the barn. "There be a wheelbarrow out back there, next ta the manure pile."

Great. Just what I wanted to do. Clean up the muck.

"Got any questions, yell fer Mark. Owns the place. He be 'round somewhere." He slapped me on the back and started for the door. "See ya tonight, My Friend."

"Wait," I called after him. "I already have a question. Why are some of the stall doors green and some red?"

His eyes got big. "Oh, yeah, almost forgot ta tell ya. Good thing ya reminded me." He motioned with his head for me to follow him. Stopping in front of a red door, he pressed his head against it as if listening for something.

I couldn't hear anything from where I stood.

As I opened my mouth to ask him what he was doing, he put a finger to his bearded lips. He reached up and quietly flipped up the latch holding the window portion of the door shut. Slowly, he opened the window a little ways and peeked inside. He nodded with a smile and whispered, "Take a look. Don't make no noise."

As he moved over, I took his place at the crack of the window. I leaned my head inside. It took me a minute to digest the reality of what I was seeing. The creature looked similar to a horse in build, except for the fact it appeared much bulkier around its girth. Its skin looked like the scales of a snake. I tried to comprehend the strangeness of this animal when it's lizard-like head reared up at me and hissed.

Maxston abruptly shoved me aside, slammed the window closed, and held his shoulder against it.

The whole building shook when the animal hit the door.

As I caught my breath and adjusted my glasses, I stood well back from the stall. "What the hell is that?" As the shock wore off at the near-miss of almost being bitten by that thing, I found myself trembling.

Maxston latched the lock on the window and checked the board across the door to make sure it held secure.

"It...it almost looked like a dinosaur," I stammered, feeling ridiculous calling it a dinosaur, which I knew it couldn't be.

"It is. And a mean one, too."

I watched Maxston's blue eyes as he guided me away from the area. "You're serious about this being a dinosaur aren't you?"

He nodded. "Ya gotta remember, this ain't yer world no more. Yer gonna see sights you be havin' a hard time believin'. Just like the rest of us, you be denyin' it fer a while."

I glanced back at the other stalls with the red paint. "What are these animals doing here? Where did they come from?"

"Live in the wild parts of this here world. Caught 'em when they was young and small. Six of 'em. We was gonna tame 'em ta pull the wagons, but they be too dad-blamed mean."

I heard a horse nicker. I turned to see a pretty buckskin horse stick it's head out of the open window of one of the stalls. It tossed its head as if asking for attention. I noticed the green paint on the stall. I guess green meant safe and red meant deadly.

Maxston walked to the stall and rubbed the horse's forehead. "Tell ya what," he said to me, "I be takin' a little trip north ta deliver some supplies 'n do a little tradin'. How'd ya like ta go along. See the country? We be back 'fore the wagon train be leavin' town. Get ya outa workin' here."

"That sounds fine with me." The sooner I got away from shoveling muck and the monstrous creatures behind the red doors, the better. "I've gotta ask you, though, how come this horse isn't freaking out, being in the same barn with the dinosaurs?"

He patted the horse on the neck. "That be easy. Horses know them dinos won't eat 'em. See, them dinos be what they call 'herbivores,' meanin' they eat-"

"I know what herbivores eat, Maxston." He had been right all along about me having a hard time believing many of the things I'd seen since I'd arrived in this world. But *dinosaurs*? Really?

The cowboy had tried to warn me about the dinosaurs that first night. I figured he'd been pulling my leg, so I didn't pay much attention. But now, after seeing that creature and almost being bitten, I intended to pay more attention.

"Special handlers come in here 'bout once a week," Maxston explained. "Clean the stalls. Have ta drug the dinos, rope 'em and blindfold 'em ta do it. Even then, we lose a man every once in a while."

Wow, I could just imagine roping the dinos was probably the most exciting show in town. "When are they coming in? I'd like to see that."

"This week, it be tomorrow. We be gone. Leavin' fer the north." As he headed for the barn door, he said, "We be gone a might. You just be ready at sunrise."

Layne Walker

As Maxston left the barn, I turned and trudged up the ladder to the hayloft. There, I lifted the pitchfork and peeked over the side into the stalls. In the shadows of the stalls, I could only see vague forms. Luckily, the loft seemed high enough that none of the dinosaurs could reach me. I began pitching the hay, sometimes getting a grunt or hiss from a moving creature below. I was kind of sorry that I wouldn't be here to watch the cleaning of the stalls.

On the other hand, I was growing excited about the upcoming trip with Maxston. It would be better than cleaning up stalls. As long as I was going to have to wait a few weeks for the wagon train, I might as well spend my time seeing more of this unusual world. Also, I felt relieved that it would be an opportunity to get out of town and avoid Hannah.

* * *

Five days later, I estimated Maxston and I had covered close to one-hundred-and-twenty-five miles. Four pack-horses trailed behind us. Two of the packhorses would be left with one of the villages we would be meeting. These two horses were used to haul skins, furs, and dried meats from this northern region to North Town. Later, like now, they were returned with goods and supplies that the village needed.

As we traveled into the colder regions, the tall pines, snowcapped mountains, and pockets of lakes reminded me of one summer when I was in high school and my family had taken a vacation to the Northwest Territories above British Columbia. This area looked similar, but for the mountain peaks not reaching great heights. So far, I hadn't seen any mountains in this world as high as the Rockies or the Sierra's in my world.

Now that we'd gotten out of the mountainous areas, we were coming into a treeless expanse that looked more and more like the arctic tundra. I couldn't believe how fast the topography changed as we moved northward. While the landscapes looked generally similar to those of my world, the different terrains sat much closer in proximity.

I threw the hood of my heavy fur coat up over my head and pulled the collar tighter around my neck to keep the icy breeze from burrowing down my back. Not having had a shave since leaving town, my whiskers were starting to grow long. I wore fur leggings over my jeans and fur-lined moccasins over my feet. Maxston had supplied me with plenty of winter clothing, for which I was much obliged. Unlike my previous horse trip going to North Town, this time I was riding on a real saddle with stirrups. My rear was sore, but not blistered.

During midday, the temperatures would rise to the low fifties, but during the night, the temps dropped considerably. I'd seen ice on the water of the lake near our camp when we'd gotten up this morning. Now in the late afternoon, the winds seemed to take a blustery turn for the worse as we continued on.

I wondered how much farther north Maxston had planned to take us. With the grasses running out for the horses and wood not being available for our nightly fires, I didn't see how we could keep going forward with only the bare tundra in front of us.

Maxston sauntered along on his horse just a little ahead of me.

I had to trust that he knew what he was doing.

Suddenly, I smelled smoke. I shifted in my saddle to scan the area for signs of a village or town…maybe a campsite.

"Good, they ain't moved," Maxston said over his shoulder. "Thought we be havin' ta travel two more days before we met up with 'em."

"Who are *they*?" I asked, surprised that anyone would want to live in this desolate area.

"Inuit."

"Inuit?"

"Yup…you know…Eskimo's."

"Oh, right." I got this sneaky feeling that Maxston came here for some ulterior motive. "So, I suppose there's someone special you came all the way up here to see."

"We come all the way up here," he replied tersely, "ta deliver supplies these people need, like medicine, coffee, 'n sugar."

Yeah, right. He just wasn't going to admit that he might also be seeing a woman.

"If'n ya want, I can be arrangin' for ya to have a roll under a pile a polar-bear skins with a willin' lady."

"No!" I blared. I'd just gotten myself away from one messy entanglement. I didn't need another.

A single dog barked, soon followed by the yaps of a whole pack.

I studied the area more closely to look for people. I saw signs of the village. Low rounded domes, covered with hides, blended well into the surroundings. I hadn't noticed them from the distance before.

"Well, they know we be a comin' now. Don'tcha be alarmed if'n they act a might hostile to us at first. They be wary of strangers 'til they know if we be friend or foe."

In our heavy coats and hoods, making it hard to tell who we were, we slowly ambled forward.

A string of men, women, and children started out on foot in our direction. I could understand the men coming out to meet us, but I wondered why they allowed the women and children to take a chance that we could be dangerous. As we drew closer, I understood. Even the women and children carried weapons of some kind: a spear, a bow, or a heavy stick. They all held themselves in an obvious manner of being prepared to fight.

A little nervous about facing them, I sat stiffly on my horse, making sure they would not misinterpret any of my moves as being a danger to them. I was glad my gun was hidden under my fur coat.

Maxston pulled his horse to a stop some thirty feet in front of the moving mass. He held up one hand. "Greetin's from North Town. I bring ya supplies and yer packhorses. Also have news of the world ta share."

My anxiety about meeting these weapon-toting people diminished quickly as they approached.

They lowered their weapons and showed no hostility on their wide, round faces. In fact, most of them smiled. A few turned back and headed toward their village as if they trusted that these two lowly white men would be no problem.

Most of the people wore leather or flannel clothing, like being out on a warm afternoon in the middle of winter. They seemed much more adapted to the cold than I was as I sat with my heavy coat snuggled closely around me.

A short, very fat man, almost as wide as he was tall, came forward. He wore a buttoned-up flannel shirt with rolled-up sleeves. His leather pants had been tucked into his high-top moccasins. On his head, he wore a well-worn hat that looked like it might have once been a white fox. Graying strands sprinkled his black hair, which he'd pulled back into a single braid that hung halfway down his back and bounced from side to side as he waddled forward. I presumed he was the chief.

He stopped a few feet in front of Maxston's horse. "Hey Maxston, how's it going?"

I was shocked at his casualness and easy English, which he spoke better than Maxston. I had expected him to talk to us in some form of pidgin English that the Eskimos might use.

Maxston slid off his horse. "Good, good. How ya been, Stranded Seal?"

"Ornery," he said in all seriousness. "I've been out of coffee and tobacco for two weeks now."

"Sorry. Couldn't be makin' it sooner. Ya know Master Benjamin. He got other things fer me to do. Things he sees more important, 'course."

"He never has thought much of us." The man shrugged. "We've learned to deal with it...you know that."

During this conversation, the crowd of people who'd stayed with Stranded Seal remained standing behind him, their eyes going from me to Maxston to the bundles strapped on the packhorses. Their faces had a healthy weathered look from being out in nature a long time.

Maxston took the lead ropes of two of the packhorses and handed them to Stranded Seal. Like a switch that had been flipped, his people immediately surged forward, jabbering away in English and some other language I couldn't understand. They took the horses and headed for the village in a festive, happy mood, leaving Maxston and me alone with Stranded Seal.

Maxston introduced us as we made our way to the village, where, on closer inspection, I could see the dome-like tee-pees, as well as a couple of wooden structures made of logs.

When Maxston said Stranded Seal's name, I couldn't help myself. I blurted, "I hope you don't mind me asking, but I'm curious about your name. How did you get such a name?"

He patted his considerable girth. "I'm fat as a seal, but I can't swim like one. I can't swim at all. So, I'm stuck on land forever."

"I see," I said, nodding my head. "*Stranded Seal.* It makes sense now that I think about it. By the way, how come you speak English so well?"

"Along with my people, I came in from 1985."

"Wow, that's pretty close to my time, relatively speaking. I'm from 2015." I looked at the group of people heading back to the village. There had to be at least forty or fifty of them. "How did all of your people end up here at the same time? Did you all walk into the web together? How did that work?"

"We were living in a small town in the Northwest Territories of Canada. We lived like normal white people in clapboard homes and regular neighborhoods. Every year, we would take a week-long, ritual trip and live like our Eskimo ancestors. On our last trip, we ran into the web as a group, all of us together.

"When we realized we could no longer go east to return home, we sent scouts to the west and to the south. I was one of the scouts who journeyed southward and, luckily, ran into Maxston one day. He returned with me to our camp and explained what had happened, that there was no going back home. It took a while for us to accept this notion, but the group finally decided to live like they had been meant to live: at one with nature.

"Luckily, some of the elders still remembered the old ways. We learned from them and managed to survive quite well alone here all these thirty-six years." He leaned over and put his hand to his mouth, as if he were whispering a secret to me. "To tell you the truth, I think it sucks, but it's what the tribe wants."

"If you hate it, why do you stay? Couldn't you just go live in town and leave the tribe on their own?"

He shook his head. "I wish it were that easy. See, I come from a long line of chiefs and, whatever I decide to do, the tribe has to follow. If I go to live in town, they will feel they have to go live in town. I can't do that to them. They like it out here, living like our ancestors."

I felt sorry for him. "Bummer, Dude," was all I could think to say.

We reached the outskirts of the village and stopped as two young boys of about ten ran up to greet us.

"They will take care of your horses," Stranded Seal said. "Get whatever you need off them and come with me. I'll get you settled into a hut."

I grabbed my backpack and slung it over one shoulder.

The "hut" turned out to be a few hides sewn together and thrown over a framework of wood, antlers, and what looked like long leg bones from caribou or deer. Someone had stacked a pile of wood and bones against one wall. A fire pit, surrounded by rocks, sat in the dirt in the middle of the floor. Thick furs covered the remaining floor. I worried about getting dirt on them, but Maxston told me not to worry about it, so I didn't. As I stepped into the hut, I felt like I was walking on a mattress.

I threw my backpack, now containing a change of clothes and personal items, including my boots, into a corner on top of the furs, then we stepped outside. I peeked back into the hut and debated about whether or not I should leave my prized possessions in my backpack untended. "I'll be right with you," I called to Maxston, who was heading into the main part of the village.

He lifted an arm in response.

I hurried back into the hut, opened my pack, and fished out the wallet, keys, and cell phone. I stuck them in my coat pocket. If something happened to the rest of the stuff, I didn't care, but I wasn't going to lose the only links to my home. Even if I were being foolish, I couldn't help myself.

Chapter 10

Apparently, our arrival in the Eskimo village was cause for a celebration. In the center of the village, the people greeted us with smiling faces and good cheer. Maxston and I were taken inside a large building made of logs. There, we stripped off our coats and carried them with us to our seats.

An older woman showed us to a place of honor next to the chief's family. A large wooden platform, raised a foot off the ground, formed the table around which everyone sat. The furs lining the floor gave us some cushioning for our seats. I appreciated the furs for keeping our rears out of the dirt and adding some warmth to the ground.

On Stranded Seal's left sat a woman as fat and round as the chief himself. I figured her to be his wife. Maxston was seated next to her.

On Stranded Seal's right sat a girl of about twenty-five or thirty who looked just like Stranded Seal's wife. While she wasn't nearly as big as Stranded Seal or his wife, she looked like she was well on her way to breaking the two-hundred-pound mark. I was placed next to her.

As I lowered myself onto the furs, she smiled, showing me her yellow-stained, cavity-ridden teeth. I could see her interest in me sparkling in her eyes. *Oh, God, this is going to be a long night.*

"Hi, I'm Janice," she said, holding out a balloon-like hand as she tucked her multiple chins tight to her chest and giggled.

Like a good guest, I shook her hand. "It's nice to meet you, Janice. How come you aren't named after an animal like your dad, Stranded Seal?"

She leaned close and whispered, "That's not his real name. His real name is Peter Cavanaugh, but he hates it. Doesn't go with his image of being the big chief."

I almost laughed out loud. Here, I'd thought we'd run into a tribe of real Eskimos, but they were nothing more than fakes. Well, I couldn't say that for sure. Most of them seemed to have strong Eskimo features.

"Are you staying long?" Janice asked hopefully.

"No," I blurted way too quickly. "We're leaving in the morning." I had no idea if this was true or not, but I didn't want her to think I was going to be available.

"I come with a big dowry," she said candidly, staring at me with her large brown eyes.

Is she trying to railroad me into getting involved with her? I shifted in my seat, not at all comfortable with this conversation. For one thing, I preferred my women small and delicate. For another, I found this woman's attitude to be disgusting and overbearing. "Um, I'm married already. I have three kids, too."

"I don't mind being a second wife."

I turned on her, asking a little too unkindly, "Why me? You don't even know me. There must be some lucky guy here in the village you've known and had your eye on. Someone who would know more about your life than I do."

She rolled her eyes. "Yeah, right. As if any of these bozo's were good enough for me. I want someone who can take me away from here, not someone who will make me stay and have his kids, cook meals, and clean house. Booooring."

"I thought you couldn't have kids in this world."

"Just a matter of speaking. For sure, I won't clean and skin whatever he kills while he's off drinking homemade hooch with his buddies. I want to live in a real town with electricity and indoor plumbing so I won't freeze my-" She leaned to the side and patted her expansive butt. "...cute little bottom off every time I have to go to the bathroom."

"Gavin," Maxston hollered from down the table.

Thank God, he saved me from having to come up with an appropriate response to her comment. I leaned forward so I could see him on the other side of the family. "Yeah?"

"Stranded Seal here invites us ta go on a three-day huntin' trip with the tribe. They be leavin' in the mornin'. Sounds like fun, don'tcha think?"

Janice clapped her hands in delight. "Ooooh, goody. We can spend more time together."

My mouth dropped open.

Maxston saw the look on my face. "This be an honor ta be invited, Gavin. Would be rude ta turn the chief down."

Everybody around the table stared at me as they waited for my response.

I groaned and fell back in my seat. "Yeah, Maxston. Sounds great. I can't wait."

If I'd known about Janice and this village prior to the trip, I would've bowed out in advance, but now, it was too late. It looked like I'd be spending the next three days warding off the unwanted advances of Janice, unless I could figure out a way to avoid her. Being stuck in North Town with Hannah now seemed like a more appealing problem.

* * *

"Mommy, why did Daddy leave us behind?" my seven-year-old daughter asks with tears in her eyes.

"I don't know, Sweetheart. Maybe he stopped loving us and decided to find a new family. I'll bet he's flirting with some chief's daughter right now."

I shifted in my sleep. I knew I was dreaming, but in my exhaustion, I couldn't wake myself up.

"But what about Hannah?" my daughter cries. "She said he was the one she's been waiting for all these years."

How does my daughter know about Hannah?

Oh, yeah, I'm dreaming, I remembered.

Erica's concerned face appears alone on a large movie screen in front of me. She wears her sandy-blond hair back in a pony tail, her bangs hanging just above her tired blue eyes. Her face looks drawn. "He is the one for her. He just hasn't admitted it to himself yet. He even feels guilty every time he thinks of her, which is quite often, isn't it, Gavin?" Her eyes narrow as her face expands until it covers the

Layne Walker

whole screen. "Are you having fun, Gavin?" her lips yell. "Do you still remember us?"

The face transforms into my father on my wedding night. "Gavin, you will have a long and prosperous marriage if you remember two things. First, never make your wife take the garbage out. That's a man's job. Second, don't give in to Janice's advances. Hannah is the one true love for you."

Hannah? I thought I just married Erica.

My father continues. "Let your dreams of being in Hannah's arms carry you through this tough time. Think of her often, and Janice will sense your love and leave you alone."

The face changes again, this time becoming the cowboy I talked to just before I met Hannah. "What a fool ta go traipsin' all over the country when ya'll got a good, beautiful woman waitin' on ya ta come home. Cancel the trip ta South Town. It's too dangerous. Hannah is waiting for ya. Come claim her as your own."

I rolled over, waking briefly, but my heavy drowsiness pulled me back into the dream.

Now the face turns into my oldest daughter, who is nine. "Daddy, is Hannah my new mommy? Where's my old mommy?"

The face of my youngest daughter appears and speaks in Master Benjamin's voice. "Goodman Gavin, thou canst never return home again. Accept thy fate. Surrender to thy new world with thy new family."

Janice's face emerges and takes over. Her fat cheeks, folded chins, and sex-crazed eyes fill the screen. "I won't ever give up on you, My Love." She puckered her small lips, making kissing sounds. "I love, love, love you."

While the face remains Janice's, her voice shifts to that of Stranded Seal's. "According to our customs, you are now Janice's husband. You did not properly ward off or discourage her advances. Welcome to the tribe, Son."

Three sets of huge bare arms enfold me into rolls of blubber, blocking the light, and smothering me.

Gulping for air, I call out, "No. I can't stay. I have to go." I wrestle to get free as I sink deeper into the blubber. I

90

fight the constraining arms to get back to my family, to see the faces of my children again, but I can't break loose. I can't breathe. I start to lose consciousness.

"That's right, Gavin," Erica's voice whispers from a distance. "Give in. Come home to me."

Gasping for breath, I jerked upright on the furs which had been covering my face. In the darkness, sweat drenched my long-john-type woolen pajamas and forehead. Feeling weak, I could hardly stay sitting up, but I refused to lay down and fall back into the dream again. *What a nightmare.*

"You okay?" Maxston asked from across the room.

I couldn't see him in the pitch blackness. The fire had obviously long gone out. Not even a few embers glowed. "Yeah, I'm fine," I managed to get out between breaths. "It was just a bad dream...about my family." I heard him get up.

"Sometimes them dreams, they can tell us what we really be feelin'. Might want ta talk ta the shaman. He be purty good at interpretin' my dreams. Might make ya feel better."

"No thanks. I understand this dream just fine. I need to stop screwing around and find a way back home to my family."

Maxston, having slept in his clothes, coat, and all, headed out the hut flap. "Gotta pee."

I sat with my eyes closed for a few moments. The icy chill of the morning began to freeze the soaking-wet pajamas Maxston had given me. I hurriedly got up, stripped off the nightclothes, and groped around in the dark for my glasses, jeans, and shirt. Now I knew why Maxston slept in his clothes.

After I got dressed, I pulled on the fur leggings and fur-lined moccasins for extra warmth. It was too dark to read my watch to see what time it was. As I considered whether or not to lie down again, I could see the faint light of dawn just coming through the partially open smoke hole at the top of the hut. *Good, I don't think I want to go back to sleep and dream again. Time to get up and face the day.*

I strapped on my gun and threw on my fur coat. I ducked out the low entrance of the hut. I could see my breath turn to fog. My hands about froze. I put them in my pockets and hurried toward the designated latrine area. Once again, I felt grateful for the extra clothing Maxston had given me.

While North Town had built outhouses for privacy, here, the community had simply dug a long hole in the ground. A person squatted and hoped to keep his balance so as not to fall into the person next to him. I could fully understand why Janice wanted to leave this primitive place and move to a real town with plumbing. I decided to wait to do anything more than pee until we got out of camp, where I could find a little more privacy.

By the time Maxston and I arrived at the large log building in the center of the village, the people were milling around in their heavy coats with a big fire going and numerous metal coffee pots sitting on the fire or placed off to the side, allowing the coffee grounds time to settle at the bottom of the pot before pouring the liquid into the cups. Maxston and I grabbed a couple of cups and stood in line.

For breakfast, we ate leftovers from the night before. By the time everything had been cleaned up, less than an hour had passed and dawn had broken. Excitement ran through the villagers as they prepared their children and their packs.

While I had expected to be traveling by horse, I watched a team of dogs being hooked to a sled. I turned to Stranded Seal and asked, "How are those dogs going to pull the sleds with no snow on the ground?"

"The runners are greased with seal fat. They'll slide across the ground just fine. North of here, about five miles, we'll hit the ice and snow. From there, we'll really make good time." He seemed to be in a cheery mood. I figured it meant that, deep down, he really did like living like his ancestors.

Janice and her mother made a big deal about me traveling with their "family" group. "We have the biggest sled in the village," Janice boasted. "Plenty of room for you to sit next me if your feet get cold." She smiled affectionately. "I'll keep you reeeeal warm."

I'll bet. In a firm tone, I told her a little white lie. "Maxston and I made a pact when we left North Town. We swore we'd always stick together, even if we were with other people."

Maxston reaffirmed my lie when he said, "That be right. We be travelin' mates. Ain't gonna let nobody separate us." In a voice only I could hear as we turned away, he said, "But still think ya ought'a think about sleepin' with her. It be gitting' awful cold at night. She be keepin' ya nice-"

"Don't even say it," I broke in with a hard glare. "I'll be just fine on my own. If I get too cold, I can always curl up with one of the sled dogs."

Maxston roared in laughter. "That be pissin' her off good. Choosin' a sled dog over her. Man'd have ta be braver than me ta do somthin' like that." He wandered off, leaving me to myself.

As I watched the villagers make the final preparations, I told myself I would rather be heading south, toward…oops, I almost slipped and said *home*. Could I really be thinking of North Town as *home*. Anger flooded me as I remembered my dream and all the people trying to tell me that Hannah was the right person for me. No, I needed to get to South Town. Only in South Town would I find the information I needed to get back to my real home, my real family, my real life in Lake Havasu City.

For now, I hated being stuck here in the tundra, forced to go on this trip that would further delay the answers I was seeking. My whole body felt flushed with frustration.

I briefly thought about saddling my horse and galloping off toward the south on my own, but I couldn't do that to Maxston. He turned out to be the best friend I had in this world. I needed him to get me safely to South Town.

Dejectedly, I strapped my backpack across my back and started walking with the procession heading north.

* * *

Over the next two days of the hunting trip, Janice continuously pestered me, turning what might have been a-once-in-a-lifetime experience into something I wanted to forget, and probably never would.

No matter what I did or said to discourage her or chase her away, she clung to me like a bloodsucking tick. At the meals, she squeezed in next to me before anyone else could sit down. As we drew lots to separate into groups for the hunting sprees, she made sure she tagged along with my team, even if she had drawn lots to be part of another team.

Her incessant flirting morphed into lurid descriptions of what she would do to me in bed. The images made me sick to my stomach. Nothing I said to her seemed to deter her attention to me.

Other members of the tribe seemed amused. In fact, they started taking bets on whether or not she'd get me to give in before we got back to the village.

Maxston, alone, bet that I would hold out. He threw his coins into the pot like everyone else.

At one point, I convinced Maxston to talk some sense into the girl. That did no good.

I begged Stranded Seal and Janice's mother to speak to her on my behalf, stating indisputably that I had no intention of getting involved with her in any way.

If anything, Janice grew all the more insistent that our time together would run out soon and our opportunities for a rendezvous would pass all too quickly.

By the second afternoon, I was warn to a frazzle by her constant badgering. So far, I'd managed to sleep apart from her in a portable tent I shared with Maxston, but I knew she was going to press harder and harder for me to spend the last night with her. I also knew it would be extremely rude and humiliating to her for me to go sleep with the dogs to show her I meant business, but the thought passed often through my mind as the afternoon wore on. If nothing else, I reasoned I would be better off cuddling up with a polar bear than with Janice.

Maxston and I walked some distance behind Stranded Seal's sled as the tribe moved across the solid ice to find a new area to set up camp for this last night of the trip. We had hit the furthest reaches of our hunting expedition the previous day. This portion of the trip was taking us back toward the village for a little more hunting before we camped for the night. We would return to the village in the morning.

Janice seemed to be in a particularly good mood as she flitted around me like a moth around a light. She danced and skipped, taunting me all the while with disgusting threats. "Just you wait and see. See what I've got in store for you...all kinds of goodies for when you climb into the furs with me. I'll-"

I gritted my teeth, trying not to listen to the words or the cruder descriptions that continued to spew forth from her mouth. All this time, I fought back my anger, but the rage was growing inside me to such a degree that I thought I could kill the woman if no one was looking.

Maxston fidgeted next to me as he put up with Janice's pornographic descriptions. He nudged me. "Gotta talk to Stranded Seal. See ya later." He took off, leaving me completely alone with Janice for the first time since we'd left the village.

With Maxston gone, Janice really poured it on. She blabbered on and on, pawing at my coat, circling around me, walking backwards in front of me as she looked up into my eyes to tell me all her sick fantasies. "...and then, I'll..."

In angry frustration, I stopped in my tracks and blasted her. "I could *never, ever* be interested in someone as obnoxious as you are, or someone who smells as badly as you do. I don't find anything appealing about you. Don't you get it? I don't want you. I don't want to have anything to do with you."

She laughed, her brown eyes glittering in the sunlight. "You'll change your mind after one night in my bed. You'll see. Just give me a chance. I'm the best."

I rolled my eyes and let out a frustrated sigh. I walked a little faster to catch up with the others and avoid being alone with her much longer.

As I hurried along, Janice moved faster, too, to stay just ahead of me. She trotted backwards in front of me as she extolled the virtues of a woman with a lot of meat on her bones. I had to admit, for a big woman, she could move fast.

The parade of sleds ahead of us turned, bearing to the left across the field of white ice. A chilly breeze crossed my face as the dusty snow on top of the ice blew lightly over the expanse. Not far to my right, a crevasse in the ice, about eight or ten inches across and a foot deep, ran for a long stretch ahead of us. It looked like someone had taken a knife and tried to cut the ice in half, but ended up with only a crack.

Putting a little distance between me and the crevasse, I placed my full attention ahead on the sleds and avoided looking at the desperate woman in front of me. I scanned the horizon, hoping to see a polar bear, caribou, or something interesting as I blocked out Janice's words, but the crudest ones tumbled, unwanted, into my mind anyway.

Janice started dancing behind me. With her gloved hands, she patted my butt, then grabbed me around the waist and hugged.

Aggravated, I roughly pushed her off.

She skidded backwards, caught herself, then laughed. Her eyes filled with a playful challenge as she came charging toward me again.

I shifted to the side to avoid her.

Instead of grabbing hold of me as she had intended, her foot slipped and slid. She hit the edge of the crevasse. Her legs twisted as she slid into the crack, deeper than I had originally thought it to be. Trying to catch her balance, she fell sideways, her leg bone snapping loudly as she fell. Writhing in pain, she screamed and called out, "Mommy, Mommy."

I knelt down next to her. "Don't move. You'll do more damage to your leg if you keep thrashing around."

By now, the tribe members had stopped the dogs and sleds, and many were running in our direction.

Janice's mother and father were the first to arrive. Stranded Seal rudely pushed me out of the way as though I had been responsible for his daughter's injury.

"What happened?" Maxston asked as he came up behind me.

"She was trying to grab hold of me when she slipped and fell into the crevasse. There was nothing I could do." Strangely, I felt guilty, like all this was my fault, that if I'd been more careful, none of this would have happened.

One of the men, probably the "shaman," bound her leg in a support made of animal bones and strips of animal hides. Several men lifted her out of the crack and placed her in the family sled that had been brought to the site of the accident.

"She must go back to the village," her mother said, glowering at me.

Janice whimpered, no longer paying me any attention.

After a discussion among some of the tribe members, the man who had bound Janice's leg agreed to travel back to the village with Janice and her mother to help care for the girl's leg and general well-being.

Despite the tragedy of the situation, I felt relieved that Janice would no longer be following me around and taunting me with her pesky flirtations. I could finally eat a meal in peace. As I watched her sled pull out for the village, a great weight lifted off my shoulders and I started to enjoy myself. That night in camp, I laughed, sang songs, drank the homemade liquor, and had a blast.

As things turned out, I didn't have to sleep with the sled dogs after all.

* * *

Early the next day, we returned to Stranded Seal's village. As the villagers unloaded their booty and settled into their huts, Maxston and I packed up the horses and prepared to make our journey south. I was happy to be getting away from Janice's cloying attention.

Maxston was happy, too. He'd collected a bunch of coins on the bet, being that Janice didn't get me for a romp under her furs. Maxston even offered to split the winnings with me, since I was the one who'd gone through hell so he could win it.

I accepted the split, now having some currency of my own to spend in this world. I also realized that Maxston had been in my presence every day and night. I'd been wrong about him coming up here to be with a woman, and I was glad I hadn't made any bets about that.

As we pulled out of the village, I turned in my saddle to wave goodbye to Stranded Seal and his family.

Janice blubbered like a newborn.

I wondered if her tears would freeze, and in turn, cause her eyes to freeze shut. *Actually, that wouldn't be such a bad thing. Then, she won't have to watch me ride out of her life.*

Chapter 11

Instead of returning on our original trail, which would have taken us southeast, Maxston angled us to the southwest. "Got someone I gotta see," he remarked.

Ah, ha, here it is, I thought. *I knew he'd been intending to see a woman all along. I was just wrong about where she was.*

We'd been gone for over a week. I was getting impatient to get to South Town and a little nervous about the wagon train leaving without us if we were late.

"Don't worry yer head off, Son," Maxston said. "We got us plenty a time 'fore the wagon train be ready ta leave North Town. Cain't leave without me, ya know."

I sat back in my saddle and tried to relax. I hadn't had any more dreams about my family. That was a relief. I felt guilty enough for being gone so long. I didn't need their ghosts nagging me about not loving them anymore.

Despite the fact that everything was out of my control, and even though I couldn't make things happen faster, I still felt I wasn't doing everything possible to get back to them. No matter how hard I tried, I couldn't convince Maxston to take me to South Town alone. I couldn't make the wagon train leave earlier. I just wasn't going to get to South Town and talk to Howard Blackman until the timing fell into place. I could only hope that, once I got there, he held the key to getting me home.

As much as I loved my family, I found myself trying not to think about them as we traveled. I found it too depressing. If I were going to find a way home, I needed to stay healthy, not only physically, but also mentally. I only let myself feel depressed at night when I curled up in a ball and cried myself to sleep, knowing the bright light of morning would perk me up again so I could face another day.

I continued to keep close tabs on the few meager possessions I'd brought with me into this world. This included my gun, of course, which I always carried on my hip. My watch stayed on my wrist, day and night. Still carefully stashed away in my backpack were my cell phone, my wallet, and my key ring.

I thought about the key ring. It contained four keys, each one symbolic of a different part of the world I'd been taken from.

The first key, my truck key, represented my escape vehicle to take me away from town and the pressures of society and my family.

The second key went to the door of my office. I prided myself on my business: the best home inspector in town, always on time, always giving the customers my honest appraisal, going out of my way to learn more about the business, offering my customers valuable information and advice. It'd been a good livelihood for the last ten years.

The third key belonged to our family car, the vehicle we'd taken on many drives and trips, giving us many fond memories. I missed Erica sitting in the passenger seat and navigating with the maps, while the girls played games or sang songs in the back seat.

The last key meant the most to me. In fact, it meant more to me than the other three. It was the key to my house, the key to my home, the place where my wife, my kids, and my heart resided. My heart so longed to use that key and open that door again.

I wasn't about to leave those keys or any of my possessions behind or allow them to get lost. They were the closest tangible objects I had to remind me of my family. Unlike many men, I didn't carry a picture of Erica or the girls in my wallet. All I had were a couple of twenty's, my driver's license, two credit cards, and my library card. The more I thought about not having a picture of them, the more it seemed kind of sad.

* * *

One afternoon a few days later, as our horses clopped along through a meadow filled with tall grass, colorful flowers, and a bubbling stream, a grizzly bear lazily stood up about fifty yards away from our position. The bear had apparently been dozing in the sun. It roared its displeasure at having its nap interrupted by two humans and four horses.

Maxston briefly paused the horses, which stirred restlessly as we watched the bear.

Although feeling a little nervous myself, I couldn't help but admire the magnificent animal. It stood at least ten feet tall with glossy, silver-tipped hair and claws six inches long, curving out from its dinner-plate-sized paws.

Before the bear became more threatening, we departed. The horses seemed to be relieved that we were moving along.

* * *

The next morning, we approached the top of a small hill. I heard a faint roar, a familiar sound that I couldn't place. As we crested the hill, the blue vista of an ocean spread out in front of me. A steep, rocky cliff separated us from the beach. The pounding of the waves against the shore had formed the familiar roar. I could taste the salt on my tongue and smell the slightly fishy scent of the sea on the light breeze.

I should've realized we were getting close to the ocean by the birds and the vegetation. Seagulls, pelicans, and egrets had been flying overhead for at least the last half-hour, but I hadn't put much thought to their significance.

Because the weather had gotten warmer, I now wore my jeans and boots. I could've used a light jacket over my long-sleeved shirt, but the fur coat bogged me down too much. I'd strapped it on one of the packhorses.

"Have ta find a way down there," Maxston said, peering first to the north, then to the south.

"Wouldn't it be easier to travel up here along the cliff?"

"Nope. Beach be a straight shot ta where we be goin'. Need ta get down there."

He sounded a little testy, so I didn't question him further.

Maxston eventually found a path down the rocks without the horses balking too badly. At one point, it took some coaxing to get them down a steep area, but for the most part, the horses seemed fairly surefooted and managed just fine.

Once on the beach, Maxston led us out to the damp sand along the shoreline where the packed ground would make it easier for the horses to travel.

I glanced down the coastline. I did a double-take, shocked to discover that it looked like someone had lined the beach up with a ruler. It was straight as an arrow for as far as my eye could see. Same for the shore in the other direction.

Maxston caught my surprise. "Told ya it be straight, did I not?"

"Yes, you did, and I didn't believe you." I checked the line again. It looked like an aberration of nature. "Even now, it's hard to believe. How can this be? There's no way that the shoreline could have eroded into such a straight line."

"Don't know, don't care," he said as he started the horses southward down the beach. He'd been acting like this all morning, like he had other things on his mind and didn't want to talk or get involved in a discussion.

I didn't feel it was my place to ask about it. I figured, if he wanted to talk, he'd bring up a topic first.

As we rode along, I watched the ocean, looking for signs of jumping fish, dolphins, or maybe even a whale. That's when I noticed something else didn't seem right. I'd never spent a lot of time at the ocean or on a beach in my world, but I had spent enough time to know a little bit about how the ocean acted. Ocean waves tended to be random, coming into shore at different intervals, heights, and sizes. The waves on this ocean came in uniformly at precise intervals. Too precise to be natural. As crazy as it seemed, they looked like man-made waves.

The horizon looked different, too. The horizon ended where the sky and the ocean met, but the sky looked funny...phony somehow. I had the weirdest feeling that, if I were to get in a boat and sail out to the horizon, I'd run into a wall of some kind.

I kept staring at the distant skyline as we rode down the beach. At one point, I swore I saw movement in the sky. It wasn't that the sky really moved or that something flew by like a bird. No, it was more like I was looking *through* the sky, like looking through a tinted window into a car and not being able to see the details, but noticing something move. A shiver went down my spine.

I continued looking at the sky, but I could see nothing more out of the ordinary. I blinked a few times to clear my eyes. I wondered now if my mind had played a trick on me, or if I had really seen the movement.

I wanted to ask Maxston if he'd seen anything unusual, but he seemed to be in his own little world. I didn't want to bother him about something that sounded so crazy and might have just come out of my own fears and concerns that I'd been carrying around.

As we moved along the beach, I continued to watch the sky for the next hour. I saw no movement again, so I chalked it up to my overactive imagination and soon forgot about it. I had other more important things to worry about.

* * *

In the afternoon, Maxston suddenly dropped the lead rope to the packhorses, kicked his horse in the ribs, and took off down the beach as fast as his horse could run.

I looked around to see who was attacking us, but could see no one anywhere. *The old man must be heading to something or, more importantly, to that someone he wanted to see.* I rounded up the packhorses and followed Maxston at a slower pace.

After traveling a hundred yards down the shore, I caught sight of a row of dugout canoes pulled up on the beach. This explained Maxston's behavior. We must have arrived at that place where Maxston's mysterious *someone* lived.

I stopped the horses at the canoes and looked around. I saw no signs of people or a village. Thick shrubbery and a copse of deciduous trees, which looked like dwarfed cottonwoods, sat a ways back from the shore. A few palm trees rose above the greenery. I figured the town or village had to be further inland. The hoof prints of Maxston's horse had turned in that direction.

As I rode toward the trees, an older man, wearing only a breechcloth and long, black stringy hair, stepped out of the brush and waved to me. He looked like an American Indian. He called out, "Hello." In heavily accented English, he spoke some gibberish, slaughtering Maxston's name and pointing to my horses. When he held out his hand for the reigns, I figured he intended to take the horses.

Hoping he would understand me, I spoke slowly. "Just show me where you want the horses. I'll take it from there." I didn't feel right handing the horses over to the first Indian to step out of the brush. The last thing I wanted to do was end up horseless and have to walk back to North Town. Maxston wouldn't be too proud of me, either.

The man grinned and waved for me to follow him. He sauntered along slowly as he led me on a winding path around numerous thickets of bushes and trees. The terrain in this section of the country consisted of rolling hills with a sandy loam, partially covered with grasses. Scattered in clusters were leafy eight- or nine-foot trees and heavy brush.

We finally reached a clearing with an empty pole corral. From the looks of things, the corral hadn't held animals for some time. I saw no tracks in the dirt and no recent droppings, just dung clumps half-buried in the dirt. They looked so old they appeared petrified.

"I help," the Indian said as he opened the gate so I could ride into the corral without getting off my horse.

Before entering the fenced-in area, I glanced around nervously. I half-expected more Indians to jump out from behind the thick bushes. My eager "helper" seemed friendly enough, but I found myself disconcerted about being alone with the horses and all our personal belongings. It would be impossible to replace our gear in this wilderness.

With a hand motion, the Indian urged me to enter the corral. His bare skin sagged with age. Well, he *had* mentioned Maxston's name, or at least, it had *sounded* like he'd said Maxston's name. It had sounded more like, Magshon.

I hesitantly rode forward.

The gate closed behind the packhorses. I climbed out of the saddle and jumped to the ground. It suddenly dawned on me that Maxston's horse wasn't here. "Where's Maxston?" I asked as the Indian walked toward one of the packhorses.

"He busy. See you later." He winked as if he'd just told me a good joke. He started undoing the ropes on the packsaddles. Removing my fur coat and one of the packs, he set the items over the fence of the corral, then started to untie a sack.

"What are you doing with my stuff?" I said. Maxston hadn't told me he was delivering goods to an Indian village, and most of the stuff was ours for the trip.

"Go to home," he said, adding a few undecipherable words. He grinned, nodding his head vigorously as if he knew I'd understood.

I interpreted him to mean he was going to take the items to his village. I wished Maxston was around so I could confirm that this was okay.

Before I knew it, the Indian had set all the pack supplies from the packhorses outside the corral. He turned and yelled something in his language.

Almost immediately, a bunch of near-naked kids popped up from behind bushes and shot out from around trees. Some even seemed to appear right out of the dirt, as if by magic. Between the ages of maybe six to twelve, the kids laughed and carried on as if they'd just pulled off the best practical joke of the year.

The older Indian laughed, too. He pointed to the packs. On his command, the kids swiftly grabbed something from the pile of goods and took off running.

"Hey, wait," I hollered, starting after them. "Where the hell are you going with that stuff?"

They disappeared before I got out of the corral. Not one item had been left behind.

Exasperated, I turned and stared at the older Indian.

A big grin remained on his face. "It okay."

Luckily, I had my own backpack strapped to my saddle so they hadn't gotten away with my treasured things. I just couldn't imagine them rummaging through the pack and stealing the only possessions dear to me.

The Indian started to remove the halters from the packhorses. He threw them over one of the poles of the corral.

Well, at least the old Indian is still here. I guess I'll catch up with the supplies eventually. I undid the straps on my horse's saddle, removed the saddle, and placed it over one of the rails on the fence.

When we had all the gear off the horses, the Indian said, "We go now."

I looked around. "We need to get the horses some food and water. They need to be rubbed down."

"Other man do." He opened the gate for us, then latched it closed.

He moved along a winding trail at a lazy pace, like we had all day.

I was anxious to catch up with Maxston and find the supplies. Twitching my fingers impatiently, I ambled along behind him, my boots eroding his barefoot prints in the sand.

Chapter 12

Although we hadn't traveled far, it seemed to take forever to get to the point where my guide stopped. "Home," he said.

We stood in a clearing with scattered clusters of green trees and woody bushes all around us. A few Indian men and women sat in the shade of the trees. They grew quiet, stood up, and watched us from a distance. I saw nothing that appeared to be a village with teepees or living quarters, just trees, brush, and dirt.

A couple of young Indian women, wearing nothing but scraggly skirts made out of tree bark, carried baskets over their heads and made their way past us down the path. They looked up at me and giggled. Children, probably the ones who had absconded with my belongings, suddenly appeared. They all stopped in a group and watched me with large brown curious eyes.

My Indian guide pointed to a spot in the middle of a clump of trees. "You home." It looked like a tall pile of twigs, tree branches, and dried brush.

I studied the pile closer and saw a pattern begin to take shape. The mix of dried materials formed a dome-like hut that reminded me of an upside-down cereal bowl. The structure had been built around some of the living limbs from nearby trees, melding the hut into the brush and natural vegetation, not obvious to the naked eye. As I looked around at the other groups of trees, especially where the Indians stood in the shade, I could see similar huts.

"You home," the old man repeated, moving toward the structure and pulling on a section of the domed formation. A door opened outward. He stepped inside and motioned for me to enter.

I took off my hat and ducked my head low to pass under the door frame. The place couldn't have been more than ten or twelve feet in diameter. Being over six feet tall, I had to keep my head bent to prevent hitting it against the ceiling. Even the highest point of the domed roof, a square-hole opening in the center, would not allow me to stand at full height because of the close branches on the roof.

I immediately recognized the packs and sacks from the horses, all lined up against the hut wall. A feeling of relief washed over me that I had them back in my possession now. Next to the packs sat a pile of blankets, woven with intricate Indian designs. A small fire pit had been dug in the center of the dirt floor, directly under the hole in the roof.

"Me go now," the Indian said, leaving through the door.

"Wait," I said, anxious to be able to find him again if need be. "What's your name?"

He grinned from ear to ear. "Magshon call me José. You no can say real name." He took off before I could ask where I could find him.

The first thing I did was kneel down and check the gear and packs to make sure nothing important was missing. As far as I could tell, everything was there.

My stomach growled with hunger. I was growing more anxious to find Maxston. I pushed open the door and ducked outside.

Now that I could recognize the huts in which the Indians lived, I had a better sense of how clever these people had been in creating theses structures, so well camouflaged into the trees and brush.

As I walked into the clearing, I saw more activity. The group of children, the youngest ones completely naked, ran around the area, playing some sort of game with each other. It looked like "tag." When they saw me, the little ones ran to me excitedly, shouting words in their own language.

One of the older boys in the group stepped forward. He wore a breechcloth. Around his neck, he'd hung some kind of animal tooth attached to a leather strip. He said in a falsetto voice, "We show you village. José say."

A small female child, wearing only a dirty face and a big smile, pulled me by the hand to lead me down the path.

I stumbled along, towering over them and staying alert for signs of Maxston or José.

Along the path, women sat outside their huts and worked with their hands, doing weaving or sewing. One older woman wove nuts and seeds into a fancy pattern on a buckskin shirt. I stopped to take a closer look at the beautiful handiwork. I imagined her skillful craft to be highly valued in this primitive culture.

As with the young girls I'd seen earlier, most of the girls and women wore skirts of various lengths made from strips of woven bark. The skirts looked ratty. Some of the skirts were missing so many pieces of bark in between sections, they left nothing to the imagination. None of the women wore tops, but some of them wore strings of beads, nuts, or shells around their necks. They all wore their long, black hair pulled back into a single braid.

As I strolled along the path, a few children stayed in the lead, while the other kids ran behind me in a parade of giggles, still tagging each other in a playful way.

I couldn't imagine how it must be to live a long time as a child, to grow up really slowly, but these kids all looked happy and content. Even though they would have to depend on someone else to take care of them, they would get to live the carefree life of a kid all those years. *Wow, that would be something. I wonder if their minds develop faster than their bodies. Another question to ask Maxston.*

I glanced at the prepubescent boys and girls in the group. Those poor souls were stuck for long years at the awkward teenage stage. They could no longer enjoy the greater freedom of being a child, and yet, had to wait a long time to be accepted fully into society as an adult. I wondered if this caused psychological problems for these kids. They seemed more subdued than the younger children, but still, they joined in the glee of the situation, showing this stranger around town.

I watched a young mother pick up a tiny child as our parade came down the street. Worse than being a teen, I thought, would be the problem of coming into this world as a toddler, needing to be fed and clothed by someone else for a long, long time. I wondered just how long that might be for that young mother.

Then, it suddenly struck me what a burden these babies and children would be to their parents or caretakers, to have to live with a child for a hundred years or more, children that took a long time to become independent on their own.

I thought about my girls. Maybe it wouldn't be so bad if they stayed the same ages they were now. They were a fun, happy, creative bunch of kids. Maybe that wouldn't be so bad, at least from my perspective as a parent. But I sure wouldn't want to have to take care of a screaming baby and change diapers for an endless number of years.

Now, the children led me into a busier section of the village. Under one large tree, several old men had gathered in a clutch to chew tobacco or some kind of grass. In another area, to the side of the dirt path, a group of younger men squatted in a circle around the sand. One of the men drew lines in the sand, as though making a map to show a location. Most of the men, young and old, wore breechcloths like José. A few, however, also wore a woven belt around their waists. These belts held things like a knife, a small throwing stick, or a coil of rope made from a vine, braided hair, or plant fibers.

Everyone looked up at me as I passed by with the children. The older men chewing tobacco nodded their heads in a warm, silent welcome.

I'm sure I must have been a sight with my factory-made clothing, cowboy hat, and boots. Plus, I stood over a head taller than anyone I'd seen. Living far from the civilized towns, these people probably weren't used to strangers visiting their village.

Soon, the children were turning me around, pushing me in the opposite direction. I took the clue that we had reached the end of the village, which made me realize it wasn't all that big.

As we made our way back, I counted maybe fifty huts, each snuggled neatly into a copse of trees and bushes along the path. The clever way the huts blended into the environment continued to impress me. Even from a short distance, I had a hard time telling the huts apart from the bushes.

As I made my way back through town, I stopped in the middle of the children. "Maxston," I said, pronouncing the name slowly. "Do any of you know where Maxston is?"

"Maxston, Maxston," the children repeated over and over, jumping up and down with delight. But no one pointed out a direction in which I could find him.

"Where?" I said, opening my palms, trying to make my question clear.

The children laughed and continued to lead me down the path a short ways. Then, suddenly, they all disappeared, as though they had fulfilled their task and now had other things to do.

I wandered back along the path alone and wondered if I could identify my own hut. When I came to the place where I thought I'd started, I studied the huts carefully, not sure which one was mine. I didn't want to alarm anyone by walking into the wrong hut.

I adjusted my glasses and studied the dirt. I could see the footprints of the children's bare feet, and also the prints made by my boots. I managed to follow the boot prints to the front of a hut. Sure enough, when I peeked inside to make sure it was mine, I saw the familiar packs still sitting against the wall. I decided to pull some fresh branches off a side tree and place them in a pattern across the front of my door so I'd recognize my hut the next time.

Now what?

I wandered across the way to a couple of old women weaving blankets. "Maxston?" I asked. "Do you know Maxston? Do you know where I can find him?"

The women looked at each other with little smiles on their faces. One of them spoke to me with words I could not understand.

"Maxston? Where?" I pointed down the path to show them what I meant.

The women remained smiling, shook their heads, said things in their own language.

"José?" I tried.

They shook their heads. Maybe they didn't know Maxston called the old Indian José.

After trying to get information from a few other Indians, I sat down in front of my hut and leaned back against the wall to wait for word from either Maxston or José.

Down the way, a couple of middle-aged men sat in the shade and carved on pieces of wood. The women next to them ground some kind of meal and chatted. The children played in the dirt, then would disappear down the path for a while.

The family life made me think about my wife and kids. I wondered what they were doing at that moment. Were they thinking of me, too? Were they worried about me? I couldn't imagine them not being frantic over my disappearance. It had been nearly two weeks since I'd been gone. Were my in-laws still at the house? Probably. They would've stayed to help Erica with the children until some sign of me was found. Erica would lean on them emotionally to get through her grief.

My mind abruptly screeched to a halt. *Wait a minute, I'm thinking like I'm dead and gone. I'm not.* I stood up to break the momentum of my thoughts.

The Indians across the way all looked up at me.

I'm right here, healthy as ever, I told myself. *I'm gonna get to South Town. I'll find a way home...no matter what I have to do. It might take a while, maybe not before Erica and the kids bury an empty box, but everything will be fine once I get home and explain my story.*

The smells of cooked food, drifting from around the village, were beginning to drive me crazy. I held my stomach to quell the churning pangs. I thought about asking one of the women for something to eat, but no one seemed to understand English.

I paced in front of my hut impatiently and looked at my watch: 4 o-clock. It'd been three hours since I'd last seen Maxston. *Where the hell is that guy?*

José suddenly appeared in front of me. "Magshon say you come." He motioned for me to follow him.

It's about time.

Chapter 13

José took me to a hut on the other side of the village. This hut had been hidden from the path the children had taken me through the town. It sat on the other side of a huge tree.

As José led me around to the front of the hut, none other than Maxston sat on a huge brown bear rug with a drink in one hand and a beautiful older Indian woman next to him.

He smiled when he saw me and lifted his drink. "'Hey, Gavin, 'bout time ya showed up. Where ya been all this time?" He winked at the woman, who, unlike the other women in the village, wore a full dress made of buckskin. With feathers strung in her long black loose hair, she looked like the counterpart of Maxston.

"Oh, you know," I said sarcastically, "taking care of the horses, wandering around the village, biding my time, starving to death. By the way, thanks for leaving me on my own with a bunch of people I can't even talk to."

"Sorry 'bout that. Been a long time since I seen my girl here. Couldn't wait one more minute." He patted her leg. "This be Caroline, my wife. Caroline, meet Gavin Clark."

I should've acknowledged Caroline right away, but I was too shocked. I glared at Maxston. "I didn't know you were married," I spit out. I couldn't believe he'd kept that kind of information from me, especially since he'd intended to introduce her to me.

I looked at Caroline. *Caroline*. That couldn't be her real Indian name. It had to be Maxston's pet name for her. I couldn't believe for a minute that this beautiful, intelligent-looking woman with golden skin and large ebony eyes would be married to the likes of Maxston, a burly, ornery man with a dull sense of humor.

I glanced back at Maxston and asked in a skeptical tone, "You're married?"

He nodded his head.

"To her?"

He nodded again.

"What about the other woman?" I blurted. "The one in North Town you went to visit? Is she your *wife*, too?"

He chuckled and shrugged his shoulders.

Glancing at Caroline, I suddenly hoped I hadn't gotten Maxston in trouble by mentioning the other woman in his life.

"Hello, Gavin," Caroline said in a sultry voice. "Maxston here has plenty of girlfriends, but they're all little children at the North Town orphanage." She held out her hand. "It's nice to meet you. Maxston has told me so much about you, I feel like I already know you."

Stunned by her excellent American-sounding English, I stepped back. I also felt ashamed of myself for automatically assuming Maxston had gone to see a woman. I'm sure I had the stupidest look on my face Caroline had ever seen.

Her round dark eyes smiled at me while her lips wavered to hold back a laugh. She winked at Maxston.

My mind struggled to figure out how this Indian woman could be living in this primitive Indian village and speak such perfect English, as well as demonstrate such good manners. "I…I'm sorry," I stammered, stepping forward and shaking her hand. "You...you took me by surprise. I wasn't aware you spoke English."

Her laugh rang out in melodic tones, sounding perfectly proper. That is, if there were such a thing as a proper laugh. This was a classy lady

"Oh, Gavin, what you must think of me. Let me guess. You presumed I was one of the women of this tribe, a barbarian, one who could speak only gibberish and would spend her whole lifetime taking care of her man and babies."

I gave an embarrassed smile with a little shrug. "Well, yeah, something like that. You speak and sound more like I do, which leads me to think you must be from close to my timeline."

"Close, yes. I'm from 2065."

My mouth dropped open. *The future? How could someone be here from the future?* Once again, I must've had that stupid look on my face.

Caroline smiled politely. "Please, sit down with us."

As I sat on the bear rug, Maxston said, "Don't tell me ya think yer the last in the timeline ta get brought in, do ya?"

I stared at him, trying to gather my wits. "I *was* the last one. I just came here. It's still 2015. I mean, only a couple of weeks have passed. I can see people being brought in from a time after you arrived, but I just got here. Someone from fifty years in my future wouldn't be brought in for another fifty years. It doesn't make sense."

"Tried to tell ya," Maxston stated. "Time be different here."

Caroline's eyes softened. She spoke with sympathy in her voice. "I know how you feel. I felt the same way when I found out about others who had come from my future."

Still dumfounded, I asked, "How far into the future are these other people?"

"Three hundred years, as far as we've been able to discover. And sadly, the further into the future they lived, the harder it is for them to adjust." She pressed her delicate hands into her lap. "Think about it. Aren't you having a hard time adjusting to a world without electricity, cars, cell phones, fast foods, and all the other conveniences you had that made your life easier?"

I nodded.

"Someone from the 1800's, like Maxston, fits right into this rugged, undeveloped world. Master Benjamin, too, and others who lived before his time find it easy to adapt quickly. Life hadn't gotten so complicated for them. They had no extraordinary conveniences.

"Now, imagine someone from one, two, or three hundred years in the future. What would their world be like? It would probably be as different as your world was from Maxston's. They would be far more advanced than even my world of high technology and push-button amenities."

I could see where she was going. "Yes, and at least in my time, some people still hunted, fished, and camped. I got out into the great outdoors a little. I know some people in my world who just flat-out wouldn't be able to survive here. So, I can image what it would be like for futuristic people to have to put up with smelly outhouses and lack of electricity." I thought about all the prominent, high-society women and men in my world—the rich actors and actresses, the popular singers, the wealthy entrepreneurs, the ones who lived in mansions filled with servants who tended to every little detail in their lives. I realized that all these people, unless they'd come from a hard background, would probably never make it here. It just dawned on me that these were very likely many of the people living in shanties on the outskirts of North Town. They couldn't get back and they couldn't die, so they walked around in a cloud of confusion.

"How long have you been here?" I asked Caroline. "In this world, I mean."

"Twelve years this month."

My mind reeled with so many questions, I didn't know where to start. I quickly did the math. "If you came in 2065, that means it would be 2077 in the future. But it's only 2015. How can any of that be?"

"You are correct that your time is 2015," she stated, "but mine is 2077. Each person's timeline is different. It doesn't matter *when* you came in, only how long you've been here."

Wow, this was getting more confusing by the minute. "How can anyone keep track of anything if everybody is on a different timeline?"

Two elderly Indian women, carrying woven baskets, stepped around the hut and stopped in front of us. Three young girls followed them. Two of the girls carried a pole between them with a leather bag suspended from it. Steam rose from the bag. The oldest woman said a few words in her language to Caroline.

"They've brought dinner for us," Caroline translated, as she motioned for the women to go ahead and serve us.

One young girl, not more than seven years old, handed each of us a wooden bowl, while the two girls with the pole moved closer. One of the elderly women used a ladle, made from the skull of a small animal, to dish soup from the bag.

Bits of meat, as well as what looked like potatoes, carrots, and onions, poured into my bowl.

The smell of the food made my mouth water. I hadn't eaten since early morning, so at this point, I didn't care what kind of meat this was. I was going to eat it.

The old woman lifted a small leather bag from her basket and opened it. Surprisingly, it contained the white grains of salt.

I glanced at Caroline. I felt certain she had been responsible for making improvements to the tribe's diet in the years she'd been here. It interested me that she hadn't taught them English. I wondered if it was because she felt it was wiser to honor their culture and allow them to live the way they chose.

The women served us half a loaf of bread that looked like typical wheat bread. We were given a jar of honey to put on the bread. The women quickly left us to enjoy our meal.

I put my questions aside and delved into the meal with the other two.

* * *

As we finished up our soup, I took a closer look at Caroline's full-length buckskin dress. It had been made from patches of deerskin, sewn together with thick threads. A wide belt, woven from heavy strings, wrapped around her thin waist. Attached to her belt were several items: a knife in a leather pouch, a small beaded bag, and some kind of fork-like tool that had been carved out of wood.

Curious about her background, I said, "Caroline, you seem well educated. What did you do in your world?"

"I was a paleontologist, specializing in the early inhabitants who lived in the southwestern United States and northern Mexico 10,000 years before my time. They were called the Kumeyaay. They were my ancestors. In fact, it wouldn't surprise me if José is my great-grandfather ten times removed."

This fascinated me. "Aren't you afraid you'll mess up the future. You know, the whole idea about going back in time and killing-your-grandfather-thing?"

She laughed. "What future? The future in this world is *now*, just as the past is *now*. All our pasts, presents, and futures are taking place simultaneously. Anyway, no one can have kids, so how would it affect me if I killed José?"

"Hmmm, I see your point."

She laughed again. "At least, that's what my friend in South Town says. He works in the government offices."

My ears perked up at the mention of South Town. "You have a friend in South Town?" I said eagerly. "Does he know the head scientist? Would he be able to help me get in the door?"

She seemed to pick up on my thoughts. "He works in the same building with the scientists, but he's a file clerk in the records department. His name is Hector Rodriguez. He's from 2021, really close to your time. I'll write a letter of introduction for you, if you like. He's a nice guy. He keeps me informed of all the latest news."

"Oh, okay," I said, feeling a little disappointed that Hector wasn't in a higher position. "I'd like to see this guy Howard Blackman first. I'd rather deal with the top man. Someone who directly knows what's going on and can give me some decent answers."

"Suit yourself," she said, "but the offer will still be there if you change your mind."

I set my soup bowl aside. Having satiated my hunger, food no longer mattered. I was starving for news of any kind that could get me closer to Erica. "So, tell me, what have you heard lately? What are they doing? Are the scientists making any progress on getting us back to our own world and our own times?"

She shook her head. "No, not that I'm aware. However, of interest is a rumor brought to me last month about a guy making it back home."

My eyes got big.

"I wouldn't put any faith in it, though," she said quickly. "Hector hasn't been able to confirm it, and I don't know how anyone would know if someone made it home or not." As I started to ask for details, she held up a hand, cutting me off. "Hector did tell me that the group who takes credit for this outrageous claim is an off-shoot of the main scientific community. In fact, they're based in North Town so they can do their thing without the scientists in South Town interfering with them. They're pretty far out, from what I hear. They've come up with this idea that we're part of an alien experiment. Kind of like a giant ant farm."

Ant farm? I blinked. "Are they serious?"

"They claim we're in a glass-like enclosure of some kind. Word is, if you travel to a specific place on the east coast, you can see outside the glass. They claim that, every now and then, an alien comes close and looks inside. They even say they have pictures."

Wow. This sounds scary. An alien experiment? "The other scientists must know about this place," I said. "Surely, they've checked it out to verify that it's true or not."

"Hector says he's seen the photos. He couldn't tell, one way or the other, what he was looking at. The forms were blurry, as if the pictures had been taken through a white, flimsy veil. He said he wouldn't put any stock in the photos or the claims."

I pushed my glasses up on my nose. The idea of being an alien's experiment sounded completely unbelievable. But then again, what if it was true? People had claimed for years that they'd seen flying saucers, and even tried to prove it with photos. Still, no one believed them.

White veil. The words rang a bell with me. They reminded me of the invisible spider web, the feeling of moving through a veil of white wispy material. True, the substance had been transparent, but the word *white* seemed to relate to it as close as I could imagine a color. Now, I wondered if this white veil prevented us from seeing outside the world we'd gotten ourselves trapped in.

For a moment, I remembered the glimpse of the hazy movement against the sky across the ocean. A shiver went down my spine. Could that have been an alien? Oh, my God, how could this be?

Up until now, Maxston had been quietly listening, letting us talk. "Been to that coast they talkin' 'bout," he said somberly. "I seen...well...somethin'. Don't know what. But I seen it. Don't know I believe what they say."

Caroline brushed back a long lock of her dark hair and continued. "These renegade scientists have come up with the theory that the aliens have crowded many elements of our world together, to see if different species from different time periods would be able to live together in a place where they are forced into a smaller world." Her dark eyes became animated, as though the idea fascinated her. "Imagine, all ages of mankind living with every creature that had ever lived on earth. How would humans interact with dinosaurs? Would they exterminate them? Would they tame them and use them for work animals? Would they make food out of them? Or...would the dinosaurs exterminate mankind?"

I'd seen a real dinosaur in the barn in North Town. I couldn't deny they existed in this world. The idea that aliens might have thrown us all together in a melting pot had some credence, considering the strange things and people I'd seen. That is, if I could believe in aliens.

Caroline went on with her imaginative ideas about what this world could reveal to someone of a scientific mind who wanted to try an experiment with living beings. "How would a twentieth century man deal with a race like the Neanderthal man? Would he treat these primitive men like a different species? After all, we have this belief that Neanderthal man was closer in essence to the great apes than to modern man."

The sun was going down and the temperature was dropping. A breeze brought a blast of cooler air in off the ocean, causing all of us to shiver.

"What about you?" I asked Caroline as I rubbed my arms to keep warm. "What do you believe about all this?"

"I believe...," she said as she shifted closer to Maxston, who put his arm around her, "I believe we were chosen for a reason. Whether we were chosen by God, aliens, or some other force, I don't know. And to tell you the truth, I don't care. I decided ten years ago, when I realized there was probably no way out, to live my life the way I wanted to live and not worry about how I got here or why I'm here."

"You came from an advanced society, yet you're living here with a tribe of archaic Indians. Wouldn't you rather be living in South Town, where they're supposed to have indoor plumbing and electricity?"

"Not really," she said with a chuckle. "I lived in South Town for a number of years. It's too politically oriented for my taste." She motioned toward the village. "These simple people are a part of me, a part of my past. How many paleontologists get to live among their work?" She snuggled into Maxston's arms. "No, I'm happier here than I'd ever been in South Town."

As I looked at the two, I couldn't resist asking her, "So, how come you married this wild man?" I tipped my head toward Maxston.

"Wild man, my ass," Maxston yelled in fake anger.

Caroline laughed, glancing fondly at the man. "I met him in South Town. He'd brought a load of supplies in from the north. He intrigued me from the start. I about embarrassed him to death when I asked him out on a date." She laughed again.

A scowl formed on Maxston's face, like she was saying too much and he didn't like it.

"The differences between our two cultures," she continued, "became a serious challenge. He'd never heard of Women's Lib, and I wasn't about to stay home, barefoot and pregnant, so to speak. When I learned about this tribe living out here alone, I decided to visit and study them for a month or two. Maxston brought me here and chose to stay at the village for a while." With a wry smile, she put a hand to her mouth and loudly whispered, "He thought I needed to be protected."

Maxston guffawed and rolled his eyes. "Ya don't need ta tell this story, ya know." He gave her a pleading look, but she plowed on ahead anyway.

"One day, we were out with a hunting party, tracking a wounded bear. Maxston and I were by ourselves when the bear came out of a clump of brush and charged us.

121

Maxston's rifle misfired. He was sure we were going to be killed. I'd learned to shoot a bow in my world as a child. I got so good, I did competition shooting. For this hunt, I was carrying a bow José had given me, so I nocked an arrow and let it fly."

"Yeah," Maxston said dryly, taking over the story. "She get lucky. Arrow hit the bear right in the eye. Went clear ta the brain." He chuckled. "Damn bear dropped dead at my feet, chin layin' on my toes. I 'bout messed myself."

"To this day," Caroline said with amusement, "he swears he would have been able to fight the bear off with his tomahawk and knife." She gave him a light punch. "But, I'll admit, that was the biggest grizzly I'd ever seen, before or since. It measured twelve feet tall with paws fourteen inches across. It would have torn him to pieces with one swipe of those eight-inch claws."

I looked at the bear rug under us. "Is this it?" I asked with amazement at the size of the skin. It would take an elephant gun to stop something this size.

"Yeah, but I'd a taken him apart, bit by bit," Maxston said, puffing out his chest. "I be part bear myself," he bragged, trying to sound tougher than he really was.

Caroline affectionately ran her hand down his beard. "That bear brought us together. We married here in the village and we've been married ever since. I never went back to South Town to live."

I had a thought, ignoring Maxston's past resistance to going it alone with me to South Town. "Hey, Maxston, we've traveled hundreds of miles and nothing bad has happened to us. Why do we need to wait for the wagon train, anyway? They can get someone else to be the wagon master. Why don't you and I just take off from here and head for South Town?"

His face grew dead serious. "Numbers, Gavin. Strength in numbers. Nobody goes south without strength, less'n ya want ta die."

"Maxston's right," Caroline said, sitting up and putting the bowls and honey jar into the basket that the women had left. "Some of the most dangerous animals in this world live in the middle of the country. When I came through, I was glad for the wagon train and the many people who had traveled with us. Were it not for the numbers and the training with weapons, we wouldn't have made it. Not with an attack by a T-rex and another attack by a band of velociraptors."

"So what do they do?" I asked. "Have an army of men armed to the teeth to escort people on every trip?"

"Just about," Maxston said. "Army be the wagon drivers, wranglers, and helpers. Everybody on the trip be trained ta fight. You be no exception. Best ta be prepared."

Sitting in this quiet, peaceful, boring Indian community, safe and sound, the trip to the south actually sounded adventurous and exciting to me. "What kind of weapons do they use? I wouldn't mind shooting a T-rex."

"This ain't goin' ta be no joy ride," Maxston said gruffly.

Caroline nodded in agreement. "The people who try to make it on their own, without the wagon train, go off to die. And believe me, if you go it alone, you *will* die."

For some reason, maybe something in the soup, I just couldn't get into the seriousness of it right now. "Hey, maybe this world is just a figment of our imaginations and, if we die, we'll go back home to our real worlds. Maybe that's the test, to see how long we'll live here before we do something stupid and get killed."

Both Maxston and Caroline glared at me.

"That be the stupidest thing I yet heard ya say," Maxston said, shaking his head at me like I was a naughty child. "Promise me, ya won't do somethin' stupid, like run off to try to get ta South Town on yer own."

As much as I'd gotten attached to Maxston and liked the guy, I couldn't make a promise I wasn't sure I could keep. If I had the chance of getting to South Town and back to my family more quickly, I'd abandon him in a heartbeat. Rather than tell a lie, I decided on a compromise. "Tell you what, Maxston. I promise to tell you upfront if I decide to do something stupid. At least, that way, you'll have an opportunity to try and talk me out of it."

"Fair 'nough," he said, getting to his feet. He helped Caroline rise. "Time ta hit the sack. We be takin' off day after tomorrow. Get a couple a day's rest 'fore we head back ta North Town."

* * *

I made my way back to my hut in the twilight. I curled up on my side between a bunch of blankets. I thought about Erica and the girls. I wondered what they were doing at that moment. Were they worried about me? Did they think I was dead?

I pictured Erica going through my things, cleaning out my drawers and closet, throwing my clothes away. She'd probably sell my tools and guns. I just hoped she'd keep something to remember me by.

I sighed, feeling a tear come to my eye. I hoped she wouldn't move on too soon. I hated the thought of finally getting back home, only to find another man sleeping in my bed.

I turned over and silently cried myself to sleep.

Chapter 14

The next morning, I woke to the sounds of children laughing, dogs barking, and men and women speaking and shouting in a foreign tongue. It took me a few moments to remember I was in an Indian village.

Getting up, I rubbed at my eyes, wishing I had some water to wash my face. I wondered where they got their fresh water supply in this community. I'd slept in my clothes, so I pulled on my boots, put on my hat, and strapped on my gun. Everyone had looked at me like I was some kind of enigma around here, so it didn't seem to matter if I carried the gun. Maxston always kept his rifle with him.

Ducking outside, I squinted in the sharp sunlight and had to shade my eyes with my hand. I heard my name being called.

José sauntered in my direction. "Good," he said. "You up. You come with me. Fish day. Work day."

I nodded and followed him, moving along at his lazy pace. My stomach was already calling for food. I hoped the itinerary included breakfast.

José took a path that headed straight toward the ocean. Other villagers, also heading toward the ocean, ran around us in a more excited frenzy. Some men carried nets. Some carried ropes of various widths and lengths. The children carried rocks about the size of golf balls.

I soon found myself at the top of the beach. I looked back. This trail had seemed much shorter and more direct than my winding jaunt to the corral and the village the day before. Thinking about the corral, I said to my companion, "José, I need to check on the horses and make sure they're okay."

He pointed to the surf, where it looked like the whole village had now congregated. "Go there. You go there."

I saw Maxston in the crowd, so I hurried over to meet up with him.

"Mornin' sleepy head. 'Bout time ya get yer lazy butt outta bed." The twinkle in his blue eyes told me he was enjoying giving me a hard time.

"What's going on?"

"Be once a week. Whole tribe fishes. Everybody helps, even guests." He pointed to the dugout canoes that had been sitting on the beach the day before. "Gonna be in one a them dillybobs fer the next four ta five hours. Ya better take care a yer business while ya can. Grab you a plate a grub from that fire over there. Ya got fifteen minutes 'fore we go."

He took off before I could ask him about the horses. I figured he must have already taken care of them, or maybe asked one of the Indians to feed and water them. I looked back up the beach toward the area of the corral. I shrugged. *Well, maybe the horses are just fine. If no one else is worried about them, I won't worry either.*

After wolfing down a quick breakfast of fresh soup and bread, I found a secluded spot in the brush to take care of my morning business. I arrived back on the beach just as Maxston looked up and yelled for me.

"Hurry up, Son. If ya get left behind, you be havin' ta work with the women buildin' fires and smokin' fish. Nasty work. Be better off out with the men." As I joined him, he shoved me toward a canoe with six men in it already.

I climbed into the second-to-last seat, struggled for my balance, and just about tipped the canoe over. Luckily, the other men managed to keep it upright. Maxston climbed in behind me.

Made from a long tree trunk, the canoe looked like it had been hollowed out by building a fire in the center of it, putting the fire out, then scraping the burnt area clear. It still smelled like burnt wood. Maybe it was a new canoe.

One man handed me a wooden pole with a widened end on it. Taking the paddle, I watched the others to see which side of the canoe I should start paddling on. I'd often watched the Olympics and had seen how those teams paddled in unison. It didn't take long for me to figure out the

Indians' unified pattern and fit my strokes in with theirs. With Maxston behind me, I couldn't see what he was doing, but I had the feeling he'd done this many times before.

We crashed over the unnaturally-timed breaking waves and made it out to the more gently rolling swells of the ocean. Pristine blue skies stretched as far as the eye could see. I studied the horizon for a while, wondering if I would see the faint movement in the sky that I'd seen the day before. The idea of aliens watching us gave me the creeps. Nothing seemed out of order, so I decided to think about other things.

Being in the middle of a big body of water in an unstable, constantly rocking canoe made me a little nervous. I could swim in a backyard pool, but I didn't consider myself a strong swimmer. These people, obviously, didn't have a lifejacket for me.

I glanced back at the shore. It seemed to be getting a long ways away. I should've asked how far out we'd be going. It might have been better if I'd stayed back with the women, made some excuse to take care of the horses or something.

Not watching what I was doing with my paddle, it got tangled up with the man in front of me. It took us a minute to get things back in order. As my embarrassment passed, I settled down into the rhythm of things again.

We moved farther and farther from shore.

When my nerves got the better of me. I yelled over my shoulder. "Maxston, how far out are we going? Aren't there any fish closer in?"

"Don't tell me ya get seasick?"

"No, I'm just not that good of a swimmer."

He laughed. "Don't worry. These guys can swim. You fall in? They be savin' ya." He shouted something in the Indian language.

Muttered grunts and laughs filtered back to us.

We stopped and the other canoes spread out around us. I wasn't sure of the distance to shore, maybe a quarter-mile, maybe more. All I knew was the shore looked pretty far away, too far for me to swim. All I could hope was that we stayed upright for the whole trip.

Layne Walker

The Indians used a combination of fishing methods. The men in our canoe each pulled out a line with a bone hook attached. A foot above the hook, each tied one of the golf-ball-sized rocks. After fastening a piece of animal gut to the hook, they dropped their lines into the water and let them sink. This fishing process was new to me and somewhat interesting.

The men chattered back and forth while they waited for the fish to take the bait. After many years together, doing the same things week after week, I wondered what these men could possibly have to say to each other.

The first man to catch a fish reeled it in by pulling on the line and looping it in his hand, kind of like a cowboy coiling up his rope. When the fish came next to the boat, one of the other men carefully leaned over to gaff the fish with a hooked stick. They lifted the smaller fish right up into the canoe. After all these years of practice, they seemed to know how to keep the canoe well-balanced. If one man leaned in one direction, another leaned to the other side. When the men shifted, I just clung to the sides and hoped the thing wouldn't tip over.

I managed to get my line, hook, and sinker into the water. As I waited for some action, I watched the other canoes.

Some of the groups used the same fishing method with the hook and sinker, but another group of men moved smoothly through the water away from us, as though they were following a school of fish. Half the men sat in the canoe and paddled, while the other half stood up and threw spears into the water. A thin line had been hooked to the spears to pull the catch back to the canoe. When the standing men threw their spears and pulled in the lines, they kept the canoe perfectly balanced, like a circus feat.

On another canoe, the men used bows and arrows in a similar manner as the spear-throwers. I wondered how hard it would be to hit a fish beneath the water with an arrow that had a line attached to it. Just as I admired these Indians for their ingeniously camouflaged huts, I gained a new respect for them for their ability with their bows and spears. It seemed like for every shot that went out, a fish came back in.

Every now and then, one of the Indians would jump in the water and swim around for a few minutes. The frigid water was way too cold for the men to be using it to cool off from the day's heat. For the life of me, I couldn't figure out why they wanted to get into the freezing water. I turned to Maxston for an answer.

"They be relievin' themselves. Think it be bad luck ta just hang over the side."

Wow, I hoped I could wait until we got back. I didn't feel like taking a swim in the icy water. Nor could I imagine myself trying to get in and out of the canoe with nothing to stand on.

Since none of the men wore any coverings on their bodies, except for their breechcloths, it didn't take them long to dry off in the sun. I, on the other hand, would be drenched to the bone with my cowboy clothes.

Then I had another thought. "Are there sharks out here?"

"Never seen one in these parts. They be north a here mostly."

I hoped he was right. Once, I'd watched a show on the Learning Channel about the megalodon, the ancestor of the great white shark. The megalodon had been a seventy-foot-long, 60,000-pound predator that could swallow this little canoe in one gulp. If this world really was a hodgepodge of animals and beasts from every period, including prehistoric times, it could very well have megalodons in it.

I swallowed hard and glanced toward the shore again. It seemed farther away than the last time I'd checked.

Suddenly, the water looked dark and sinister. I could almost see a huge, triangular-shaped head shooting for the surface, a mouth full of seven-inch teeth heading right for our canoe. I took a deep breath and tried to block out the image. It was going to be a long day.

* * *

Over the next hours, the floor of our canoe filled up with fish, which now rested under our feet. I'd even managed to bring in a few myself. I'd never been one who was big on fishing, but I had to admit, once I got over the scare of being eaten by a shark, I was enjoying being out in the open air and part of a primitive practice. Truly, there seemed to be something satisfying about collecting our own food.

While the fishing was underway, I hadn't paid much attention to our surroundings. At one point, I looked up and was surprised to see a patch of white on the horizon. At first it gave me a fright that it could be a shark, but it looked too boxy. "Hey, Maxston." I waited for him to catch my eye. "What's that?" I pointed to the white patch.

"Ship. See 'em ever now 'n then."

I frowned. "You didn't tell me there were ships. Do they make trips up and down the sea? Can't we take one of them instead of the wagon train? Wouldn't that be faster? And a lot safer?"

"Can't get on a ship, 'less'n yer a scientist. Or got ya special permission from Howard Blackman. Rarely gives a man permission." He saw my next question coming and answered it before I could get it out of my mouth. "Nope. It ain't worth tryin'. Take ya a month ta get an answer. By that time, the wagon train be sittin' in South Town. Sides, if ya take a ship, ya still gotta get from the water ta town. Takes almost as long ta do that as ta take the wagon train."

My hopes dashed, I slumped back in my seat. It was at least nice to know this world had ships. It made me wonder about other things in this world. "Maxston, you said this landmass is only 250,000-square miles and that it's perfectly square. What about across the sea? What about other countries like England, Australia, Japan, and China? Are they out there, too?"

"Don't know. That be somethin' you can ask the big-wigs in South Town. Maybe they can tell ya."

I looked toward the horizon. "What happens if you sailed a ship due west? Would you sail until you hit the eastern coast of this country, or what?"

"Like I said...don't know. Never bothered ta find out. It ain't important ta me. My world be on land, not water. More importantly, I ain't sure I wanna know."

I could *not* agree with him on that. I wanted to know what was out there. The more I knew about this world, the better chance I had for finding a way out of it. I intended to discuss this ocean with Howard Blackman when I got to South Town.

Around high noon, we paddled back to shore. I felt a great relief when I got out of the canoe and stumbled again onto dry land.

We took a break on the beach, ate dried meat and bread, and washed it down with water from skin flasks. While we ate, the women and kids unloaded the fish from the canoes. The kids seemed to make a game of it, seeing who could haul the most fish to the baskets. Some of the women cleaned the fish, while others filleted them with sharp flint knives and spread the meat out on wooden racks. A few other women dug long pits in the dryer parts of the beach. After building fires in the pits, they helped the other women set the racks over the fires to smoke the fish and dry out the meat.

I didn't look forward to going back out onto the ocean to spend the rest of the day fishing with the men. Unfortunately, even though I was a "guest," I knew it would look bad if I stayed back with the women. Everybody else in the village was working hard, even Caroline as she helped the women. I figured I should make the same effort.

* * *

As the sun set that day, we pulled our canoes out of the surf and dragged them onto the beach. My cowboy hat and long-sleeved shirt helped to prevent me from being sunburned, but I could see that the backs of my hands had turned bright red.

I couldn't remember a time of ever being so tired. My eyelids drooped. I wanted to shut my eyes during dinner with Caroline and Maxston. They seemed to understand and dismissed me early.

As soon as I laid my head down on the makeshift pillow I'd formed from a rolled-up blanket, I fell asleep.

Surprisingly, I didn't dream about Erica and the kids this time. Instead, lovely Hannah floated into my mind with her golden hair, sky-blue eyes, and mesmerizing smile. I slept peacefully, like a baby.

Chapter 15

Early the next morning, before leaving the village, Maxston and I went down to the water and took what passed for a bath. We stripped off, rubbed sand on our bodies to remove the dirt, then used some kind of soap that stunk like moldy wood. When finished, my skin felt squeaky clean, but it also itched like crazy. While I was at it, I washed my clothes. I'd washed my socks and underwear a few times previously, whenever I'd had the opportunity, but my jeans and shirt hadn't been laundered since I'd gotten stranded in this world. They were so filthy, they could almost stand up by themselves.

José gave me a pair of buckskin pants and a matching shirt to wear while my clothes dried. "You keep," he said.

Patches of deerskin had been added to the bottom of the pants to accommodate my height. Same for the length of the sleeves. Someone had prepared the buckskins specially for me. It surprised me how comfortable the material felt against my skin. The shirt hadn't been fancily decorated with beads like Maxston's, but it suited me just fine.

The Indians had the packhorses ready as we reached the corral. I draped my wet jeans and shirt across the packs to allow them to dry while we rode.

I was in a good mood, excited to leave, to get on with my goals. If my calculations were correct, the wagon train would be ready to leave shortly after we got back to North Town.

Maxston seemed sad as he tied a pouch to his horse's saddle.

I figured he didn't want to leave Caroline behind.

As though reading my mind, he said, "My woman be comin' along."

"Why do you seem so down, then? I thought it was because you'd be missing her."

"I be sad every time I head ta town. Rather be out in these here wild, open spaces. In town, everybody be fallin' all over each other, gittin' in the way."

As I thought about it, I had to admit I held the same sentiment. I didn't look forward to the stench of the town, the poverty and depression of the confused people, the clutter of the houses, the dark government offices at the old fort. Being out in the open country had lifted my spirits, though it hadn't made me completely forget my anxiety about getting back to my wife and kids.

We met Caroline on the beach. She sat tall and proud on her chestnut horse, which she'd kept in a corral near her hut. Caroline had tied her long black hair at the nape of her neck with a beaded strip of leather. Instead of the dress she'd been wearing around the village, she wore a plain buckskin top and pants for riding the long distance. Her eyes sparkled with excitement. In contrast to Maxston, she bubbled over with joy. "It's been a long time since I've been to North Town," she said. "I'm looking forward to a change of scenery. Even though I love it here—I love the simplicity and naturalness of the people and the wilderness here—I need a break from the village. I miss intellectual conversations and having more direct access to what is going on in the other communities." She laughed. "Who knows, I might even tag along when you go to South Town. I'd like to visit old friends and see what kinds of changes have been in the making in South Town."

I liked the idea of her coming along. Not only was she beautiful to look at, but her laughter and spirit would make a pleasant companion, giving me someone to talk to when Maxston wasn't in the mood to speak.

* * *

As the trip got underway, we passed from the ocean retreat into flat wooded areas, then out onto open plains of high desert.

Caroline entertained us with anecdotes about her own time period, growing up under the auspices of her advanced culture with her desire and interest in studying her ancestors and history. She told us a number of amusing tales about people in South Town after she'd first arrived, then how she'd grown disillusioned pretty quickly with the lack of progress in the scientific community. They'd had only a limited amount of technology with which to work, so even though the advanced scientific minds had come together to sort out the abnormalities of this world, not much progress had been made. She admitted she didn't expect to find much more accomplished in the last ten years. She knew that from the letters that she'd recently received from Hector.

As I observed Caroline and listened to her stories, it seemed strange to me that she'd been born in my lifetime in the year 2005 when I was twenty-four. In my world, she was younger than me. In this world, she was older. Another one of those tricks of time.

One evening at the campfire, after we finished our meal, I prodded Caroline with some of the questions on my mind. "I was wondering about kids. If their bodies grow slowly, what about their minds? Do their brains expand with information faster than their bodies grow? I mean…what I'm trying to say is, do they become wiser than their years?"

"That's an interesting question," she said. "I've only been here twelve years, but I have noticed the phenomena that children don't age quickly. You can observe the changes in babies the most, since babies show the most obvious growth from being in the crib to being a toddler. It's more difficult to see the changes in an older child or a teenager. The studies that have been done by the scientists in South Town have concluded that children age about one year in our world to ten years here. In other words, it takes about ten years here for a child to move from being a one-year-old to being a two-year-old in our world."

I leaned toward her with rapt interest. "That seems amazing. What about their minds? Do they learn that slowly, too? If a two-year-old child has been around for ten years, does that child learn to talk like a ten-year-old?"

"No, and that's another strange thing about the time distortion in this world. The children don't seem to get any smarter for being around all those years. Their minds seem to mature as slowly as their bodies."

"It must be difficult on parents to have to raise the children for so many years. It seems like that would get to be a burden."

"Yes, I believe it could be a burden." She glanced briefly at Maxston, who was chewing tobacco and watching the fire. "This world can also be a burden for those who wish to have children and can't. In either case, it's a long time to have something you don't want, or something you want that you don't have."

And a long time, I added in my mind, *to miss the ones you love if you can't get back to them.* "So, if children only age about one year to every ten years, what about adults?"

"The scientists estimate that we age at the same rate as the children. It's just not as obvious. I've hardly noticed any changes in my own body over the last twelve years. I feel the same as I did when I came into this world. Well, if anything, I'm a lot healthier and heartier because I don't live in a polluted society or eat foods that are manufactured. I've found myself actually feeling stronger as I grow older."

"Do you think that people would die if they grew old enough?"

She shook her head. "That I can't tell you. No one has seen it happen in this world, at least so far. If it takes a person one hundred years to add ten years of life in our world, we could all live a long time here. I guess we'll know if people will die of old age two or three hundred years from now, since nearly everyone is documented when they come in, as well as when they die."

My eyes widened in surprise. "How can that be? No one documented me."

Maxston chuckled. "Praise the Lord, Goodman Gavin. Thou be on the records."

I shot a look at him. "You mean I was documented when you took me to Master Benjamin?"

"Yup. And you be documented when ya die. If'n anybody sees ya die or finds yer body."

It hadn't dawned on me that someone was keeping a census of the people who came into this world. "How do you know when someone comes in?"

"There are scouts," Caroline interjected, "living in different towns and vicinities, assigned with the purpose to watch for newbies. It's pretty easy to identify them. They are always confused and disoriented. They usually look more polished and fresh in their clothing and behavior. They haven't yet taken on the dullness or hardness of living here over a period of time. Basically, they haven't yet bought into this world nor accepted the fact that they won't ever be going back."

Erica and the girls flashed into my mind, along with a painful ache in my heart.

"It's not a perfect tracking system," Caroline added. "No one knows where people will pop up, and people die without anyone being around to report it. So, the system works the best it can under the circumstances."

I stoked the fire with a stick. "How long has this world been here? Does anybody know?"

Maxston rustled around as he opened his pouch for more tobacco. He sat back and listened, seeming to enjoy the interaction without speaking.

Caroline responded, "The scientists haven't figured out how long this world has been here, but their best estimate is that mankind showed up about one hundred years ago. They seem to think the first place to have appeared was the fort at North Town. With it came soldiers from the Civil War era. From what they can tell, some of these people have been here maybe a hundred years. Of course, they've hardly aged that much. These people still have the old records from the fort. Someone had kept good documentation. They continued to document the progress of the people in the fort after it had been dislocated from its time."

"Have any of those people died?"

"Well, yes, but not of old age."

I stopped to think about what it must have been like for the Civil War soldiers to suddenly find themselves in this strange world with no connection to any other civilization.

They must have sent scouts to the east to look for their command center. That had to be shocking. "What about South Town?" I asked. "Did people from North Town migrate there and start that town?"

"Strangely, South Town cropped up shortly after the fort appeared. It was a little mission town from Mexico. No one kept records when it first appeared, so it is unclear as to when it had actually come into this world. The scientists feel pretty sure it hasn't been here longer than North Town. Some of the scientists from the more advanced eras started showing up there a little later. They brought the society together and created a central economic and political structure. This eventually developed into a semi-metropolitan area where many of the newcomers migrated. More people seem to appear in the southern section of this world than in the north. Plus, a lot of the northerners who want a more advanced trade system and living conditions will travel to South Town to settle there."

I found myself intrigued with all this information, wondering how this paralleled the development of my own world as people cropped up in sections of different countries, living off the land, forming the basis of more advanced civilizations for the future. "What about the Eskimos and your Indian village? Why don't those people live closer to the towns where they can get more supplies?"

"Like ta have their own space," Maxston answered. "Like ta live without the bullshit of the government."

"Plus," Caroline added, "it's actually safer out in those isolated areas than it is in the towns where newbies come in and create havoc until they settle down. If someone shows up in the outer areas, the Indians and Eskimos will take them in and give them a home until they decide to move elsewhere. The new people in those outer areas seem to make an easier transition until they can get their bearings."

"I still don't get how this timeline thing works. How can you be here for twelve years, Maxston for forty-four years, and Master Benjamin for fifty years, but you are all from different time periods?"

Caroline smiled. "Anyone who can figure that out probably has the whole key to this strange world. It's just a fact. We learn to live with it."

Eager for more answers, I plowed on. "What about other countries? You know, like France, Russia, China? Do they exist in this world?"

"I can't answer that. I don't know."

"What happens if someone sails a ship due west? Does the ocean connect to the other side of this landmass? I saw the ship of the scientists out in the waters when we were fishing? Could it reach another country? If it goes all the way north and this land is square, can it cut across the waters to get to the other side?"

Caroline shook her head. "I don't know any of that." She seemed to grow sad. Her manner became more somber as she turned toward the fire and doodled with a stick, stirring the outside embers.

I wasn't sure if she really didn't know the answers or had just gotten tired of not having them.

Maxston stared into the fire as though his mind had traveled thousands of miles away.

Caroline threw down the stick and stood up. "Well, I'm exhausted. I'm going to turn in for the night. I'll see you in the morning."

Maxston got up and joined her.

"Goodnight," I said after them, feeling like maybe I'd chased Caroline away with my questions. Something had changed in her manner. I had the feeling she knew more than she was saying about this world, but didn't want to tell me. Maybe she thought, if I knew the truth, I would freak out. It gave me the creeps to think this little piece of land might be the only island of humanity that existed in this world.

* * *

The trip to North Town took three days. Over the course of the journey, I found myself thinking less and less about my family. It wasn't that I didn't love them and miss them. It just seemed like I was getting more and more involved in this world, its beauty, and its strangeness—how the different terrains melded into each other and changed so quickly. Here, it took a day to cross a desert when, in my world, it would take a week. My reveries about the people in this world and their problems, how they experienced arriving here, and how they survived making a new life for themselves, distracted me from my concerns about Erica and the girls. So much was going through my mind about what I'd been seeing and what I was yet to see, I didn't have time to dwell on the past or what I was missing.

Having been here for over two weeks now, things seemed more and more normal. Hell, I'd even started thinking of North Town as my home. Occasionally, I'd consider how the human mind was such an adaptable thing. Mine seemed to be adjusting rapidly, making me feel like I belonged in this world. I had to keep reminding myself that I *didn't*. I kept telling myself that, once I was on the wagon train heading south, I would get back on track and concentrate on my mission to find my way back to my *real* home.

The closer we got to North Town, the more nervous I grew. At first, I wasn't sure why, but I soon realized that it all stemmed around Hannah. All through the trip, especially when I would lie down at night, images of her beautiful face and soft curves would float into my thoughts. A part of me wanted to see her as soon as I got into town, but another part of me told me it would be better if I avoided her completely. She wanted us to be together. She wanted marriage. I couldn't give that to her…at least not right now.

Hell, what am I thinking? Not right now? *I must be crazy. It's just not going to happen. Well,* I told myself as I calmed down, *if—and that is a big if—I can't get back home to Erica and my kids…well…I might think about a life with Hannah.* But marrying Hannah would only happen after I'd exhausted all possible avenues of finding a way back to Erica.

As we rode into the outskirts of town through the shabby-looking streets, I realized what I feared most about seeing Hannah again. I feared that she would capture my heart so fully as to distract me from my ultimate goal.

Chapter 16

We pulled up in front of Maria's boarding house and got off the horses. I dusted off my buckskins.

Maxston said, "Grab yer gear. I be takin' the horses ta the stable. You two get the rooms."

I had only my backpack containing my stuff. I detached them from the saddle and threw it over my shoulder.

Caroline grabbed the one bag she'd tied behind her saddle.

"Gavin, you're back," a sweet voice said from across the street.

I turned to see Hannah approaching in my direction. Gretchen, Sven, her sister, and two brothers followed closely behind her. My worst fears had manifested.

"I missed you so," she blurted.

Great. This is all I need right now. I pushed my glasses up on my nose. "Hi, Hannah. It's good to see you." I felt like a trapped rat as she and her family formed a half-circle around me.

Maxston caught my eye briefly, then took off with the horses.

Caroline walked next to the building and waited, for which I was glad. I didn't want Hannah to think that Caroline and I were together.

"Now that you're home," Hannah said, "you vill be coming to dinner tonight?" It wasn't really a question, more like a demand. She looked pretty in a light-blue dress with homespun white lace trim. She wore a matching bow in her hair.

Compared to the cleanliness of her clothing and that of her family's, I suddenly felt grimy in my dirty buckskins. I feared I was beginning to look like most of the derelicts outside of town. "I…um…I'm not sure." I didn't want to hurt her feelings, but my gut feeling told me, *Don't go*.

Sven's feisty little body stepped forward. He wore a scowl on his face. "You not be shunnin' my little girl, now vould ya?"

"Oh, no, not at all," I said nervously. "It's just that…" My mind raced for an excuse that would be plausible and acceptable by this high-strung little man. "Look, it's been a long day. I'm tired. I'm dirty. All I want to do is go up to my room, clean up, and sleep. I wouldn't be very good company. Why don't I come tomorrow night instead?"

He continued to glower at me.

Hannah put her hand on Sven's arm. She looked at me and said, "I understand." Disappointment showed on her face. "I vill expect you at six." She turned and walked away, followed by her sister, brothers, and big-boned mother.

Sven remained glaring up at me. After several moments, he turned and left.

Caroline stepped up next to me. "Looks like you may have a little problem."

"Yeah, I think I do. All I wanted to do was to be Hannah's friend. Already, it's spiraled out of control. I can't wait until we leave for South Town. At least then I won't have to see her every day." I closed my eyes and brought Erica's face into my mind. "I just want to go home…to my wife and kids."

Caroline grabbed my arm and escorted me into the boarding house where we signed up for rooms and arranged for baths.

A little while later, soaking in a tub of hot water, I leaned back, closed my eyes, and enjoyed the soothing respite from the rest of the world. I washed out my buckskins and wore my jeans to dinner with Maxston and Caroline. Then, I crashed on my hay-stuffed floor mattress and fell soundly asleep.

* * *

The next morning, I awoke to the sound of someone banging on my door.

"Gavin, get yer butt outta bed," Maxston yelled. "We got us work ta do. Meet ya out front."

Annoyed at the disturbance of my deep sleep, I dragged myself off the mattress. Why couldn't he give me a day to recuperate from the trip before throwing me back into work. I thought about the work I'd done in the barn that one day. I had to admit, it hadn't been all that bad, even with the dinos in the stalls. The work was boring, though. I hoped Maxston had something else planned for me. I dressed in my washed-and-air-dried buckskins, strapped on my gun, and stuck my hat on my head.

After a quick breakfast, Maxston led me in the direction of the barn. I felt disappointed, since it looked like I was going to be cleaning up muck again.

As we came around a bend, we saw a big commotion at the barn. Two wagons sat in front of the large open door. A crowd of people milled around, some going in and out of the barn.

"What's going on?" I asked as we stopped in the middle of the street.

"Looks like yer in fer a treat. Ta day's the day they be cleanin' the dino stalls." He grabbed my arm and got me moving forward again. "Let's be goin'."

Horses blustered and whinnied. Dinos squealed. Men yelled. I couldn't tell if these noises came from nervousness or fear.

I halted in my tracks. "Hey, wait a minute," I called to Maxston, now ahead of me. "You're not expecting me to help these guys are you?"

Maxston turned around and shot me a look. "It be yer job, ain't it?"

My mouth went dry. "Um…I'm not real comfortable-"

Maxston broke out laughing. "Yer sure a fun one ta tease. Ya know that? I be just joshin' with ya. Only ones allowed ta work with them dinos be the men trained ta work with 'em."

While I relaxed with relief about the dinos, my jaw clenched in anger at Maxston for joking with me. I trudged after him, careful to avoid the piles of manure in the dirt.

Inside the barn, we stood against the wall to stay out of the way. Maxston put the butt of his rifle on the ground and leaned on the barrel. I'm not sure I would be that trusting. Apparently, he felt confident the gun wouldn't discharge and blow his arm off.

Suddenly, a scream ripped from halfway down the barn.

Every head turned in that direction.

A group of men shot past us and made for the barn door.

That's strange. Unsure whether or not I should be afraid, I asked, "Maxston, what's going on? Why's everybody leaving?"

His blue eyes stayed narrowed straight ahead. As a loud crash sounded from halfway down the aisle, he picked up his rifle. One of the red doors bulged as if it had been slammed by something big from the other side.

All I could picture was the hissing snake-headed creature I'd seen behind one of the other red doors. A chill ran down my spine. I didn't know if I should run or not.

"Might wan'ta get behind me," Maxston said gravely as he lifted his rifle and put it to his shoulder.

I jumped as the red door bounced again with a loud bang.

This time, the door broke completely off its hinges and flew into the aisle. An angry dinosaur fell into the aisle behind it. It quickly got its bearings and stood up on its four legs, its scaly body shimmering in the light from the open barn door. It swung its head back and forth until its beady eyes locked on Maxston and me.

My fear rooted me to the ground. I couldn't move.

Maxston took a step forward, putting me behind him. He calmly cocked his rifle, took aim, and fired. The deafening blast echoed inside the confines of the barn.

My ears rang. The smoke from the rifle hung in the air like a light haze, but I could see the dinosaur lying on the floor.

Maxston loaded his rifle again. "Hated ta do that, Son. But when one of 'em gits out, ain't got no other choice."

I could barely swallow. "Does this happen often?"

"Nah. Just twice before." Still loading his rifle, he took the time to put one hand to his mouth and yell, "*Clear*!"

Immediately, men started coming back into the barn. It hadn't occurred to me until that moment that we had been the only ones left inside.

Maxston finished loading and stuck his rifle in the crook of one arm. He walked toward the dead dino. The rest of us followed at a cautious pace.

Maxton had hit the dino right between the eyes.

From inside the stall, a man yelled, "Joshua's been killed. We gonna need Master Benjamin and Clyde ta come in quick-like and witness the scene in case his body goes away."

"I'll get Master Benjamin," one man said.

"I know where ta find Clyde," another responded.

In case his body goes away, I thought. That sounded strange. Not like the man meant the body would be picked up by an undertaker or something. "Who's Clyde?" I asked Maxston. "And what did he mean by Joshua's body going away?"

"Head doc," Maxston said. "'Bout the body. I be explainin' that later. This place gonna be busier ta work in than a soup kitchen at noon on Christmas day. Ya might as well come with me fer the day."

I followed him outside. We stopped next to a group of men discussing the situation.

"He was new ta the job," a red-haired, freckled-face man said. "Bet he didn't check ta make sure the dino had been drugged before he went into the pen."

"Bad way ta go," said the man next to him. "Tore ta pieces on yer first day at work." He shook his head sadly.

A man with a scowl on his face and wearing some kind of brown uniform came running up to us. He carried a modern, bolt-action rifle and looked like he wanted to pick a fight. "Who shot the dino?" he shouted.

"I did," Maxston stated flatly.

The man glared at him. "Are you authorized to dispatch a rogue 'saur?" The man stood about Maxston's height and just inches from his face.

Maxston looked at him calmly. "No, Sir, I ain't. But I be authorized ta dispatch irritatin' little pipsqueaks like you."

"Are you threatening me?" the man asked, standing on his toes to look taller.

Maxston didn't budge an inch. He remained completely relaxed with a half-grin on his face. "Only if yer gonna make an issue of me doin' yer job fer ya."

"We'll see what Master Benjamin says about this when he gets here." The man turned away stiffly, full of unresolved anger.

"Who is he?" I whispered to Maxston.

"Foreman. Be his job ta keep track a who's in the stalls. If there be a problem, he be the only one allowed ta kill a dino. Wonder why the bugger weren't where he was supposed to be?"

Master Benjamin—pilgrim hat, white collar, black breeches, and all—came running up the street. The foreman rushed forward to meet him and to plead his case. I couldn't hear their words, but from the tone of Benjamin's voice and the change in the foreman's demeanor, it seemed obvious that the foreman had gotten a reprimand for not doing his job right.

The foreman pointed at Maxston, apparently telling Benjamin who'd shot the dino.

Benjamin's voice raised. "Be it not for Goodman Maxston, more kind folk here shall have met the Lord this day. Praise God, Goodman Maxston presented himself in thy stead."

The foreman glared at Maxston then stomped off.

Benjamin came to join us. "Good morrow, Goodman Maxston, Goodman Gavin." He bowed slightly as he tipped his hat to each of us. "The wretched foreman, I fear, hath earned the town's disfavor. Another man shall be assigned to stand his watch from this day forth. Tis sad, the loss of another good man." He wrenched his hands as he looked toward the barn.

"Yes, it is," I agreed.

"Bigger problems loom before us," Benjamin said to Maxston. "The Sioux hath struck down Goodman Allen Jessup's party, the group of scientists traveling hither from the east coast. Only Goodman Jessup, the guide, hath survived. Pray tell, all those men now be dead or prisoners."

Maxston's eyes narrowed. "Don't make no sense. Sioux ain't never done nothing like that since before the treaty. Suppose ya want me ta go get 'em back fer ya. Find out what be going on with the Sioux?"

"Thou art the best man. Thou knowest the Indian Badger. If he listens to anyone, it will be thee. Nay, I know not why he broke the treaty. I fear now he willst kill any man I send in my name."

"Was Allen injured?" Maxston asked. "If not, I'd like ta have him come along with us."

Us? I wondered if that meant *me*. I didn't like the idea of fighting renegade Indians.

"Praise God," Benjamin said, "the good man, wounded only slightly he was. His arm, an arrow but creased. He resteth. The poor man walketh long nights by foot without his horse."

"I wan'ta talk to him," Maxston said. "And I wan'ta leave as soon as possible." He looked at me. "Yer gonna come, too."

"Me?" I looked behind me to make sure Maxston was talking to me. "Why? What good could I possibly do?" At this point, I really didn't want to go on another trip, even a short one. I had the wagon-train ordeal just in front of me. Worse, this confrontation with the Indians sounded like it could be dangerous. Real Indians on the warpath: torturing, kidnapping, and killing people.

Benjamin's eyes brightened at Maxston's idea. "Yay, so be it. Thou, Goodman Maxston, hath a talent for making a man doeth as thou wisheth." He smiled. "I know not in truth, but thou hath shown me that very talent firsthand, many a time."

"I have other plans," I pleaded, turning to Maxston. "I promised Hannah I'd come to dinner tonight. If I don't show up, not only will she be upset, Sven will think I stood her up. He'll come looking for me. I don't want to deal with that problem. Do you?"

"Leave it ta me," Maxston said offhandedly. "I be speakin' to 'em, tell 'em you be comin' with me on a very important mission. A matter a life or death." He winked. "She be thinkin' yer a hero when ya return."

"What about the wagon train? Isn't it suppose to leave any day now? Shouldn't we be thinking about that?"

Benjamin interjected, "Pray tell, the train shall not go forth from this town without Goodman Maxston, thy wagon master. The train willst wait for thy return."

Great, another delay. I still didn't want to go. I started to protest.

Maxston raised his hand and interrupted me. "Go to yer room. Get yer stuff. Meet me at the stable in an hour. I be going' ta the store ta get a few things." He took off abruptly, not giving me time to object.

Master Benjamin turned to talk to the people who had been patiently waiting for him so he could deal with the death of the worker.

Once again, I found myself packing my meager belongings in my trusty backpack and heading out into the unknown, all the while wishing I could, instead, find some way to get back to Erica and my kids.

Chapter 17

Since we didn't have packhorses to follow us, we made pretty good time, covering around thirty miles across the plains before the sun set.

Our companion, Allen Jessup, turned out to be another mountain man. He wore buckskins, long hair, and a shaggy beard. He carried a black-powder rifle like Maxston. I got the feeling he and Maxston might have known each other in their other world.

I now, too, carried a black-powder rifle like these two mountain men. Maxston had secured me one from the fort before we'd left. It wasn't a modern rifle like I was used to, so I wasn't familiar with how to handle it. I figured I wouldn't be able to shoot very fast with it, but having it rest in the crook of my arm gave me some confidence. The rifle would give me a longer range than my pistol.

As we rode, Allen told us the details about what had happened. He'd been asked to escort a group of five male scientists from North Town to the east coast. The scientists had done tests on the coast, taking photos of the ocean and sky, doing measurements, studying the flow of the tides. He didn't understand what they'd been doing, but they'd gotten excited about something, made some kind of discovery, and were heading back with the information. They'd been on the trail for days, making good time when the Sioux Indians ambushed them.

I thought about the photos of the sky Caroline's friend had told her about. I wondered if these scientists had gotten more evidence to support this world being some kind of experiment. I asked Allen, "Do you know what they discovered?"

"Nope. I just know they be findin' somethin' they think be needin' ta get back ta town. Wanted to get goin'."

For Maxston, Allen listed the names of the three men he was sure had died. After that, Maxston went into a state of depression or something. He wouldn't talk to either one of us. He kept to himself, staying behind us on the trail. I had the feeling he might have known one or more of the men who'd been killed.

The country reminded me of the plains of Kansas and Oklahoma: rolling hills, scattered oak trees, an occasional tree-lined stream. Not much to see for miles.

At one point, we came over a hill and saw a herd of buffalo spread out before us. Thousands of them leisurely stood or rested across the expanse of the plain. Rather than disturb or stampede them, we backtracked, swinging wide around the huge herd.

We made camp next to a small stream. Maxston seemed to perk up a little and joined us in a fireside chat about the countryside and wildlife.

The next morning, within an hour, Allen had led us near the location of the attack.

I hung back. I'd read enough books and watched enough movies to know what some of the Indians did to people they killed. I didn't want to see any mutilated bodies or gory remains.

As Maxston made his way toward the site, he said, "Bodies be gone."

I wasn't so sure. I rode forward slowly, ready to bolt at the first sign of blood and gore. When I reached the site, I looked around. I saw nothing. No bodies. No blood. I got off my horse with the other two. "Are you sure this is the place?" I asked Allen.

"Sure as my name," he said.

It was just as Maxston had said: all the bodies were gone. It seemed even the blood had been cleaned up. I wondered if the Indians took them someplace or buried them.

Allen said, "Oh, oh. We better be gittin' ready fer an attack." He pointed to the north where some thirty Indians lined up on the top of a hill. They looked just like Indians on a warpath in the movies.

"Them Injuns won't attack us," Maxston said confidently.

"Why not?" I asked, nervously watching more Indians line their horses up along the skyline.

"'Cause Badger knows better than ta attack me."

That sounded stupid to me. "What if he doesn't know it's you down here?"

"He knows. I'm the only one Master Benjamin be sendin' out here after an attack like this." He took the reins of his horse. "Let's be mountin' up. Head fer the village. Gotta feelin' them Injuns'll be right along."

I didn't have Maxston's confidence. As I settled into my saddle, I checked my holster and made sure my pistol was easy to get to, if I needed it. I kept the rifle ready in my arm. *God, what if I'd come into this strange world just to get killed by Indians? There'd never be an epitaph about it for me back home in Lake Havasu.*

Allen seemed to be wary, too. He looked around often, as though waiting for the attack to begin. Since the previous attack with some of his party killed, he had reason to be on edge.

As we rode toward the village, the Indians flowed off the hill and formed a half-circle behind us. They stayed back a half-mile or so, but I had the feeling we were being herded like sheep to the slaughter house. Before we'd even gone a mile, another group of Indians appeared in front of us. They lined up like the ones behind us, in a half-circle. When we drew up in front of them, the two half circles closed in on us. I glanced nervously around at the half-naked warriors. Their painted faces looked fearsome at first. On a closer glance, I saw not anger radiating from their eyes, but excitement.

One warrior, wearing an elaborate headdress with feathers, urged his horse forward. He stopped in front of Maxston and said something in a foreign language that I assumed was Sioux. As he spoke, he also moved his hands in a feminine-like motion, as if he were using sign language.

Maxston let him talk for a minute, then said, "Cut the crap, Curtis. Speak English or I be findin' somebody else ta talk to."

The Indian shut his mouth and glared at him.

Curtis? I looked at Maxston in surprise.

Maxston leaned toward me, as if he were about to say something confidential, but he spoke loud enough that everyone around us could hear. "Calls himself Badger. Real name be Curtis Allbright. He come in the year 1974. A real educated man he be."

"Go on, Maxston," Curtis said in a whiny tone, "tell him the truth and ruin everything." He turned his attention to me, his eyes slowly going up and down my body, as though he was checking me out. He finally came back to my face and gave me a little crooked smile.

It gave me the willies.

"Ya see, Curtis here be out with his tribesmen and women, reenactin' a big huntin' trip. They run into the web. Got themselves trapped. But, lo 'n behold, Curtis be smart enough ta know somethin' be wrong right away. Took control a some three hundred people. Managed ta keep 'em from panicking. Managed ta stay in charge of the tribe since then even. But, ya gotta know, he's…he's…." Maxston seemed to be choking on his words.

Allen remained jittery, keeping his eyes down, not looking at Curtis.

"Go ahead and say it, Maxston," Curtis said, still eyeing me intently. "I'm gay." He threw out his bare chest and lifted his head high. "And proud of it, too."

Maxston's face flushed. He grimaced and squirmed in the seat of his saddle. He could hardly keep his horse still.

Despite the unease I was feeling from Curtis's attention, a sound erupted from my throat at the look on Maxston's face. I couldn't hold back my laughter. To cover it up, I pretended I was coughing. I bit my tongue to get control of myself.

Because Maxston had come from a time when being gay was not openly discussed—ever—he cowered in discomfort at the state of affairs.

When I finally felt I could contain my laughter, I said, "If I remember right, in your culture, someone like you was referred to as a *berdache*. They often became shamans or medicine men. Is that not right?"

"You are right," Curtis said in his slightly high-pitched voice. "Now, we are known as *two-spirit people*, not *berdache*. We are no longer looked at as being weird or strange. We're revered and treated with respect. My tribe members have accepted me as their shaman. I have more power and authority than a normal chief." His attitude hadn't come across like he'd been boasting. He'd simply stated the facts.

I didn't miss the fact he'd used present tense either. I interpreted that to mean he wanted us to know his current tribe had the same beliefs they'd held hundreds of years before.

Maxston, still slightly shaken, stirred himself to come back to the subject of our trip. "If that be right, then tell me why some of yer boys decided to attack a party of scientists, killin' three of 'em and takin' two hostage. Only survivor be ol' Allen here." He swept his arm back to indicate Allen, who hung out behind us and kept silent.

Allen looked about as skittish as a stray cat who'd accidently wandered into a dog show.

While some of the Indians muttered unintelligible words, I hoped Maxston's blunt accusations wouldn't make them angry enough to kill us.

Curtis seemed offended. His eyes narrowed. "None of our warriors had anything to do with that raid. We have a treaty. We honor it."

Maxston leaned forward on his horse in a threatening manner. "Yeah? Then what the hell happened ta the scientists?"

"Strutting Elk!" Curtis called out. "Get up here."

From out of the circle, a rail-thin little man rode forward on his horse. He wore a band across his forehead with a single tall feather sticking out of it. Red and white war paint marked his face. His small black eyes seemed alert and nervous.

"Tell him what you saw," Curtis demanded.

Strutting Elk cleared his throat and spoke in perfect English. "We were out on a hunt. We'd just made our way into the hills when we heard a commotion. We saw a bunch of men with extra horses that looked like Indians heading our way. They were dressed just like us, but we didn't recognize them. They weren't our people."

"How many of them?" Maxston asked.

"Ten, twelve. They were acting kind of strange, like they were on dope or something." Strutting Elk seemed to be growing more nervous the more he talked. His horse milled around a little.

"Tell him what happened next," Curtis said to Strutting Elk, but Curtis's eyes watched me. He gave me another little smile.

I blushed and looked at Strutting Elk.

"They seemed like they were in a hurry, so we hardly said any words. As they rode off and we went a little farther, we found the massacre site."

"Did you see the bodies?" Maxston asked, seeming to grow more interested.

"Yeah. They were still there."

"How many?"

"Five."

Maxston glanced back at Allen. "Looks like they got 'em all, would ya say?"

Allen's face fell, his eyes down. He nodded.

Maxston glared back at Strutting Elk. "What then? Did ya bury the bodies or did they disappear?"

That was a funny question to ask.

Strutting Elk swallowed. His eyes grew wider. "They disappeared. All five of 'em. Right before our eyes." He glanced over his shoulder to get agreement from some of the other Indians in the circle. "Didn't they?"

Several of the men nodded and grunted in concurrence.

Disappeared? What are they talking about?

Curtis interrupted. "We think they were fake Indians, trying to discredit us or to make us take the blame for the slaughter. After the bodies disappeared, Strutting Elk and his hunting party went after the Indians, but they couldn't find them."

"Is that right?" Maxston said, directing his question at Strutting Elk.

"Couldn't find their trail. Like they disappeared into thin air, too, just like the dead men." The little man's body shuddered.

"Go on," Curtis urged, "tell them what you think."

"They were aliens," he blurted. "They were aliens pretending to be Indians."

Maxston chuckled. "How long ya gonna go on believin' aliens are controllin' this world? You be a fool."

"They were aliens," Strutting Elk shouted. "They can make people disappear, you know."

Maxston grunted.

All this talk befuddled my mind. I asked Maxston, "What do you mean about bodies disappearing? What's going on?"

"Tell ya later." He turned to Curtis. "What do *you* think about all this?"

"I don't know," he said in his squeaky voice, his dark eyes looking into the distance toward the hills. "I don't believe in the alien thing, but I don't see how those Indians, riding around and looking like us, could just disappear from the face of the earth. Must have left the area pretty quick." His eyes wandered back to me, settling there as he spoke to the group. "But one thing that always scares the hell outta me is knowing about dead bodies disappearing. Just can't get used to that. Wouldn't believe it myself if Strutting Elk here and his party hadn't sworn to it. They had no bodies to show."

"Well," Maxston said impatiently, sitting high on his horse, "I got a sneaky suspicion we ain't never gonna find out." He looked around at Allen. "What'cha think, Allen? You positive all this happened? You be missin' five men?"

"Just as I told ya. Them scientists, they be dead. I seen 'em. Three of 'em dead. Don't know 'bout the other two."

Curtis spoke to Allen with sympathy. "All five disappeared, Allen. We have eye-witnesses. I'm sorry. I wish the hunting party could have come upon the scene sooner. Maybe we could have prevented that from happening. I'm just glad you escaped."

Allen kept his eyes down. His shoulders sagged. The scientists had been his responsibility. He'd failed to keep them safe. That regret would be hanging over his head the rest of his life, and that could be for a long, long time in this world.

To avoid catching Curtis's eye again, I glanced around the hillsides, wondering if the fake Indians had hidden somewhere in the area. Why would they dress up like Indians and kill the scientists? Why would their bodies disappear?

Maxston gave a brief farewell and abruptly turned us around to head back toward North Town. I could feel Curtis's eyes burning into my butt as we pulled away.

I studied the Indians as we rode past them. It struck me that some kind of pattern was coming into focus for me. Here were a group of Native Americans, people who had been living in the Twentieth Century like all modern men, probably well-educated, and yet, they had been forced into a situation where they were now living like their ancestors. The same thing had happened with the Eskimos in the tundra. It seemed like such a strange coincidence. Just another question to ask.

* * *

As we rode back across the plains, I asked Maxston the question I'd been dying to ask. "What about the bodies disappearing from the massacre site? Why'd they say they disappeared? What happened to them?"

He stared straight ahead with his lips tight, just like he'd always done when he wasn't going to answer me. Finally, he said, "It be somethin' I don't like talkin' about. Makes me feel…weird."

It was hard for me to imagine a strong, self-confident man like Maxston feeling *weird*. "What do you mean?"

"It be like…I dunno…like questionin' God or somethin'."

"Just tell me what happened to them," I said, growing a little miffed. "Do they turn to dust? Or disappear in a puff of smoke? Come on, tell me."

He he-hawed around, then said, "Cain't tell ya why, but before the hour passes after death, a body just...well... just disappears. Poof. Gone. Even the blood be gone."

Wow. That's strange. No wonder Maxston feels weird talking about it. It did seem to explain one thing for me, though: why there were no bodies or signs of blood at the massacre site. Of course, the Indians could have buried them and cleaned up the ground. But there had been no signs of graves or digging or overturned soil.

I tried to piece together what I'd learned so far. People in this world aged real slowly. As far as anyone knew, no one had died of old age, yet. People died by being in an accident or being killed in some way. That meant that people could possibly live forever, if nothing killed them.

The idea of disappearing bodies intrigued me. Back at Caroline's Indian village, I'd joked about dying being a way to get out of this world and back to my own world. What if I hadn't been so far off? The thought started to fester in my mind. I mean, if people died and their bodies disappeared, where did they go? Did they reappear somewhere else? Did they go home?

I recalled the death of Joshua in the barn the day before. A man had said something about his body going away. No, he'd said *in case his body goes away*. "Maxston, did Joshua's body disappear in the barn yesterday?"

"Didn't stay 'round ta find out."

I interpreted that to mean this thing was unpredictable. "Are you saying that it might not have disappeared? That not everybody disappears?"

"Yep."

"Why just some? What makes the difference?"

He shot me a harsh stare. "Where ya goin' with this, Son?"

"I want to figure out what's going on."

"You ain't thinkin' this be a way ta get back home again, do ya?"

Well, yes, it's been crossing my mind just now."Tell me, how do you know which bodies will be taken and which ones won't?"

"Don't nobody know."

"So you have to wait an hour to find out if a body is going to disappear or not?"

Maxston shook his head in annoyance, his scruffy beard rubbing against his buckskin-covered chest. He swatted his hand at me like I was a fly as he tightened his lips.

"Come on, Maxston, tell me more. What's the big deal? I'm going to find out sooner or later what's going on. Why not tell me now?"

"Ya be a real pain in the arse, ya know?"

"Tell me."

He squinted his blue eyes me. "I'll tell ya one thing. The ones kill 'emselves. They not be taken. Never a one disappears."

Suicides. That's interesting. If a person kills himself, his body remains in this world.

"Plus the ones go lookin' ta get killed," Maxston added. "If ya walk into a dino pen on purpose, knowin' the dino will attack, ya won't be taken either."

I tried to get my mind around these ideas. "So, people who kill themselves or decide to be killed don't disappear. Their bodies stay in this world to be buried, like they are really dead. The ones who get killed by accident or murder—not by their own intention—they can disappear?"

"I told ya. Only some. Body disappears…that be the knowin'."

"What do the scientists in South Town say about it? Do they have any ideas why it happens? Why the bodies disappear or why only some bodies disappear?"

"No. They cain't explain it neither. Just happens."

This all seemed so random and confusing, as confusing as stepping into the web. But still, there were patterns in this world, patterns about aging and patterns about suicides not leaving this world. There had to be a pattern to the bodies that disappeared and the ones that didn't. A chill stirred my bones. Even though the idea of dying to get back home seemed farfetched, the thought excited me and scared me at the same time.

"There's got to be a reason why some bodies disappear and some don't," I insisted, determined to get Maxston to give me more information.

He sighed loudly. "Give ya one theory, but nothin' ta back it up, ya hear?"

I nodded. "Go on," I prodded when he didn't speak.

He pressed his lips together again for a little while. "The ones disappear. Seem ta be different. Seem ta be smarter, maybe. Like the scientists that died. These be the renegade group. Ones against the government of South Town. Knew one of 'em. He be a friend…real smart. He be wantin' ta get outta this world real bad."

"Wow. That's too sad. Maybe he found out something when he was on the coast. Maybe he found the answer." I wondered if he *did* get out of this world, now that he was dead and gone. "Did this scientist friend ever say anything to you about what's going on? Did he think we were living in an ant farm? An alien ant farm?"

"We be differin' on that point. This cain't be no ant farm. Won't believe it."

My mind whirled with new possibilities. This death thing had my full attention. I couldn't help but think that disappearing bodies could be a key to the whole thing. But how to get killed. And how to be sure that my body would disappear. And how to be sure that I would go back home if it did.

"Now, don'tcha be gittin' yerself killed," Maxston warned, as though reading my mind. "Just 'cause ya think it might get ya home. There be no proof the killin'll work. What if ya end up someplace that be worse than this?" Maxston seemed as uncomfortable with this topic as he had been with Curtis being gay.

I decided to keep quiet for now, but I knew my questions about death and disappearing bodies would haunt me all the way to South Town.

Chapter 18

We reached North Town the next day. Much to my delight, Benjamin announced that the wagon train would leave the next day.

After having dinner with Hannah's family, I spent a few hours with her on the porch. I probably looked pretty scruffy with my growing beard, but I hadn't had time to see a barber. I felt strangely sad when I had to leave. I figured the sadness came from Hannah looking so much like Erica, who I was missing deeply.

I had to admit that I liked Hannah. She was a sweet, warm-hearted young woman, easy to talk to, and as comfortable to be with as Erica. To tell the truth, if I thought I would end up being stuck in this world, I probably wouldn't find a better woman than Hannah to be with.

I had to be careful, though, because the more time I spent with her, the more time I wanted to spend with her. It seemed like a vicious circle that could suck me in and make me lose sight of my goal, which was getting back to my world, my wife, and my kids. The coming trip to South Town fell right into place because I needed to get as far away from Hannah as possible.

The next morning, as the wagon train prepared to move out, I looked for Maxston, who had arranged for my horse. I expected to ride along with him and Caroline at the front of the caravan.

"You be ridin' in the cook's wagon," Maxston told me. "You be helpin' him 'long the way. Yer duty fer the trip. If he be needin' somethin', he can call on ya." He pointed toward a barrel-shaped, sluggish-looking man who was loading things from a cart into a wagon.

"A cook's helper?" I whined. "I don't know anything about cooking for over a hundred people."

"You be learnin' real fast."

I didn't like the dour look on the face of the cook, my upcoming traveling companion. Maxston ignored my further protests, so I trudged over to the cook's wagon and helped him load up the sacks of food. Right off, the offensive odor coming from the cook made me nauseated.

The grubby-looking man didn't talk much, and when he did, it was only to grumble and complain. "Didn't want to come on this damn trip," he lamented. "Master Benjamin, he forced me ta be here."

Within the first five minutes, the cook had gotten on my nerves with his griping and smell. "Tell you what," I said to him, "I would prefer to walk alongside the wagon for most of the trip...so I can stay in shape."

His heavy brow furrowed over his deep-set eyes, like he didn't believe me. Like he thought I was crazy.

I'm sure a man of his size couldn't appreciate someone wanting to stay healthy, but more importantly, no way did I intend to listen to the man bemoan his fate for the next three weeks. Of course, I realized I couldn't walk clear to South Town, a 250-mile trip, but I could avoid the man as much as possible by staying off his wagon.

All together, we had twenty-four freight wagons, six private buggies, and a number of men on horseback. The horseback riders weren't part of the wagon train per se. They were traveling with us as guards for protection. Three of the wagons carried cages containing the last three dinosaurs from the barn. After Joshua had died and Maxston had been forced to kill the dino, the town council voted to release the rest of the dinos into the jungle. They had taken the animals out of their natural habitat, and rather than just kill them, decided to return them to the area where they'd found them in the first place.

I had learned along the way that Joshua's body had not disappeared. He had been buried in the town cemetery. This fascinated me no end. I wanted to understand why some people's bodies disappeared and others didn't. Nobody could tell me much about Joshua, other than he'd been in town for two or three years, living close to the slums. He had no family. Benjamin had told me Joshua had taken the job with the dinos to improve his lifestyle. After stumbling around in confusion for years, he'd started getting himself together. His sad story left me feeling depressed.

As I finished loading up the cook's wagon, I remembered from the discussion in Caroline's village that Maxston had said something about every traveler being taught to fight. I'd pictured it as being a few days of military-type training. Well, I must have missed out on it, because I hadn't been given any kind of training. In fact, training hadn't even been mentioned. I just hoped everyone else knew what they were doing and there were enough of them to handle it.

I now had the black-powder rifle. Maxston had let me keep it. I'd asked for a more modern gun and learned that modern firearms were rare. Maxston told me that I should count myself lucky I had my pistol. For that, I did feel lucky.

Just before heading out, Maxston announced to everyone that we'd make about ten miles a day on the 250-mile trip. He claimed some days we would make more miles and some days less. It would all even out in the end.

As the train pulled out, I felt relieved to finally be on the road to South Town. Hopefully, my growing list of questions would all be answered.

I had been in this world for three weeks now. Thoughts of Erica made their way into my mind. I couldn't imagine what she must be going through with me never coming home and the rescue teams not being able to locate me. Had they found my truck? For sure, then, they knew I'd been out on the desert, but my body would never have been found. It made me sick to think of what Erica must be going through and what she had to be telling the girls.

I suspected that, by now, Erica and Brian had worked out some kind of agreement about running my business. I just hoped they would keep things going for while longer and wouldn't give up on me never coming back.

I ached to get home to calm Erica's fears and let her know that everything would be okay. But again, I had to force the thoughts out of my mind so I could continue functioning.

* * *

The first night in camp, the cook had me racing around and doing multiple things at once. He nagged and grumped as I ran from one side of the fire to stir the pots of stew, to the other side to throw bread dough in clumps on the cast-iron pans for biscuits.

The wagons had formed an enclosed circle for protection. Guards rode along the outside to watch for wild beasts and marauders. From what I'd heard, an occasional band of Indians or other renegades took advantage of people traveling, but not usually a train this large.

"Git me a bucket a water," the cook complained in the middle of my other tasks.

As I hauled the bucket from the wagon, I saw my biscuits burning. Hurrying to deliver the water so I could take the biscuits off the fire, I tripped on a rock. The water spilled over the cook's chest and lap as he came towards me.

He gasped in shock.

I stepped to the side to get out of his way and knocked one of the pots of stew into the fire.

"Git outta here," he screamed. "Yer fired!"

Stunned for a moment, I stared at the mess: the charcoaled biscuits, the stew sizzling out the fire, the spilled water forming a mud puddle on the ground, and the cranky cook ranting and raving about bad help. I turned and headed past the wagons to find Maxston and Caroline.

Sitting down next to their fire, I told them the woeful tale about my mishaps and how I'd lost my job.

Carolyn's eyes sparkled with delight at my story.

Maxston laughed. He gave me a knowing look. "Had a feelin' you'd do somethin' like that. Planned a backup job fer ya."

Great, I thought. *Wonder what kind of trouble I can get into next.*

"From now on, yer gonna be my sidekick. You be helpin' me run this here shebang. Take charge of the guards. Make sure they be on duty 'n all. Make sure nobody goes a wanderin' outta camp alone. Person can get into a might of trouble bein' on his own out here."

While the idea of the new job pleased me, the thought of Maxston assigning me the cook's job when he knew it wouldn't suit me made me frown at him. "Why did you make me help the cook in the first place?"

"That be Master Benjamin's idea. Didn't want ya ta have a fun, easy job like bein' my sidekick. Said ya needed ta do somethin' productive." He laughed and shook his head. "You ain't no cook. And I sure'n as heck ain't gonna trust ya ta help with the dinos. Bein' my helper…well…it be the only job I got left open fer ya."

I chuckled at his merriment. "Well, I'll try not to screw it up too badly."

He leaned over and whispered loudly to Caroline, "I hate ta say it, but he already be screwin' up." He winked at me. "Ain't my helper supposed ta keep the fire stoked?"

I happily threw another log on the fire.

* * *

The next few days passed quickly. Riding out in front with Maxston and Caroline was almost like being by ourselves. Sitting on a horse all day didn't bother me anymore. I'd been on horseback so much since I'd come into this world, it seemed like second-nature. I was feeling as comfortable on the back of a horse as a tick on a hound dog.

One afternoon, as the three of us came over a hill, Maxston yanked his horse to a stop so fast it surprised me. Caroline and I pulled up beside him. All three of our horses pranced in place nervously, wide-eyed and snorting in fear.

"There," Maxston said, pointing into the valley, which stretched about a mile across. A narrow stream ran through the middle of the verdant pasture.

I squinted, trying to make out a golden-brown shape next to the stream. As I watched, the shape seemed to be moving slightly, back and forth, back and forth.

Caroline's horse whinnied in fear.

The object next to the stream suddenly stood up and looked in our direction.

"What the hell is that?" I asked. "I'm thinking it might be a mountain lion, but it looks way too big."

"It's a Smilodon," Caroline said. Seeing the confusion on my face, she added, "More commonly known as a saber-toothed tiger."

"You're kidding me, right?" For some reason, the idea of seeing something that had been extinct in my world for thousands of years excited me. I strained to look at the thing again, but it was too far away to make out the details. I found myself wishing I'd had a pair of binoculars in my backpack the day I gotten sucked into this world.

The saber-tooth tiger let out a roar, causing the horses to mill around in a panic. Our firm hands on the reins barely kept them from bolting and running away.

I swallowed, glad we had a lot of distance between us and the tiger.

"There be not many of 'em," Maxston said. "Kinda rare ta see one. It don't be my choice ta run into one. They be a might unpredictable. Let us mosey on outta here 'fore it decides ta take a closer look." He looked frightened. Even when he'd faced down the dino in the barn, he'd remained calm, cool, and surefooted. If he didn't want anything to do with this tiger, then neither did I.

"If it sees the horses runnin'," Maxston warned, "it be a chasin' 'em so walk 'em away slow-like."

Thus, we forced our horses to walk slowly until the tiger was out of sight.

"Shame," Maxston went on. "Was plannin' on campin' there tonight. We be havin' ta push on. That thing probably wouldn't attack the camp, but I ain't takin' any chances. Let's get far away. That beast be certain ta attract wolves, n' we don't want them things, neither, ta come sniffin' around camp and lookin' fer an easy meal."

"Wolves?" I asked. "I can't imagine wolves attacking a saber-tooth tiger."

Caroline jumped into the conversation. "*Dire wolves.* They're twice the size of the wolves you know from our world…and twice as mean. They've been known to attack parties of twenty or more men. They are fearless, and they move so fast, it's hard to get off a shot at one." She shivered. "I'm more frightened of the wolves than I am of anything else in this world. That tiger will eat its prey as quickly as possible because, as soon as the wolves detect the kill, they'll move in and take it over. The tiger risks its life to stay around long."

"Would they attack our camp?" I asked, wondering about the thin walls of the flimsy canvas tent I slept in.

"Nah," Maxston said with a little too much force in his tone, leading me to distrust his words. "Our camp be too big. Fearless they may be, but they ain't stupid. Might attack smaller trains, but not ours."

Oh, great. I might as well look forward to a sleepless night ahead of me. "How big is their territory?" I asked, wondering how many nights I'd lose sleep before I felt safe enough to lose consciousness.

"Couple a days we be outta their domain," Maxston said, putting his horse into a gentle trot.

I matched my horse's speed to his. "How can you be sure?"

"'Cause then, we be in the jungle. Even the wolves ain't stupid enough ta go farther than the edge of the jungle."

I pondered the situation. *The wolves aren't stupid enough to enter the jungle, but we are?* If the wolves were the meanest things in these parts, what was waiting for us in the jungle? The dinosaurs? I began to get a sense of why the cowboy had refused to travel alone with me and, in fact, why he'd claimed he wouldn't travel at all but with a *big* wagon train with lots of protection. I began to wonder if we had enough protection with the group we had in tow. I felt glad now that I hadn't just flitted off to South Town on my own without anyone knowing about it.

"Don'tcha worry 'bout it," Maxston said, picking up my concern. "Trust me. I'm tellin' ya, everything it be okay. Right now, we be needin' ta get back to the wagons. Tell 'em ta change direction. I got another spot in mind. If we catch 'em soon enough, we can make it ta the spot before dark." He pushed his horse into a gallop.

Caroline's chestnut horse stayed up with him. Her long black hair whipped behind her in the wind. In their buckskins, they looked like a couple of Plains Indians on the run.

Trailing behind them, I kept watching over my shoulder and expecting to see the saber-toothed tiger chasing us down. Luckily, the animal never showed.

We got the wagons turned in the right direction and arrived at the night's camping spot with plenty of daylight left to comfortably set up camp.

I kept watching the horizon for fear that the tiger would show up. Or worse, the wolves would come into sight and stalk the camp.

"Relax yerself, Son," Maxston insisted. "We be far enough away from them tiger's kill ta be safe."

Yeah, right. I couldn't help but notice that Maxston had gone out of his way to make sure there was plenty of firewood in the camp and that he'd assigned a larger number of guards to keep watch for the night.

Chapter 19

Early one morning a few days later, we reached an area where the country drastically changed right before my eyes. We'd had no mishaps from the saber-toothed tiger or the wolves, but I'd not slept well. Even now, I remained on edge, worrying about the jungle that the dire wolves would not enter. I stayed constantly alert for movements of any kind of animal or beast as I rode out ahead of Maxston and Caroline.

Now, I sat on my horse on the edge of a hill leading down into a green valley with scattered trees and bushes that formed the outskirts of a thick jungle forest, which stretched as far as the eye could see. Compared to the scrubby hills we'd been traveling across, this valley appeared to be a thriving oasis, filled with all sorts of jungle-like-looking vegetation, including palm trees and ferns.

Some sort of enormously tall trees, popping up here and there across the forested area, towered above the palm trees and bushes like sentries watching over the land. Closer to the forest, these trees grew thick in number, forming groves among the other vegetation and blocking out the sun's light. The thought of what dangers hid in the shadows of those trees sent a shiver through me.

Loud caws from the call of a few birds echoed through the dense vegetation. A monkey screeched in the distance.

This is where Maxston had claimed the dinosaurs lived, anywhere here along the northern parts of the jungle. It's true that I'd now seen the dinosaurs that we carried on this trip, but the scaly, snake-headed creatures didn't look anything like what I'd seen in the books or in the movies. I believed that T-rexes really existed in this world at the word of Caroline and Maxston, but I sure didn't want to run into one of them.

A road of sorts, nothing more than a two-tire track in the dirt, wound its way into the thicket. I followed it with my eyes until it disappeared into the shadows of the lush greens. This was the path to my future, the path that would eventually end at South Town, the place where I intended to get the answers to all my questions. I gulped at the thought of the long trip still ahead to get me from here to there, especially with the ominous dark, eerie jungle said to be one of the most treacherous areas we'd pass through.

I dared not venture alone into the wild tangled mass that sat before me. I waited for Maxston, Caroline, and the wagons to catch up.

Once we joined each other and set off on the road into the valley, we moved slowly and cautiously. The road turned out to have more twists and turns than a good murder mystery. We traveled through the sparser patches of vegetation on wide trails that wound around the shaded areas. This kept us in the direct sunlight where the sun beat brutally down upon us. The rising temperature had to be reaching eighty, ninety, or more degrees. The humidity increased rapidly, thickening the air with a sultry stickiness.

Within a short time, I began sweating profusely. I longed for the shade of the thicker vegetation. I took off my hat, wiped my forehead, and fanned myself. The growing beard on my face added to my discomfort. I wished I'd had my shorts and t-shirt instead of the full buckskin garb.

I didn't understand why we were riding in the open when shaded areas were within our easy reach. Coming up next to Maxston, I asked, "Why can't we travel over there in the shade?"

"Cain't," he said, sweat beading on his forehead and around his mustache. "Need ta be in the open fer safety." He seemed agitated, his eyes constantly roaming the area ahead of us and all around. His rifle sat in the crook of his arm, ready to pick up quickly.

Caroline stayed alert, too, sometimes waiting along the trail, scanning the outlying shaded areas, letting a few wagons pass before catching up with us again. She carried a large rifle in her hands. She seemed more jittery than I'd ever seen her.

I was on edge, too. I made sure all the guards were on duty, sticking to their assigned places alongside the wagons. They had their rifles at the ready.

I still couldn't figure out why we couldn't travel in the shade, but I didn't want to press Maxston for an explanation. Since no one else seemed to be bothered by it, I kept my mouth shut and my eyes open for any apparent dangers as I suffered in silence.

* * *

At high noon, Maxston called a halt to the wagon train for lunch. He directed the wagons to stop away from the trees as much as possible. A few copses ended up in the middle of the circle of wagons, but the guards checked them thoroughly for wandering animals or beasts that might be hiding there.

Grateful for the little bit of shade, I guided my horse to one of the copses where Maxston and Caroline had unsaddled. Since early morning, this was the first time I'd been out of the sun. Even though the muggy air remained thick and hot, it felt good to not have the heat beating directly down my back.

As I got off my horse, I said to Maxston, "Man, I'm already dreading the travel this afternoon."

"We ain't be travelin' no more ta'day," he said. "Spendin' the night. We be movin' on in the mornin'."

"Why?" I asked. "Why waste a half-day's traveling time?"

"Time ta let the dinos go. This be close ta where we caught 'em. They can find their way home from here." As he headed toward one of the wagons, he added, "Keep yerself and everybody else close ta the wagons. This be dangerous territory. Nobody goes for a walk alone. Don't think anybody will, but ya never know."

I nodded.

Sure enough, after lunch, the frenzied activity of getting the dinos ready to be released began. The specially trained handlers busied themselves with the preparations, engaging many of the other people on the wagon train in helping them with the safer tasks. I asked if they needed my help, but they told me they had things under control. I hadn't realized that so many people on the trip had actually been recruited to help release the dinos. I hoped they would be paid well for their service.

The guards kept vigil all around the outer edge of the campsite.

Feeling like I was in the way, yet having nothing else to do, I found myself a cup of water at the cook's wagon and sat down alone. As I sipped the lukewarm liquid, thoughts of this whole crazy ordeal drifted through my mind. I started thinking about Erica and my kids. How were their lives going now? Had they gone on as much with their lives as I had gone on with mine, facing whatever struggles came along, dealing with the problems, looking for solutions, wishing for me at night, but fearing that I would never come back, and in that fear, blocking out the pain so they could make new decisions about the future?

As I caught myself dipping into a deep depression, I shook myself and stood up. *Don't go there.*

Maxston was busy with the dinosaur group.

Looking for Caroline, I wandered from wagon to wagon. I couldn't find her. I figured she might be resting in a wagon. I returned to the cook's area.

The dinos began screeching in ear-piercing shrieks. The men had started working directly with them to get them out of the cages.

Fearful about being too close to the place they were being released, I walked to the other end of the wagon train to keep my distance. I noticed clumps of bushes that sat by themselves just ten feet from the wagon area. The bushes stood between two and five feet tall. Surely, nothing bigger than a jackrabbit could be hiding in those clumps. The guards had found nothing in the trees that ended up in our inner circle.

Farther from the camp, the brush got taller and thicker, but with all the racket being made by the men and dinosaurs, I didn't think anything dangerous would be hanging around. I chuckled to think that we probably scared off any dinos within five miles.

"I'm going to take a leak in those bushes over there," I lied to the nearby guard. I really wanted to be alone, just to get away from everyone and all the screeching going on.

The man nodded. "Don'tcha wander far," he warned as his eyes glanced down at my rifle, as though reminding me to keep it ready.

"Right." I crossed the open space and entered the bushy cluster. Nothing ran out from the bushes.

The guard kept a close eye on me.

I gave him a thumbs-up that all was okay, then moved a little deeper into the brush to where he couldn't see me.

My depression seemed to hover just above my head. I tried not to think about my family, as cruel as that seemed to me. I had to maintain my health and my sanity if I were ever to find a way home.

I hated to admit it, but I'd begun to have doubts about getting out of this world. What the hell made me think I could get home anyway? Even Caroline, the intelligent woman that she was, much smarter than I, had been here for twelve years. She was still here. The scientists in South Town, who I figured came from a time period closer to mine or maybe into the future from me, should have been able to figure out a way to get home by now. They, too, were still here. How come they hadn't left yet?

Why hadn't anyone found the solution? Why, why, why? Or had they? What about the rogue scientists? Had they found the secret? And why did their bodies disappear when they died? I still wanted to know what had happened to their bodies when they disappeared. Did they go home? Unfortunately, I couldn't be sure what the significance of that meant, nor whether or not my own body would disappear were I to be killed.

Despite all my doubts, it still stuck in my craw that there had to be a way out of this world if there was a way in.

Unless, of course, the powers-that-be in South Town *had* learned the a way out and were keeping it secret. *Yeah, right, maybe they're in cahoots with the aliens, or whoever or whatever brought us all here in the first place.* I found myself getting giddy at the thought. Everything seemed just too fantastically crazy.

A crash in the brush to my right brought me out of my reverie. I stopped dead in my tracks. I had no idea I had wandered into an area of thicker vegetation. All around me were tall ferns and flowery bushes, so tall and thick I couldn't see beyond them. I wasn't even sure in which direction I would find the camp.

Suddenly, a low deep rumble came from the thicket just ahead of me. Whatever it was, it was *big*.

My breath caught in my chest. My pulse raced so fast I feared I'd have a heart attack. I had no idea which way to run to escape. I looked at the ground for my footprints in the mud under the vegetation. Almost numb with fear, I followed them back the way I'd come. I tried to step quickly and quietly, but every time I put my foot down, I stepped on a stick or a twig or a leaf that made what seemed like more noise than a herd of elephants.

I couldn't see anything behind me. Growing more panicky, I broke into a jog, weaving my way along my footprints and getting closer and closer to camp and safety. When I thought I was in the clear, I stopped for a minute to catch my breath and listened.

Whatever was following, it grunted every time its foot pounded the ground.

I picked up my pace to a running speed, breaking through the overhanging branches and ferns. How could I have gotten this far from the camp? Did I take the wrong path? Follow the wrong footprints? Did the handlers pass this way?

A big animal behind me roared, gaining on me.

I increased my speed, hoping I was heading in the right direction. The vegetation began to thin, looking more familiar. Seeing a flash of white canvas from one of the wagons in the distance renewed my hope.

Layne Walker

I shot a quick look over my shoulder. A hungry T-rex, fifty feet behind me, gained ground with every step. My luck may have run out.

I screamed like a girl. Energized by fear, new reserves of energy burst through my body. Dropping my rifle, useless against such a large predator, I sped ahead, racing for my life.

Screams and shouts came from the camp. One man after another stepped in front of the wagons and lifted his rifle. Flashes of light sparked at the muzzles as they shot at the T-rex.

Maxston stood next to one of the wagons. He had his black-powder rifle cradled in the crook of one arm. He yelled something.

I wondered how he could just stand there and watch while I was about to be eaten alive.

When I came within twenty feet of him, he lifted his rifle to his shoulder. It roared to life and belched a cloud of smoke that engulfed him. I knew then that he'd loaded his rifle with extra powder, just in case he'd have to shoot a big dinosaur, like the one chasing me.

I didn't slow down until I was well into the camp. The crowd of people and rifle shots surely would have turned the T-rex away. I turned around, panting, leaning over with my hands on my knees to catch my breath.

Dead ahead, the T-rex lay on the ground, it's monstrous body lying just short of the wagons.

Maxston strode toward it, reloading his rifle as he walked. He had to be insane approaching the monster before making sure it was dead. As he covered the last ten feet, he pointed his rifle at the T-rex's head. He kicked its head with his foot. When it didn't respond, he touched the barrel of his rifle to its eye.

I'd heard that checking the eye was one of the best ways to tell if an animal was dead. Being the most sensitive part of an animal's body, it would flinch at the touch, should there be any life left. Apparently the thing was dead.

Maxston cradled his rifle in the crook of his arm and proceeded to walk around the T-rex.

My body shook from the adrenaline rush. I continued to gasp for air. Seeing the cook's wagon next to me, I stumbled to the water barrel for a drink to quench my overwhelming thirst. Because I was shaking so badly, I spilled half the cup of water down my beard and all over the front of me.

Everyone in camp meandered out to look at the dead dino.

I wanted to look at it, too, but I didn't trust my legs to carry me that far without collapsing. I sat down on the ground, wrapped my arms around my knees, and dropped my head on my arms. I concentrated on getting my racing heart back to something resembling a normal beat. I sat there for what seemed like a long time when someone walked up to me and stopped.

"Are you okay?" Caroline's voice said sharply.

I kept my head down as I answered, "Yeah, I think so." My voice quavered and broke like a young boy's.

"You shouldn't have been out there," she said in an angry tone.

It suddenly dawned on me that I'd placed the whole wagon train in a dangerous situation. I was just beginning to realize how lucky we'd been that things hadn't turned out much worse. "I...I know. I'm really...really sorry," I stammered, knowing it sounded so feeble. I lifted my head and looked at her. "I really am sorry. I shouldn't have gone out there by myself. I shouldn't have gone out there at all. I didn't realize how dangerous it could be. I just...I needed some time to myself. I was thinking about my wife and kids and I..."

Her dark eyes softened. "I know," she said sympathetically, almost as though she had left someone special behind when she'd come to this world. I'd never thought to ask her about it.

The voices of my fellow travelers joked and laughed as they milled around the fallen T-rex. It was obvious they were letting loose in the aftermath of the tension.

Maxston's cobalt-blue eyes looked in my direction.

I cringed. I dreaded facing him. He was, no doubt, furious at me for pulling such a stupid stunt like leading a T-rex back to the camp.

Caroline must have read my mind. She put a hand on my shoulder and said, "I'll have a talk with Maxston. Maybe I can get him to go a little easy on you."

I shuddered, but nodded in appreciation. I doubted she'd have much of a chance to soothe things over. If Maxston got it into his mind to yell at me, no one could stop that headstrong, stubborn old man. I wouldn't have to wait long either.

As Maxston walked in my direction, Caroline met him halfway. While she spoke in a low tone, Maxston kept nodding his head, all the time looking past her at me.

I felt like a kid about to be punished by my dad.

Maxston moved around Caroline and headed my way.

She stepped in front of him and placed a hand on his chest to stop him.

When he took her hand off his chest and roughly shoved her aside, I knew I was in big trouble. Maxston had always treated her with the greatest respect. He had to be pretty angry to treat her that way. What was he going to do to me?

I had the urge to jump up and run away, but my legs weren't up to moving. Plus, I had nowhere to go but into the bushes again. It passed through my mind that Maxston might shoot me in the back if I tried to run.

Preparing to take my punishment like a man, I clamored to my feet and squared my shoulders. "I know...I screwed up, Maxston. I'm really sorry. I...."

The look on his face froze the words in my throat. His half-closed eyes and mouth drawn into a tight grimace told me he was struggling to keep his temper in check. He came to a stop in front of me.

I wisely kept my mouth shut.

Instead of rage, disappointment dripped from his voice as he said, "You be knowin' better 'n ta go wanderin' off by yerself. Thought ya were smarter than that. Thought I was teachin' ya better than that. Yer stupidity endangered every person in this camp. Yer lucky the guard came and told me ya left. Otherwise, I wouldn'ta been ready ta shoot that darn thing. Could a killed us all. And you lost yer gun, didn't ya?"

I felt like crying. It would have been easier to hear him yell at me than feel that I'd let him down after everything he'd done for me. I wanted to say something to make things better, but I knew nothing would change what I'd done.

"I trusted ya, Gavin." A look of hurt fell across his face, like he'd just been betrayed by his best friend. "How could ya let me down?"

"Maxston, you have no idea how sorry I am," I blabbered, feeling desperate to make things better. "I wasn't thinking straight. I screwed up. I was thinking about the family I left behind rather than the family I have here. You've become more to me than my best friend. I promise, I will never do anything like this again."

He stood silent, his blue eyes boring into me. He seemed to be struggling with what he wanted to say next. Whatever it was, it wouldn't be good. I sensed he couldn't forgive me.

He shook his head sadly. "Nah, ya broke my trust, Gavin. I was startin' ta think of ya as the son I never had. No son a mine would'a done such a stupid, reckless thing as leadin' a monster like that in ta a camp full of innocent people." Anger had entered his voice. It continued to rise. "Don't want 'a see ya or talk to ya. Ya gonna have to earn my trust back. You be ridin' at the back of the wagons with the rear guard. That be the most dangerous position goin' through the jungle." He turned and walked away.

A mix of feelings flooded over me: regret, hurt, and anger. The flash of anger coursed through me the strongest. True, I'd messed up…big time. But Maxston didn't need to take such extreme steps to prove to me I'd done something wrong. Maybe I couldn't easily make up for what I'd done, prove myself to be more careful, but I had no training in weapons or preparation for guarding the train. It just seemed that Maxston had a bigger grievance than was necessary for a bumbling newbie to this world.

Although I wasn't looking forward to bringing up the rear, I was at least relieved that I wouldn't have to look at the old man's face every day.

Chapter 20

Over the next few days, we passed into a true jungle with extremely tall trees, overgrown ferns, hanging moss, climbing vines, and long-leafed plants. Birds chattered and cawed. They skittered out of the trees when we came through. Monkeys bounded from limb to limb above us, screeching at us like we were intruding on their territory. Misty steam rose up from bogs-like areas where mushrooms grew profusely. The days were hot and humid. The humidity kept my clothing damp, which caused it to cling and make me itch.

The denseness of the vegetation shaded us during the day, but also gave me the creeps at night. I remembered seeing jungle movies with huge spiders and beetles coming out in the dark. I didn't sleep well.

We didn't make very good time. The prior wagon trains had forged a fairly wide trail, but a team of men still had to move ahead of us and clear out the vegetation that had grown in since the last wagon train had come through. There were no large clearings in the jungle proper. We made our camps by placing the wagons as close in proximity as possible at night while everyone took a turn standing guard on one of the shifts. That way, the guards got some rest and we still had lots of protection.

During the day, I rode at the end of the train, keeping my rifle close. Caroline had returned the rifle to me after the episode with the dinosaur. I stayed alert for unusual sounds and sights behind us and all around us. The scare I'd had with the T-rex left me more nervous than ever. I constantly looked over my shoulder and made sure I was in reach of another guard, should I see a dinosaur or beast come into view.

My backpack with my personal things hung from my saddle. I still guarded it closely. Most of the time, I wore it on my back when I dismounted to eat or to bed down for the night. I slept in one of the wagons brought for the guards. It was almost impossible to sleep on the wet ground among the thick moist plants…and spiders, if there were any.

When we camped, I did everything I could to avoid Maxston. I was sure he was doing the same. We'd made eye contact a few times, but both of us quickly looked away without saying anything.

It seemed like we would never get out of the jungle. After a full week had passed, the wagons came to a halt one mid-morning. I knew something was up. It was too soon for a lunch break.

One of the men came running up to me on horseback. "Maxston needs ya upfront," he said.

Why would he want me? I looked around to make sure the man wasn't talking to someone else. "You sure you have the right man?"

"Yes, Sir."

I took my time getting to Maxston, not because I was trying to be obstinate or testy, but because I dreaded finally having to talk to him face-to-face. I felt horrible about how I'd put everyone in danger, as well as how I'd let Maxston down. I didn't feel ready to let it go or stop beating myself up over it. I wasn't sure how Maxston was feeling about it either.

When I got to the front of the wagons, I saw a wide, slowly moving body of dark brown water. It looked like a murky river. A large flat, open-decked ferry was tied to a dock on this side of the river. A rope stretched from one side of the river to the other, where it had been fastened to a wooden dock just like the one on this side.

Directly in front of us, about fifty yards from the river, I could see the back side of a small log cabin. An outhouse stood off to one side of the cabin and a barn with a pole corral sat between us and the cabin. A brown horse lay in the corral. At first, I thought the horse was just lying down.

Then I saw arrows sticking out of its flanks, like pins in a pin cushion.

Maxston had stopped a hundred yards from the cabin. Caroline sat on her horse next to him. When Maxston saw me, he waved me forward. "Got us a small problem," he said as I approached. "Want ya to come with us and see if'n we can figure out what happened here." He turned to the group of people who had walked up from the wagons and gathered behind him. "All of ya. Stay here. Be ready with yer weapons. Culprits might still be around."

The men and women readied their guns and spread out. Their watchful eyes scanned the surrounding area.

The vegetation here was thinning out, similar to the area where we'd let the dinos go. Brush and trees had been cleared for about two hundred yards around the cabin, leaving a plain dirt staging area for people waiting to take the ferry across. Unlike the area we'd let the dinos loose, I'd been assured there were no dinos here. According to Caroline, they were only found in the northern reaches of the jungle.

"What's wrong?" I asked Maxston.

Caroline answered, "The family who runs this ferry have dogs to alert them when someone is coming. We haven't seen or heard any dogs. Plus, the family always comes out of the cabin to greet the visitors. They should be here already."

"Not ta mention the dead horse in the corral," Maxston said, nodding his bearded head in that direction. "That be a pretty good sign somethin's wrong."

The tone of his voice told me he was still upset with me, so I wasn't about to argue with him. At first, I wasn't sure what he wanted me to do. Since he seemed to be hesitating. I figured he might be waiting for me to take the lead. "Okay, so let's go see where the family is." I urged my horse forward.

Maxston's horse fell in behind me with Caroline close behind.

As I rounded the corner of the cabin, I saw a man lying in the dirt on the front yard. Two dead dogs lay near him. All three had arrows poking out of their bloody bodies. In the cabin door, a woman's body lay unmoving across the threshold.

Caroline gasped.

"Oh, hell," Maxston blurted.

I stopped my horse, I didn't want to go closer to see any of the bloody details. "Who do you think did this?" I asked.

"Got me a good guess."

The arrows gave me a guess, too. "Indians?"

"We be seein' soon enough." Maxston got off his horse and handed the reins to Caroline. "You stay here," he told her. "Ya don't need ta see this."

Oh, God. I don't need to see this either. I looked back at the bodies. I didn't want to look, but I couldn't help myself. Whatever happened here had to have happened mere hours before, if that. The blood still looked fresh and the bodies hadn't started to smell.

Caroline's face had drained of color. With wide eyes, she nodded her head in agreement and turned her horse to face the opposite direction.

"Come on, Gavin. Let's get this over with." He started toward the cabin.

"Get what over with? Can't you see well enough from here to know what happened?"

He stopped and turned his full face toward me. He pointed to the man lying in the yard. "That be Marcus O'Malley." He pointed to the body in the doorway. "That be Sally O'Malley, his wife. They got them three sons and a daughter. Need ta see if the kids be in the cabin or the barn. Or gone altogether."

I questioned why he wanted *me* to go with him. Why did he call me from the back of the train? He could have picked any other man. It didn't make sense. Well, I was the only man in the group from a future time. Maybe he thought I'd have more insight or experience with this type of thing. The idea repulsed me. I was more than willing to stay with Caroline. I reluctantly got off my horse.

Caroline took my reins. Her eyes were moist. "The girl is only ten. I hope she's in there."

Did she hope the girl was dead? That was a strange thing to hope for.

Maxston was already heading for the cabin, his rifle held out in front of him at the ready.

I hurried to catch up with him. As we grew closer to the porch, I could see the woman had short red hair.

Maxston stepped past her without a look.

I moved forward and couldn't keep myself from glancing down. What I thought was her red hair was blood. *Oh my God, she's been scalped.* I turned and ran to the corner of the cabin where I threw up. I leaned against the wall to support the weakness in my knees.

From inside the cabin, Maxston mumbled to himself as he moved things around in his search for the kids.

I wasn't about to go inside at this point.

Maxston came out with a blanket. He covered Sally, then motioned for me to follow him as he headed for the barn.

I didn't know how I could look at any dead children, but I numbly started for the barn.

When I caught up to the old man, he said, "Ain't nobody in the cabin. Just hope they be in the barn."

"Maybe they left, to go get help."

"If I be right 'bout who did this, they be either dead or prisoners. I hope they be dead."

That was a pretty callous thing to say, but I dared not asked what he meant.

Maxston opened the door, then turned to me. "Yer gonna need ta come in with me. Cain't search the whole place by myself."

I nodded. *If you see something, just don't look too close,* I told myself. *Call Maxston over and let him do a closer inspection.*

He entered through a little door, which was part of a larger door that could be swung open to allow big items, like a wagon, to be brought in.

Warily, I followed him into the dank, dim building that smelled strongly of animals, animal wastes, and, strangely, the pungent smell of fresh-cut hay. It didn't make sense to me why Maxston couldn't have searched it by himself. The barn consisted of one big open room with four stalls along the back wall and a pile of hay in one corner. Bridles, ropes, and other items hung from pegs on one of the side walls, while saddles sat on wood sawhorses along the other side.

Maxston walked straight to the pile of hay and started poking around as if the kids would be hiding in it.

At first glance, I didn't see any bodies or anything that looked out of place. I sighed with relief. I'd envisioned bodies hacked apart and strewn across the floor, the blood soaking into the dirt in globs of strange patterns.

I walked to the stalls and looked in the one on the far right. A cow...correction...a *milk* cow, lay on its side, an arrow sticking out of its head just behind the ear. Wondering why someone would wantonly kill such an animal, I moved to the next stall.

When my mind registered the sight of two small mutilated bodies, my stomach heaved. I leaned over and threw up all over the dead milk cow.

Maxston immediately hurried in my direction.

I pointed to the stall.

"Hell," he said, shaking his head. "There be only two of 'em. This be bad...*real* bad." He checked the other two stalls. Almost in a panic, he swung toward me. "Need ta keep lookin'. Find the others."

As he marched toward the door, I ran in front of him, trying to block him from leaving. "Maxston, what aren't you telling me here? Why are you so intent on finding the other kids? It's almost like you hope to find them dead."

"You'd better pray we find 'em dead. The other be too horrible ta think about." He roughly shoved me aside. As he walked back to the haystack in the corner, he called out, "Hello. If you be in here, we be your friends. Come out, now." He stood with his hands dangling by his sides, a look of sorrow on his face. He turned to me, "Go on. Ya need ta leave and give me a time alone. Go back ta Caroline and wait fer me." He ushered me to the door and practically shoved me outside. The door locked from inside.

Confused by his reaction, I stared at the door. Then, slowly, I walked away. As I reached the horses, a wailing cry came from inside the barn. I looked at Caroline.

She shrugged and shook her head, gesturing for me not to ask any questions. Tears fell from her eyes.

Next came screaming, yelling, and cussing, accompanied by the sounds of boards being torn from the stalls and pounded on the walls.

I didn't know what to do. I wanted to help. I started toward the barn.

Caroline called out, "Leave him alone, Gavin. He needs to vent his anger. If not, he'll take it out on me and you."

I hesitated.

"Trust me," she said gently. "He'll be much better off this way."

I stood next to my horse until the sounds subsided and the barn door creaked open.

Maxston strode out, looking none the worse for wear. He stopped in front of me. "Gavin, I owe ya an apology. Shouldn't a come down on ya so hard the other day. Ya have yer own troubles, just like any man comes new into this here world." He stood staring at me, as though waiting for something.

I wasn't sure what to say or do. Finally, I got out, "Apology accepted."

He reached out and grabbed my hand hanging at my side. Pumping it up and down, he said, "Friends agin?" Real pain sat behind his eyes. He seemed to be begging me to forgive him.

"Friends again," I said with a smile.

"Good. We got us a nasty job ahead. Like ta have ya next to me ta help me get it done."

"Maxston," Caroline said softly, distress in her voice. She hesitated for a moment as she looked around. Her eyes landed on him again. "Are you sure they've been taken?"

He placed his gnarled hand on her leg. "Sorry, Honey, but I be pretty certain they be gone."

She sighed heavily and closed her eyes. "God have mercy on them."

I still had no idea why they were acting this way. It had to be something terrible.

"Can I come with you?" she asked.

"No," Maxston barked. "Absolutely not. I need ya ta stay here and keep everybody else in line. Gavin be goin' with me. And a few other men. Shouldn't be needin' more 'n four or five. More 'n that, Itzamna might think I be bringin' a war party."

"You should take a war party," Caroline shot back, "He needs to learn a lesson, once and for all."

I was shocked at the venom in her voice. She'd never shown such anger. "Who's this…Atz person?" I asked.

"Caroline," Maxston said as he climbed on his horse, "you explain it ta him while I get the others ready ta go." He rode off.

I looked at Caroline expectantly. "Well?"

"I'm wondering where to begin. I guess it doesn't matter, as long as I get the story told. The people who did this are Mayans. They've been here as long as anybody can remember, maybe shortly after the fort showed up. Nobody's sure. They hate all other races. Their leader is a horrible man who calls himself Itzamna. He isn't anything like the original Itzamna who had founded the Mayan culture. The real Itzamna taught his people how to grow maize and cacao. He helped introduce other things like writing and medicine. He was a good man. This new Itzamna is a criminal. He kills anyone who isn't to his liking. He takes slaves, building his own little empire of sin."

"And Maxston is only going to take a few people with us to see him?" I said. "How nice. We're going to face a mad man with… how many warriors at his disposal?"

"A few hundred."

The taste of the sour bile from my now-empty stomach grew increasingly bitter in my throat at the thought of riding into the Mayan village with only a few men. I pictured them hiding in old Mayan ruins and jumping out at us when we arrive. "What's their village like?" I asked as I climbed on my horse.

"Just like you'd expect: stone temple and pyramid. Their houses are built more like apartment complexes than anything."

I just thought of something. I looked at the bodies on the ground. "The bodies didn't disappear," I said in wonder to Caroline. "Will they disappear?"

Her eyes got big at the thought, too. "I think they'd be gone by now if they were. It usually happens within an hour, they say."

"Have you ever seen anyone disappear?"

"I haven't seen anyone die since I've been in this world." In a sad tone, she added, "These are the first...all dear people. Maxston knew them pretty well. He's been through here many times. I think he helped them settle here."

I had a thought. "Caroline, maybe the two kids were killed and their bodies disappeared. Maybe they weren't taken."

She pursed her lips and considered the idea. "No, I don't think so. It's strange, but the people who disappear are more...well, more advanced in their thinking. I don't know that these children would have been that developed." She looked at me and said softly, "Maxston has a sense about these kinds of things. He follows his intuition, and he's usually right."

Maxston and four other men rode toward us at a gallop.

Not particularly excited about the whole ordeal, it looked like I was off to do war with the Mayans.

Chapter 21

Okay, maybe it wasn't *war*, exactly, but I felt like I was riding off to my doom. We were only six men going up against hundreds of warriors, a tribe that wanted nothing better than to wipe us off the face of the earth. Not good odds in my book.

"Don'tcha worry 'bout it," Maxston said as we rode along the riverbank heading east. "Itzamna, he ain't gonna hurt us. Knows better than ta mess with the government."

"But wasn't that family working for the government?"

"Nope. They be independent contractors." His eyes constantly scanned the area in front of us.

I had the feeling he was expecting company…and not the good kind. No matter how much Maxston tried to convince me, I knew this *company* could be harbingers of death, if we weren't careful.

When this diversion from the wagon train had first been announced, I'd been a little pissed-off at another delay in getting to South Town. After all, every day that I was in this world, meant one more day away from Erica and my kids, and one more day that they would be moving on with their lives without me. Then, I thought about the two kids who were missing from the cabin. If my kids were in that position, I hoped someone would go after them and bring them home. Of course, these kids didn't have a home anymore. *If we find them and save them, I wonder what will happen to them in this strange world.* It had never crossed my mind that there could be orphans; not only orphans, but orphans who grew up so slowly they would be children for hundreds of years.

We brought two packhorses with us to carry food, clothing, and supplies, enough for three days away from the wagons. The kids, if we got them back, could ride the packhorses I figured.

"How far is it to the Mayan city?" I asked Maxston.

"It be fifty miles. Don't want ta spend more 'n one night there. Cain't stand ta stay one moment longer than we be havin' to."

"Why?"

"Them Mayan's believe in slavery. Treat their slaves real bad. Stray dogs be gittin' better handlin'." A strange look came over his face. "I remember last time I be here." He shuddered. "Saw a man cuttin' the breasts off a woman 'cause she weren't 'big enough.' Told her if she be so small, might not as well have any. Left her lyin' on the ground in her blood. Woman took the knife he dropped 'n killed herself."

"Did you try to stop him?"

"Too late."

"Why would they want to kill one of their women if the tribe can't have children to replace their own people?"

"This woman be a slave. They replace 'em by stealin' some other folk's people." He shook his head. "Them Mayans got their own rules. Don't live by decent respect fer people."

"Wow. I can see why you're so upset about those missing kids."

He looked at me sharply. "Ya don't know the half of it. Mayans will have...they be..." He couldn't get it out.

"You mean they'll have sex with the slaves?"

"Not in a good way neither. Don't matter if it be male or female. Slaves be fair game ta anybody, anytime, anywhere, even in the town square." At my dubious look, he added, "I seen it myself. Ain't pretty."

"How old are these missing kids?"

"Boy's twelve. Girl be ten."

Visions of my three girls flashed into my mind. A shiver ran down my back. Now, I more fully understood why Maxston had wished the children had died back at the cabin and why he was so distressed and determined to take on the Mayans. "How long will it take us to get there?"

"Too long," he said, urging his horse into a trot.

* * *

The next day, a group of twenty warriors in colorful regalia and war paint met us a couple of miles from the village. They split up on their horses, half in front of us, half behind. Their cold stares and serious behavior told me that, if we tried to run away, we'd be killed before we got very far.

I'd expected to see ruins as we rode into the village. Instead, in the middle of a large central square, a pyramid-type building with many steps rose to the sky. Four blocky, two-story apartment-type buildings fanned out from the square like the rays of the sun. Each ray pointed to a northern, southern, eastern, or western compass heading. Additional smaller buildings pointed northeast, northwest, southeast, and southwest. At the end of each row of buildings, a structure had been formed at a ninety-degree angle, looking like a foot had been placed at the end of each leg. From the air, it would have looked like a big sunburst. I was impressed by the size and the amount of work it must have taken to accomplish such a monument.

Surprisingly, grass grew everywhere: in the square, around the buildings, outside the town, on tiers of cultivated land. I'd assumed that growing grass in yards had been a modern-day creation, but here it was, plain as day. Horses, goats, and an occasional cow were staked out in various places as lawn mowers. The natural fertilizer, dropped from the animals, probably kept the grass its brilliant green color. Not a place I'd want to have a picnic, though,

The warriors led us toward the pyramid. We all stopped on our horses at the edge of the town square. A group of men and women, who I took to be royalty in their fancy headdresses and ceremonial clothing, appeared on the uppermost level of the pyramid and stared down at us. I had the creepy feeling we were being evaluated. And, should we be found to be a threat, we would be killed at the slightest wave of a hand.

My eyes darted to the warriors surrounding us. They were all small men, much shorter than myself. They wore bold paint across their faces in all kinds of bright colors. None of the face designs looked uniform, and none of the men gave me any clues that would help me understand how dire this situation might be for us. I held my breath.

The group above started down the long stairway. The warriors around us seemed to relax a little. Not much, but just enough to let us know we weren't going to be killed...yet.

A quick glance at my traveling partners told me I was the only one worried. Their posture appeared relaxed and casual, as if we were watching models walking down a runway, rather than a mad man and sociopath descending from his lofty perch to deal with lowly beings.

Itzamna formed what looked like the point of an arrow, his attendants, advisors, and admirers, all in their proper places, fanning out behind him. He wore a bright-yellow robe, trimmed in red and black, making him look like a dazzling, tropical bird.

Despite the seriousness of the situation, I had to bite my tongue to keep from laughing at the ridiculous hat perched on his head. It looked like something a woman would wear on the streets of New Orleans during Mardi Gras. Long feathers of every color stuck out haphazardly, pointing in every direction. Smaller feathers lined the mask that covered Itzamna's upper face. His lips had been painted bright red with some kind of dye. It reminded me of my grandma, who used to smear me with her lipstick every time she'd come to visit.

Itzamna came to a stop. While he stood ten feet higher than us, keeping him in a position of superiority as he looked down at us, he was a little man with scrawny arms and legs. His eyes, two black points, moved behind the mask.

One of the men, standing behind the arrogant leader, stepped next to him. As Itzamna spoke, the man translated in very slow, well-spoken English. "Welcome, Honored Friend and Ally. I pray your travels have been easy and your news good."

"Good ta see ya, Itzamna," Maxston said. "Unfortunately, we ain't here for a social visit."

Hushed murmurs passed through the surrounding warriors as Maxston's statement was translated.

Out of the corner of his mouth, Maxston explained to me, "Forceful words be considered a big insult. Ain't got no time ta mess around. Neither do them kids." To Itzamna, he said firmly, "We want them kids. Ones yer warriors took from the cabin by the river."

More murmurs rose. Itzamna put up his hand and all went silent.

"Bring em out," Maxston shouted, "and we be leavin'. If not, things be gittin' ugly." He shifted his ever-present rifle so the barrel pointed straight at Itzamna's chest. At that range, there was no way Maxston could miss.

The translator boldly stepped forward to stand in front of the chief, but Itzamna put out a hand and stopped him in his tracks. It looked like the translator thought he'd take the bullet.

Itzamna spoke again, directing his words to Maxston.

The translator said calmly, "Itzamna knows nothing of these children. He is deeply hurt that his friend of so many years accuses him of such a crime-"

"Bullshit!" Maxston yelled, urging his horse up to the very edge of the pyramid. "Ya not only know about 'em, ya probably took 'em for yerself."

The translator's eyes flicked from Maxston to Itzamna. The fear on his face showed his concern about repeating Maxston's words.

Itzamna grunted at the man, demanding the translation. When he heard the words, Itzamna pursed his lips in anger. His hands clenched into fists. When he replied, his voice was sharp and filled with hatred.

The translator's voice shook. "How dare you come to my land and insult me. Have you no courtesy to wait the required time to share information? You blame me for something I know not. I should have my men kill you where you are."

I trembled, glancing around at the stoic-looking warriors. I shot a look at Maxston. He stared straight up at the chief with a hard look.

Itzamna spoke a few more words and smiled, but it had no warmth to it.

"But I won't kill you," the translator said. "I'm willing to forgive your sins for now. You will be taken to the outskirts of town and be put under guard until I decide how to deal with you."

The feathered headdress spun around with the man. He scattered his assembled minions as he barreled through them like a bowling ball mowing down pins.

Maxston looked over his shoulder at me with a shit-eating grin on his face. "Upset him a might, don'tcha think?"

"What I think is that you're going to get us killed." I moved my horse closer to his. "What the hell are you thinking? I would have acted the same way he did if you'd come to my house and started accusing me of such things."

Maxston laughed. "He ain't gonna kill us. He don't dare. He just be puttin' on a show for his underlin's. Wait 'n see, by tomorrow mornin', those two younguns be in our camp. We be gittin' ready ta head out." He turned his horse and motioned for the rest of us to follow.

The warriors led us out of the main part of their town.

I kept expecting them to surround us and, at some silent signal only they would see, lift their bows and fill us with arrows like they'd done with the O'Malley family. I turned in my saddle and looked back at the pyramid. Itzamna, along with all his cronies, had disappeared inside to decide our fate.

If I was going to die, I hoped to die being brave, like I'd always imagined in my mind.

* * *

We set up camp under the watchful eye of the guards. Surprisingly, they either didn't know what our guns were or they didn't care. They could probably shoot their bows as fast as we could shoot our guns. Plus, there were lots more of them than there were of us.

I had no doubt they would win a battle with us, so I purposely kept my hand clear of my pistol to show my good-will. I left my rifle lying on the ground next to me. I wore my backpack on my back, still keeping my cell phone, keys, and wallet with me at all times.

We lounged around all afternoon, but no one seemed relaxed. Maxston walked the outskirts of the camp site as he chewed tobacco. He kept a keen eye toward the pyramid. Scheming and planning seemed to be going on in his mind. The other men stirred restlessly, sitting down by the camp fire, getting up, going to their horses, fooling with the stuff on the packhorses, fixing something to eat, sitting down again.

I couldn't stop thinking about the two missing kids and what they might be going through. They were about the ages of my girls. I couldn't imagine how horrible it would be to be dragged into captivity and be at the mercy of a psycho.

By the time the sun set, Maxston was pacing back and forth in front of the guards like a caged tiger. He kept asking the guards, in English, when Itzamna was going to bring the kids.

The guards just stared at him.

Personally, I didn't think they spoke English and he was wasting his time.

* * *

It was an hour after dark when a commotion stirred from the direction of the pyramid. We all stood up and watched. The guards parted to let through a small group of people that included the translator and two skinny red-headed children.

A mixed buzz of fear and excitement ran through me.

In the flickering flames, the kids looked scared to death, their small bodies tight and shaking, their eyes looking down on the ground.

I couldn't tell by any physical marks that they'd been abused, but their frightened, tense reactions told me something traumatic had happened to them. They looked as though they felt embarrassed and shameful.

The translator spoke. "Itzamna sends his regards. He hopes you find the children to be to your satisfaction. These children were found two days ago, wandering in the jungle, lost, scared, and hungry. We brought them here to make them comfortable and safe."

Maxston clenched his teeth. "*Two days* and Itzamna-"

The translator cut him off. "Itzamna was informed of the children only an hour ago. The warriors had taken them to the shaman, who kept them in isolation in his shelter. He was worried about your white-man's diseases." He smiled crudely. "Your diseases are deadly to our people, you know. You wouldn't want us to die off now, would you?"

Maxston mumbled something under his breath that not even I, standing right next to him, could hear. I'm sure it wasn't anything nice. Then, he said, "Tell Itzamna we be leavin' first thing in the mornin'."

The translator nodded with a slight bow.

"You also tell him we know yer warriors killed the parents and brought the kids back here ta be yer slaves. I be makin' a report ta the proper authorities in South Town. They ain't gonna be none too happy. Fact is, I bet yer gonna get a visit from 'em. Ain't gonna be a friendly one."

The translator's eyes narrowed. "Neither I nor Itzamna had anything to do with the killing of those people or their animals."

Maxston took a step forward. "Then, how come ya know their livestock be killed? I never said nothin' bout animals."

The translator didn't miss a beat. "It only makes sense that someone wantonly killing those poor people would kill their animals, too."

This surprised me. Maybe the man really didn't know what had happened at the cabin. But my gut feeling told me he not only knew about it, he might have been part of the party to make the raid.

Maxston glared at him. "We got the arrows left in the bodies as evidence. Don't yer warriors make special marks on their arrows ta tell who they belong ta?"

The translator smirked. "If you know that, you should also know our warriors never leave their arrows behind."

I couldn't help myself, but I asked, "What if the warriors were chased off before they could retrieve their arrows? Then they'd leave the arrows behind, wouldn't they?"

The translator narrowed his dark eyes on me.

I'd hit a nerve. I smiled back at him with my best So-there! smile.

"It all be gittin' figured out," Maxston said as he motioned for a couple of the men to go forward and get the kids, who still stood next to the translator with their heads hung down.

A look of hatred flashed through the translator's eyes, as though he despised us for taking the children.

I don't know why, but I suddenly knew this man, and maybe even Itzamna, had been part of the raid killing Marcus and Sally O'Malley, their two sons, and the livestock. And I felt an overwhelming rage at his treatment of these two children "For your sake," I growled, "I hope we don't find your marks or Itzamna's on any of those arrows. If we do, I'll personally come back to deal with you, one-on-one." I wanted to grab the man right then and string him up to the nearest tree.

He stiffly held my defiant stare for a few moments, then turned away.

Maxston and I watched as the translator left with his few personal guards. I sensed that Maxston felt the same way I did, wanting to take justice into his own hands and mete out the death penalty. Unfortunately, with any aggressive move, the warrior guards surrounding the camp would cut us down before we got within ten feet of him. It was important that we got the children safely out of the area without all of us ending up dead.

Maxston turned and moved toward the children. He knelt down on one knee on the ground and spoke to them softly, trying to win their trust. They must have known and recognized him from his trips through the jungle.

Slowly, the little girl responded by letting him fold her in his arms. The boy followed suit.

Tears came to my eyes as I watched them. I hadn't imagined that Maxston could be so tender and so loving with little kids. It warmed my heart that these kids would have a better chance for going on with a normal life because of this rough-and-tumble old mountain man.

Maxston settled the kids in his own tent and stayed with them through the whole night.

As I lay between my blankets on my bedroll, I wondered how I would have handled this situation if those had been my kids. I probably would be dead now, trying to kill the Mayan leader.

Thinking of my girls made me think of Erica again. "Just hold on a little longer, Sweetheart," I whispered. "I'm coming home. I just don't know when."

Seeing Maxston's courage and determination to find these kids, inspired me to have the courage and determination to get back to my own family. I set my heart on making it back. Somehow, I'd find a way.

Chapter 22

We made it back to the ferry crossing after dark the next day. By this time, the bodies had been buried and the blood cleaned up.

It had been a long, hard ride, and Maxston had insisted we keep moving. He kept the little girl sitting side-saddle in front of him on his horse. The boy insisted on riding one of the pack horses. Maxston made sure the kids were always close and well-protected.

"Don't trust Itzamna," he'd said to me early in the day. "Wan'ta put as much distance between us and the Mayans as possible."

"I thought you said he'd never attack us."

"Not directly. Might send a few warriors to harass us fer takin' the two kids here. He be denyin' it. Say he don't know nothin' about it."

It seemed to me, Itzamna was a really messed-up person.

The kids stayed silent the whole trip. Their large eyes and nervous manners showed they were still spooked.

As soon as we got back to the cabin, Caroline took charge of them, both responding to her right away. She took them to the cook's wagon where there would be room for her to sleep with them. She kicked the cook out of the wagon, so he made his bed in a tent on the cabin property with the rest of us.

After I pitched my tent, I felt so tired, I could barely unroll my blankets and climb into them. Thankfully, Maxston had assigned other men to take care of our horses and to stand guard duty all night. Being so exhausted, I thought I'd sleep like a rock, but tortuous dreams had me tossing and turning through the night. When I woke up in the morning, I couldn't remember what I'd been dreaming. I just knew it had something to do with my family and struggling to find a way home. The dreams left me feeling heavy, alone, and depressed.

By my count, I'd been gone almost six weeks. The longer it took me to get back, the harder it was going to be to explain where I'd been and what I'd gone through. I didn't know if Erica would believe me or not. I'm not sure I'd believe someone who'd told me the weird events that had happened to me.

A husband and wife who'd been traveling with us to South Town, and who'd been planning to look for a place to settle down, volunteered to take over the ferry operation. They offered to take responsibility for the two O'Malley children, but right away, the kids recoiled, ran to Maxston, and clung to the old man like their lives depended on it. The idea of them staying with strangers, and especially of living in the cabin where their parents and siblings had been killed, must have been abhorrent to them. They probably also feared the Mayan's would show up and take them prisoners again.

Maxston soothed their fears and promised they would travel with him and the wagon train.

"What will happen to the kids?" I asked when we were alone later.

"We be takin' 'em to South Town. Got an orphanage there, less'n we can find a good family ta take 'em."

"Does this happen often that kids lose their parents?"

"More often than I wish. Got parents lose their kids, too. Hard both ways."

"The bodies of the parents and brothers didn't disappear. Why?"

"Don't know." Maxston didn't seem to want to talk about it. Under the circumstances, I didn't push the issue.

We spent the whole day getting the wagon train ready to leave for the next leg of the trip in the morning. Maxston and a few of the other handy men pitched in to do repairs on the cabin, barn, corral, ferry, and docks.

I'd done some roofing jobs with a contractor while I'd been working my way through college. I offered to work on the roof of the cabin, but without modern tools and materials, I found myself to be of little value. Two of the other men took over the job.

With nothing else to do, I sat by the sluggish brown river and contemplated the area. Bird calls, cricket sounds, and a breeze rustling through the thick tropical greenery, wrapped me in nature. Maxston had reinforced what Caroline had told me, that this southern part of the jungle held fewer dangers from dinosaurs and wild beasts than the northern section. Rarely were they seen here. I felt somewhat safe sitting alone, even though I made sure I kept the rest of the wagon-train travelers well within my sight.

I realized we hadn't seen or heard any dinosaurs since the T-rex. We just might have gotten lucky this time, at least compared to the trip Caroline had told me about. I wondered if there were seasons of the year when the dinosaurs were more active than others. We still had a little ways to go to clear the jungle, but from what Maxston had said, the worst was over as far as the dinosaurs went.

My mind began to wander. Up popped a conglomeration of thoughts about all that had been happening to me in this world. The disappearing bodies still had me stunned and intrigued. I wondered if Hannah would disappear if she were to die. Before I knew it, I found myself comparing Erica to Hannah, both with blond hair, blue eyes, and charming, wonderful smiles. Hannah was a younger version. She hadn't yet gotten that tired look in her eyes after raising a bunch of kids and having to meet the demands of keeping the family happy. *Oops. Don't go there*, I told myself, shaking my head. *This ain't gonna be good.*

I stood up and tracked down Maxston. He put me to work. Guess where? Cleaning out the stalls in the barn. I hesitated as I stood in front of the stall where the two teenage boys had been killed. The bodies were now gone, but the memory remained stuck in my brain. My stomach almost lurched again.

I worked hard on the stalls, trying to block out the gory pictures of the boys. I found a way to distract and occupy my mind by going over all the questions I wanted to ask Howard

Blackman when I got to South Town. That seemed to do the trick. Before I knew it, Maxston was calling me to quit and come to eat dinner.

That night, satisfied with a good day's work and completely worn out, I slept like a baby.

* * *

After crossing the river on the ferry the next morning, we made good time. The heavy vegetation thinned out quickly. By late afternoon, we made it halfway across a huge dry lakebed. I guessed the lakebed to be about five miles across from north to south. It stretched so far to the east and west, I couldn't see the ends of it.

Thunderclouds, building on the horizon, made me think this wasn't going to be a good place to get caught in the rain.

"Cain't be helped," Maxston said. "Lakebed be way too long ta go 'round. Not without a lot a trouble. Take too much time. Best way ta get ta South Town be straight across." Like always, he remained calm and sure, not worried about the weather, even as thunder boomed overhead and the sky darkened.

The lakebed wasn't completely flat. Random areas sat lower than the rest of the floor. Not a lot lower, maybe a few feet. These lower areas stretched anywhere from ten feet to a hundred feet across. I had no idea what had made such depressions. They looked like craters from meteor impacts, but not exactly.

Just as we happened to be crossing the bottom of one of the larger craters, the rain hit. A half-hour after the first drops started falling, we managed to travel almost all the way across. That's when a wagon got stuck in the gooey mud.

A bunch of us worked to free the wheels, but with the rain pouring down in sheets, it became impossible. The wagon sunk deeper as the surface mud grew wetter. It rained so hard, I could hardly breathe in air without taking in water, too, making me cough as if I were drowning. Maxston finally admitted defeat and passed word down the line to make camp for the night where we stood. By now, other wagons had gotten stuck, too.

We all piled into the wagons and huddled under wet blankets, all of us shivering in the cold. I sat between Maxston and the smelly cook, with the children curled up with Caroline across from us. I wasn't complaining. With most of the food supplies gone, at least we had more room to lay down than a lot of the other wagons with all the people crowded into them. Thunder cracked and lightening struck as the force of nature took over.

The rain drizzled off and on for three days. By the time it stopped, we stood ankle-deep in muddy water that had formed a standing pool in the crater. On the bright side, we didn't have to worry about dying of thirst. We'd collected plenty of water in the barrels. On the other hand, we'd been living on half-rations of pemmican and whatever breads and cooked meat had been leftover from the last time we'd had a fire.

The fourth day began with clear blue skies.

I felt like I'd been reborn. I joined in the foray as people awoke, stepped outside in the sloshy mud, and jumped for joy, everyone hugging each other. I realized how the hardships of this trip had brought us together in a family-like camaraderie. Even the O'Malley children seemed to be participating in the celebration with their shy smiles and relaxed faces. They'd stuck close to Maxston and Caroline most of the time, but slowly, they'd begun to interact with other people who went out of their way to make them feel at home.

The enthusiasm of the celebrating crowd soon dampened by the daunting task of digging out the wagons. As soon as we removed the mud from around one of the wheels, water sloshed in and washed the mud back into the hole. Finally, we gave up and waited.

The temperatures soared with the appearance of the sun. In the searing heat, I soon wished for the clouds again...but no rain. I'd been to Death Valley once, and this place reminded me of it. Luckily, our water barrels had been replenished, because we would be going through a lot of water.

The water level in the crater finally evaporated and the mud began to crack and dry out. Now we had the difficult task of getting the wagons out of the mud before it turned to concrete and cemented the wagons into place for good. Well, at least until the next big rainstorm.

We worked steadily from dawn to dusk the fifth day. Sometime around midnight, the last wagon had been freed. Filthy with mud-streaked clothing and faces, we were all ready to leave the crater.

As I lay on the damp, clammy blankets for the night, with the children sleeping between me and Caroline, I felt overwhelmed with fatigue. My disillusionment with this world began to take its toll. It seemed like sometimes I would end up over-working to the point of exhaustion, then other times, I would not have enough to do so I'd be sitting around and daydreaming about going home. I had to admit, though, my body had toughened up with firmer muscles and my physical stamina seemed to last longer. I was in better shape than I'd probably ever been. That part felt good. I resolved to create a workout routine when I got back home.

* * *

The next day, late in the afternoon, we crested the tall sloping hill we'd been climbing all day. In the distance, I noticed a haze hanging on the horizon. "Hey, Maxston, what's that?" I pulled my horse to a stop and pointed. "Is it a fire?"

He pulled up next to me. "South Town."

My heart leapt with joy. *Finally.* "When will we be there?"

He laughed. "Settle down, Son. We still be three days out from where yer wantin' ta be."

Hmmm. Roughly thirty miles. If I took off in the morning, I could be there in one long day...by tomorrow night.

Maxston looked from me to the town and back again. He somehow knew what I was thinking. "Wouldn't advise it."

"Why not? We're past the dangerous part of the journey, aren't we? It can't be that hard to get there."

"People be livin' on the outskirts a town can be a might...um, how should I say...a might *territorial*."

"You mean they don't like strangers?"

"More 'n that. A man comes in alone, he be another person ta fail and end up livin' next to 'em. Easier ta eliminate 'em when they first show up."

"You mean they kill anyone who's traveling alone?"

"Yup. Yer better off stayin' with the party. If not, you be endin' up pig feed before ya know it."

Unless I disappear.

Looking in the distance, my shoulders dropped in disappointment. *Three days.* I took Maxston's advice and stayed with the wagons. In the end, I was glad I did.

* * *

The next day we traveled through an area with farms growing everything from avocados to zucchini. No houses had been built in this area, just wooden equipment shacks every now and then. We camped in an uncultivated field. The next day we reached the far outskirts of town.

Since I'd been in this world, I'd seen an Indian village, an Eskimo village, and a Mayan town site. None of those places displayed the deplorable living conditions I was seeing here. Even the lowest of the low in North Town didn't live with the kind of squalor these people had surrounding them. They walked around in rags. It made me sick to my stomach to look at the conditions they were living in.

Shacks had been fancied out of any kind of material, cobbled together, and held in place with mud. Small logs, even down to twigs and grass, formed some of the walls, while what looked like sheets of plywood and corrugated metal made up other walls or lean-tos. It surprised me to see the sheets of wood and metal.

"South Town," Maxston said, "got things we ain't got in North Town. Even got phones and electricity."

Layne Walker

Now that he'd mentioned it, I remembered him talking about phones and electricity. I was anxious to see how they worked in this makeshift society. Here on the outside of town, though, it seemed pretty obvious to me these people didn't have such amenities.

As I rode in the lead of the wagon train, I studied the motley collection of humanity that watched us pass by. Most of them stared at us with a wild, feral look that I'd normally associated with animals. This contrasted starkly with the more hollow looks of the desperate people living on the outskirts of North Town. Those people had seemed subdued and downtrodden. These South Town citizens appeared to be unpredictable and dangerous. Their savage-like faces followed us closely.

I swallowed hard, grateful that I hadn't snuck off from the wagon train on my own. Luckily, Maxston had made an effort to warn me. I could see now how easily it would be for a loner to disappear in the blink of an eye when entering this area. Judging from the smell of the place, there may have been dead bodies lying hidden in the filthy huts. I shivered at the thought that some of these people might make food out of each other.

Caroline handed me one of her spare buckskin tops to hold over my face in order to filter out the stench. Everyone else on the wagons did the same thing.

Even with the cover over my nose, I still had a hard time breathing without feeling nauseated.

Other than the one wide road leading toward South Town central, all the other roads winding through the shacks were narrow footpaths. The main road, itself, curved left, then right, then left, sometimes even making a full half-circle. The road was at least twice as long as it need to be, should someone have made it a straight shot toward the heart of town. "Why's this road so erratic?" I asked Maxston on one particularly sharp turn.

He said, "If there be a fire, and such be the case quite often, fire clears a large swath of huts outta the way. People rebuild on the road ta avoid livin' on the smell of burnt stuff. Gives 'em fresh dirt ta live in fer a month or two. The traffic be forced to reroute over the ashes. It all takes place in a matter of hours." He lifted his bearded chin in a gesture toward the town. "Road gits better on up further, closer in we git."

"How long until we get downtown?" I asked wiping the sweat from my brow. The temperature wasn't as hot as it had been in the deserts nor as humid as it had been in the jungle, but the sun sat high in the sky and burned hot enough to make me perspire in my buckskins.

Caroline nudged her horse closer to mine. She answered through the woven scarf covering her lower face. "We won't get downtown until tomorrow. We'll spend the night at the halfway point."

The thought of having to camp in the vicinity of these feral-looking people shot a wave of fear through me.

"Don't worry," Caroline said, seeing my concern. "We're staying in a much better location than this. It's a place that's safe enough to go out and get food after dark. As long as you're with other people."

The town seemed depressing. "Is all of South Town that bad?"

"Nah," Maxston blurted. "Downtown be clean, friendly, and most important, safe. You be seein' soon enough."

I was ready for this long, drawn-out trip to be over so I could get on to my meeting with Blackman. It seemed like one thing or other was determined to get in my way.

The living conditions of the residents improved immensely as we moved further toward town. By the time we stopped for the night, the area had taken on the look of a small town from the 1950's. Lining the streets were two-story houses with front porches filled with rocking chairs and swings. White picket fences separated one yard from another. While it all looked familiar to me from photos I'd seen of my parents' childhood homes, something seemed missing. As I looked closer, I realized there were no driveways. "How do people get around town?" I asked Maxston.

"Walkin'. Ridin' a horse, or a bicycle. Mostly walkin' though."

Caroline added, "Some people have talked about gas-powered vehicles, but at this point, the infrastructure can't support them. They'd need everything from oil wells to auto makers. That won't happen for a long, long time...if ever."

"Most people ain't got much more reason than ta go ta their local neighborhood stores anyway," Maxston said. "If they need ta go downtown, they usually be takin' the whole family and make it an overnight trip."

We pulled up the horses in front of a long, skinny building with lots of doors.

Caroline got off her horse and announced, "Here we are, Harry's Halfway House. Home of Harry Harrison, who's been helping travelers stay happy for twenty years."

"Harry Harrison?" I asked in disbelief. "I knew a guy with that name once."

"Oh, yeah?" Maxston said with interest. "What happened ta him?"

"He just up and disappeared one day, never to be heard from again." *Oh, my God, this couldn't be him, could it?*

Caroline raised her brows with the same question I was thinking. "You don't think it's the same person, do you?"

"Oh, no. How could it be?" I said, confused and doubting my wish that it might be true. "That's a pretty common name, anyway."

"What do you know about him?" she inquired.

"Well, he and his wife Marge owned a bar. I used to go there from time to time. I mean, I didn't know him all that well, but I did talk to him quite a bit. Rumor had it he'd run off with his bartender, Suzy, who just happened to be a good-looking, well-built blond."

Maxston and Caroline exchanged a look.

I shook my head, thinking the whole idea had to be ridiculous. I got off my horse. "Nah, it's not him. Can't be. The Harry I knew has only been gone from my world for two years."

Caroline took the lead in walking the horses to the stable. "How can you be sure? Time works differently here. You know that, Gavin. It doesn't matter when he was brought in. All that matters is how long he's been here. This Harry might have been here a number of years, but he sure acts a lot like someone from close to your time. I think it might be him."

The idea intrigued me, but I couldn't get around the fact that this Harry had been here for twenty years, and the Harry I'd known had disappeared only two years before, at least in my time it had been two years. I really doubted it was my Harry. A part of me wanted it to be Harry so badly, to meet someone from my own time so badly, I knew I would be totally crushed if it turned out not to be him. I just couldn't let myself have that much hope.

At the stable, which sat next to Harry's Halfway House, I looked around, wondering where all our wagons were going to park. Behind me, I could see only five wagons lined up. "Uh, Maxston, where are all the other wagons?"

"They been peelin' off, one by one, all afternoon. Headin' fer wherever they been assigned. These last five be all that go on with us in the mornin'."

The news saddened me. I'd been looking forward to a big celebration at the end of the line. So much for my thoughts on having a party and how things should work in this world.

Maxston paid a little extra to have the owner of the stable unsaddle and brush down our horses. He also paid me some coins for helping to bring in the wagon train. "I be takin' the kids to stay with some friends," he said. "Till they can arrange fer a room at the orphanage. See ya at dinner."

I couldn't wait to get to my room so I could get a bath, a shave, a dinner, and time to relax…all in that order.

Chapter 23

With the outside of the hotel looking like something out of the 1950's, I figured the décor of my room would be comparable to that era. It wasn't even close.

Only eight feet deep by six feet wide, the room felt like a closet. Stained white paint peeled off the walls. The warped bare-wood floors were in need of a good cleaning and waxing. A low, narrow cot with a straw mattress, covered with a thin blanket, occupied the left wall. A scarred dresser with three drawers sat on the right wall. This left a walkway two feet wide. The entry door sat on one of the short walls. A faded painting of a deer in a meadow hung crookedly on the other. Above the painting, almost at the ceiling, was a window no larger than twelve inches square. The window let in a little bit of light, but not much, seeing as how it was filthy dirty.

A pitcher of water and a bowl sat on one end of the dresser. A candleholder with a candle sat on the other end. I vowed to find fresh water, not knowing how long this water might have been in the pitcher. The window in the room didn't open.

Like the boardinghouse in North Town, the bathtubs sat in separate rooms at the back of the building. After my bath, I dressed in my other-world clothes: my jeans, long shirt, and boots. For some reason, they seemed more comfortable for town, rather than my buckskins. I'd had a wash-woman clean them before we'd left North Town, so they were fresh for the occasion.

The barber trimmed my long locks and shaved six weeks of hair off my face. It felt wonderful. I hadn't realized how much I hated having a beard until I got rid of it. I made a mental note to buy a change of clothing before I left town. Also, I would need to buy some soap so I could clean up, even when I was on the trail. *Maybe I should get Hannah a little gift, too.*

Wait a minute. How come I was preparing a list of things that I'd need to stay in this world? Was it my subconscious mind telling me I really wouldn't find a way home? Was I fooling myself into thinking I could do something nobody else had been able to achieve? *Hmmm. Maybe.*

No, I shouted in my mind. *I don't want to think that way. No. I want to go home. I need to stay positive and keep on track.*

I pushed the thoughts of Hannah out of my head and, while I finished getting ready, put my attention on Erica and my kids, focusing on memories of fun times we'd picnicked at the park, pushed the girls on the swing in our backyard, and eaten popcorn while watching movies at home. I missed those simple times. I'd never appreciated being a family as much then as I did now.

* * *

I met Maxston and Caroline in the combination restaurant/bar area. A line of people waited inside the door. It took twenty or more minutes before we got seated at a table in the restaurant portion. Apparently Harry's Halfway House was *the* place to eat.

The restaurant was separated from the bar by a low wall that ran across the center of the room. Three doorways allowed the servers to move from one room to another. People ate in either room, but the dining room offered bigger booths with more of a restaurant feel to it. The bar...well, it was just a typical bar with lots of drinkers, loud talking, and noisy laughter.

When I opened the menu, I could see why the place was so popular. The owner served buffalo wings, nachos, fried zucchini, onion rings, and cheese sticks. Wow, to most people like Maxston, this would be just some foreign fare. To me, it was close to being home. I couldn't wait to eat the familiar food and hoped I hadn't lost a taste for it, being that all the other food I'd been feasting on in this world had been fantastic without the preservatives and chemicals.

Even though I told myself not to get up my hopes that this Harry Harrison was the man I knew, I couldn't help but look around the room for him. The man behind the bar was too young to be the Harry I'd known. No one else looked familiar.

Most of the people in this place wore clothing closer to what I'd known, sort of factory-made clothing, like cotton shirts and loose pants or jeans. The women wore a variety of dresses, tops, and skirts. Some had on long skirts, while others wore short ones above the knees. I wondered how much of this clothing came in with these people. "Where do people get their clothes?" I asked Caroline.

"Some enterprising people have put together a few factories," she said. "They've invented crude sewing machines for certain kinds of heavy work. Mostly, women are hired to do hand-sewing. Their work can be very fine and accurate, almost as though done by sewing machines. The cloth comes from several cotton-weaving factories where the finished fabric is dyed and cut." She looked around the room. Her eyes stopped at the outfit of a young woman in a flapper dress. Caroline seemed amused.

I checked out the girl. "She must be from the Twenties."

"I'm sure she brought that dress in with her," Caroline remarked. "They don't make dresses like that here."

The food arrived at the table. It turned out to be better than I could have hoped for. *Mmm, mmm, mmm.* I ate until I was so full that my stomach hurt.

As we finished at the table, Maxston stood up and looked toward the bar. The place still looked crowded. "How 'bout a drink in the bar?" He took Caroline's arm and escorted her through the throng until he found an empty table in the far corner of the room.

Unfortunately, I ended up facing the wall, across from Maxston and Caroline. I wanted to keep an eye out for Harry.

Maxston, sensing I didn't want my back to the crowd either, stated, "I need ta see what's goin' on."

Caroline looked particularly lovely. She wore her silky black hair in two braids, falling over each of her shoulders against her beaded buckskin dress. She seemed to be entertained by the noise and the people. I wondered if she missed this kind of thing after the long period in the quiet wilderness by the sea.

To pass the time, I drummed my fingers on the table as we waited for our waitress to get our drinks. I didn't really mind the wait. I was so full from dinner, the extra time helped my stomach settle. I'd look over my shoulder occasionally to see what was going on.

When the beer finally came, it tasted like a homebrewed dark ale. I sipped it slowly and leaned back in my chair. The three of us chatted about little things, nothing important.

We'd just finished our drinks when a presence came up behind me. "And how are you folks doing tonight?" a man asked. "I hope your dinner was okay."

Chills ran down my spine as I recognized the voice. I slowly turned and looked at the tall, burly man with dark curly hair. "It was fine, Harry," I said calmly, my nerves running wild with excitement. "Just like you used to make back home."

Harry studied me, blinking several times. Then, his eyes got big. "Oh, my, God." He put a hand on the wall to steady himself. "Gavin? Gavin Clark? Is this for real?" His other hand went to his chest, as though he couldn't breathe.

I thought he was going to have a heart attack. "It's real," I said, standing up and holding out my hand. "Although I wish it wasn't. All things considered, I'd rather not be here."

He took my hand in both of his and shook it hard. "I know. I certainly know what you mean. But you're here now and we need to talk. When you're done with your friends, come up and sit at the bar. We've got a lot of catching up to do." As he walked away, he kept looking back at me, almost as though he feared I would disappear in a puff of smoke if he took his eyes off me.

When he was finally out of sight, I sat down in a stupor and drained off the last of my beer. "Looks like it's gonna be a long night for me. You two might as well head back to your room. I doubt what Harry and I are going to talk about will interest you."

Maxston said, "Ya sure ya don't want us ta stick around, just in case ya need us?" Surprisingly, it wasn't concern for me showing on his face. It was curiosity. He wanted to hear the story firsthand, rather than have me retell it later.

I chuckled. "No, I'm sure we'll just talk about old times. It would bore you to death. Besides, I'm sure you and Caroline can think of something better to do with your time." I winked at him.

Unexpectedly, he blushed. "Well, I, uh...."

Caroline put her hand on his wrist and jumped in. "As a matter of fact, we can. We need to go over our paperwork and make sure everything is in order for tomorrow. Right, Maxston?" She gave him a shy grin.

"Oh, yeah...right...paperwork."

I laughed. "You two go ahead and do your *paperwork*. I'll see you in the morning." I got up and headed for the bar.

* * *

Harry had saved me a seat at the far end of the bar where it was a little quieter. He insisted on buying me a drink. He stood behind the bar across from me.

"So, Harry," I started.

He cut me off. "No, I need to ask you some questions before we do anything else." With anguish in his brown eyes, he seemed on edge.

I studied him. "Okay. Sure. What do you want to know?"

"After I...disappeared, did my wife Marge keep the bar?"

What a strange thing to ask. I'd expected him to want to know how she was doing, or how his kids were getting on, or something of that nature. "Yeah, she did. It's still doing great. I was in there just a few weeks ago." I stopped myself. "Well...actually a few weeks before I came here...to this world." I felt jittery. I couldn't figure out what was making me so nervous. It was like I was in the hot seat.

"Did she remarry?"

I had to think for a moment. "No. As far as I know, she's still single, probably waiting for you to come home."

He let out a rush of air. "Thank God." At my puzzled look, he said, "Everybody thought my bartender Suzy and I were fooling around, but we weren't." He paused and looked around. As if he didn't want anyone else to hear what he was going to say, he leaned closer and spoke quietly. "There's something most people don't know about me. I've always had an infatuation with the metaphysical world. You know, manifesting your own destiny and all that stuff. Anyway, Suzy was into that stuff big time. She'd been on retreats, learned how to meditate, do Reiki, energy healing, that kind of thing. Getting in tune with her physical body on a spiritual level. She was even learning how to heal herself using only her mind."

"I know a little about that," I said. "My sister-in-law was into that kind of stuff for a while."

"Anyway," he continued, shifting his feet, "Marge didn't want anything to do with it, but she was fine with Suzy teaching me what she knew. Suzy would stay late after the bar closed. I'd take her to her house and we'd meditate together. We even went off on a weekend retreat once."

"Wow. No wonder everyone thought you were having an affair. I didn't know you well enough to say, one way or the other, but I'll admit I did have my suspicions." I took a sip of my drink.

He stared at me. "The thing is…I really loved Marge. I wouldn't have cheated on her, no matter what."

I could see the pain on his face.

"I miss her so much. I still think about her every day."

"Someone told me your hotel has been here twenty years. You disappeared in 2013. I came in at 2015, just two months ago. I don't get this time thing, but if it's true you've been here twenty years, do you mean to tell me you're still single?"

He looked at me like I'd lost my mind. "Hell, no. What do you think I am, stupid? Suzy and I got married six months after we got here. Been happy with her ever since. She works the morning shift. I work the night shift."

Layne Walker

"But I thought-"

He shook his head. "I still love Marge. If I had the chance, I'd go back to her in an instant. Suzy understands. Hell, she had a husband and three kids that got left behind. She struggled longer to adjust than I did."

"Did you try to get back home to Marge?"

He gave me a contorted look. "Now what do you think? Of course, I did. For six months, Suzy and I did everything we could think of." He added bitterly, "In the end, it was a waste of time. Once you're here, you're here for good. You might as well get used to it."

I was curious about his experience with the web. "By the way, that night you disappeared, what happened? The police couldn't come up with anything to explain where you went."

He chuckled, leaning with his hands on the bar and shaking his head. "I'll never forget that night. It was raining so hard, the bar had been dead all night. I guess nobody wanted to go out and get soaking wet. Suzy was there, of course. We hung around until closing time. When I shut up the place for the night, Suzy's car wouldn't start, so I offered her a ride home. As we were running in the rain from her car to mine, we got caught in this gawd-awful, clingy invisible substance…the web. And, as they say, the rest is history."

It seemed strange to think he'd been caught up in the web a couple of years before I could even imagine such a thing existed. Even now, as I looked around, it all seemed unreal. I didn't want this world to become the real one for me, and the other one just a fantasy, a dream that didn't exist.

Harry took a rag from behind the counter and wiped off the bar. "I'm sure the cops had a hell of a time trying to figure out what happened."

"Yes, they did. You wouldn't believe the rumors that were going around. Of course, most people thought you ran off with Suzy and got married. The most outrageous story was one where you and Suzy had been abducted by aliens."

He laughed. "Let me guess. Glen started that one, the local Havasu space-nerd trekie. Right?"

"You got it. He claims he saw you and Suzy get *beamed-up* right out of the parking lot." I laughed along with Harry until the realization of what Glen had seen hit me. *Aliens. Oh, my God. Could it really be?* My eyes went big. I looked at Harry.

We both went silent, as though sensing what the other one was thinking.

I suddenly wondered what it would look like to someone who wasn't caught in the web. Would it look like someone was being beamed up into outer space? *Wow. One more thing to ask the scientists.*

"So, how did you end up here?" Harry asked as he took my glass and topped it off.

I didn't need another beer. Already, I was feeling the effects of the two I'd had.

He set the drink down in front of me.

What the hell, I might as well enjoy it. I took a big sip, knowing I would pay for it dearly in the morning. I'd never been much of a drinker, one or two at the most, and usually only with dinner, like tonight. I didn't allow myself to do it very often because I hated waking up with a hangover.

As I sipped at the beer, I told him my story.

Harry didn't say much, just nodded his head in understanding at key points in my narrative, like when I'd mention Hannah or Caroline. When I finished, he said, "Sounds like you've done exactly the same thing I did. Well...not exactly. I didn't go north and visit Stranded Seal's village or go to the Mayan town and save kidnapped children." His eyes smiled at me, as though I'd been on the adventure of a lifetime. "As far as being in denial and coming here to South Town to talk to the scientists, that's all the same." He paused. His manner became grave as his brown eyes stared hard at me now.

I squirmed in my seat, starting to feel uncomfortable about what he had on his mind.

"Gavin, I know you don't want to hear this, but I have to tell you anyway. Stop now. There's no way home. If there was, I would have found it. Suzy and I would have found it. When you talk to the scientists tomorrow, they'll tell you the same thing they told me. You can't go home. Don't get your hopes up too high."

"I'm going to see Howard Black, the head guy."

"Won't help. He'll tell you the same thing he told all of us. And that's not much. We can't go home."

I refused to buy his story. "Actually," I said, leaning in closer to him, "there might just be a way to get back home. You must know about the bodies that disappear within an hour after someone is killed. My gut feeling tells me it has something to do with the people who go home."

"What are you going to do?" he said sarcastically. "Kill yourself? Not everybody disappears, you know. Suicides don't."

"I know. But if I could find the answer to who disappears and who doesn't, we'll have the key to getting back to our own world."

"That's crazy," he said, picking up the cloth and wiping the counter more diligently. "There's no way you can be sure you'd go back to your own world. And what about time? It's all screwed up here. You don't know if you'd go back to your own time. Hell, I've been here twenty years. Who knows where or when I'd end up if I went back."

I shut my mouth. I wasn't going to let Harry discourage me. He could have his own opinion, just like everybody else in this world. I was going to talk to Howard Blackman and get some answers. Twenty years had passed since Harry had arrived, so the scientists would have found more clues. I wasn't going to let him or anyone else stop me.

Harry topped off my beer again. He smiled, like all was okay, but also like he knew he would win and I'd come to my senses sooner or later.

As I picked up the drink, it passed through my mind that maybe the scientists would be interested in the little beam-me-up story from Glen. *What the hell? I might have the one small bit of information that would unlock the secret to getting everyone in this world back to their own time and place.*

Chapter 24

When I woke up the next morning, my head pounded so hard, it hurt to think, let alone move. My mouth felt like cotton. I regretted not having stopped at two beers the night before. Instead, I'd guzzled down five.

Sunlight filtered through the small dirty window at the top of the room. I looked at my watch: 7 o'clock. Sitting up slowly, I swung my feet off the low bed. I noticed I'd slept in my clothes. Well, at least I'd taken off my boots.

I moved as quickly as I could to get ready. I'd been waiting for this day for a long time. Not wanting to disturb Maxston and Caroline, if they weren't up, I walked into Harry's restaurant by myself and ate breakfast. I drank coffee and chatted with Suzy, a cute, slightly overweight woman who bubbled with lots of spirit. We shared a few stories about each other from home before she had to move on to interact with other guests.

Maxston and Caroline came moseying in, joined me, and ordered their meals. I shared with them my talk with Harry and how he'd gotten caught in the web. Slowly, my head stopped pounding and I felt much better.

While Maxston and Caroline ate, I began to squirm in my seat in anticipation of the coming meeting with Howard Blackman and the scientists. My mind was a jumble of thoughts. I tried to organize the many questions I wanted to ask, but I had a hard time thinking, like the hangover still had a grip on me. I wished I had a piece of paper and a pencil to write things down and organize my thoughts. This place didn't even have napkins for making notes. I realized that napkins were a little luxury I'd never appreciated before.

By the time Maxston and Caroline finished their food, I was more than ready to leave.

Layne Walker

*   *   *

Around noon, we pulled up to a huge building and tied our horses to a hitching rail with eight other horses. A long veranda stretched the length of the building with archways over the porch. Red clay tiles formed the roof on the veranda and the building itself. The whole façade reminded me of Southwestern homes, or more accurately, the old missions in California, built by the Spanish when they'd arrived in the Americas.

An adobe-type mud had been plastered over the walls. As I looked closer, though, I could see this was not the lathe-and-plaster stucco that I was familiar with, but *real* adobe, like the kind the Indians and Mexicans used to build homes in prior history. The soft reddish-orange color of the adobe came from the color of the clay, not from a paint job.

I scanned the area. Similar adobe-style houses and stores dotted both sides of the street. I figured this was the part of South Town that had come into this world from the Mexican village that Caroline had told me about, just like the fort at North Town had been sucked into the web from another location. The housing style around here seemed quaint and attractive.

A man in a loose grey uniform stood at the main arched entrance with a rifle over his shoulder.

"So, what's this place?" I asked,

"Government offices," Maxston stated. "Where all yer questions soon be asked…and soon *may* be answered."

Excited, I strapped my backpack to my back and headed for the front door.

"Wait up, Gavin," the old man barked. "Ya need ta leave yer guns out here. Don't allow 'em inside." He took his knife out of its sheath and put it with his tomahawk in one of his saddlebags. He did the same with his black-powder pistol. He stuck his rifle in the scabbard attached to his saddle. It seemed strange, seeing him use the scabbard. And even stranger seeing him without his ever-present rifle. Without the weapon cradled in the crook of his left arm, he favored the arm, like it was broken or something. "I feel naked as a dog that ain't got no fur," he said as he fidgeted with the fringe on his buckskins.

I tied my rifle to the saddle so it wouldn't fall off, but hesitated to take off my gun. I looked at the people walking on the other side of the street. I asked Maxston, "Don't you worry about someone stealing this stuff while we're inside?"

Caroline gestured her head toward the guard at the door. "Nobody would dare touch anything on these horses. They are protected by the guard and other people watching. The laws dealing with stealing in this area are a lot stricter than they are in other parts of the town. The government keeps close tabs on activities around here."

I still didn't like the idea of separating myself from my one item of protection. It had been with me since the beginning of my transfer into this world. It didn't seem right that I would have to take it off.

"Look," Maxston said, "see that guy sittin' on that bench readin' the paper?"

Just down the veranda porch, another man in a grey uniform looked over a paper in his hands.

"Just like the guard here, he be a lawman. He helps ta keep an eye on our stuff. Anybody bothers it, these men be puttin' a stop to it."

Well, at least I had my important stuff in my backpack, so the only thing I really had to give up was my pistol. "Okay," I lied, pretending to give in to Maxston's admonitions. I wasn't about to leave my pistol out here. If something happened to it, I had no way of getting it back or replacing it. I positioned myself on the opposite side of my horse and pulled my shirt out of my jeans. I took off my holster. While I put the holster in the saddle bag, I slipped the gun into the waistband of my jeans and hid it just under my shirt. I hoped the guard wouldn't pat me down. "I'm ready. Let's go."

At the door, the guard asked us if we carried any weapons. While Maxston answered, perspiration formed on my forehead, but luckily, without a search, the guard stepped aside and let us through. I almost sighed out loud with relief, but I didn't want to give myself away.

As we passed through the door, I noticed the walls were at least two feet thick, keeping the inside air pleasantly cool. We stepped into a large foyer with red Mexican paver tiles covering the floor from wall to wall. A few colorful hand-woven rugs lay strategically here and there for an aesthetic look. Someone had taken care to make the place bright and cheery.

Indian blankets had been draped from the walls between paintings of outdoor scenes. One mural, at least ten feet long and six feet tall, portrayed a herd of wild horses running across a desert landscape. Cowboys, with ropes twirling above their heads, chased the horses, ready to snake out and snare a prize mustang.

Long windows reached all the way to the high ceiling, fifteen feet tall, allowing light to stream in all day. Hanging from the ceiling was a massive antler arrangement that formed a candleholder. A rope ran from the holder through pulleys and down one wall where it was tied off. I deducted that, lowering the rope would allow the candles to be lit, then raised to light the room after dark. A closer look showed there were no candles in the holder, but electric light bulbs. *Interesting*.

What looked like a bar, complete with bar stools, took up part of the wall to the left. A blond woman in a dark blue polyester business suit, which looked like something from the 1980's, sat behind the bar. She wore her brown hair pulled back tight from her face and wound up on her head in a bun.

Maxston took the lead.

As we approached the woman, she stood up and smiled. "How may I help you today?" Her dark-framed glasses, broken sometime in the past at the bridge, were now held together by a rawhide strip that had probably been soaked in water and allowed to dry.

Maxston said, "We be needin' a couple of things. First off, my friend Gavin here needs ta talk ta Howard. I need ta file my paperwork with the Minister of Trade 'n report some deaths."

My hands began to sweat with the mix of fear and excitement running through me. I'd finally gotten this far. I was going to get some answers. Doubts began assailing me from all the warnings I'd received. I just couldn't let them take me over. A part of me just wasn't going to believe I couldn't go home.

"Oh, that's right," the woman said, "you're Maxston. I thought I recognized you." Her eyes lit up. "You brought in the wagon train, didn't you?" She acted as though she'd been waiting for something to come in with the wagons.

"That be right," Maxston said as he winked at her. "I be hearin' there be a special man ridin' along with us on the train."

She blushed and dipped her head. "I saw him last night."

Caroline whispered to me, "It's her fiancé. He was sent to North Town for six months as part of his new job training in management. Now, he's back for good and they can get married."

The woman leaned over and looked past Maxston. "Hi, Caroline. It's been a long time."

Caroline smiled. "Hi, Cindy. Nice to see you again."

I could understand Cindy's excitement about her fiancé. "How long have you been in this world?" I asked her.

"Thirty years."

"That's amazing. Your suit looks like it's only a few years old." I wanted to learn how to prolong the life of my own clothing. "How do you keep it looking so good?"

"When I got transferred to this world, I was on my way to the dry cleaners with two week's worth of pantsuits. I wear each suit until it gets so ratty it starts coming apart at the seams. Then, I get out another one and wear it the same way. Polyester lasts a lot longer than some of the other fibers, like cotton. I had six pantsuits to start, and each one has lasted relatively eight years. I only have two more left after this one. Then," she added, scrunching up her nose in distaste, "I'll have to start wearing whatever rags I can find around here. I'm not looking forward to that."

So much for learning the secret to preserving my clothes.

Caroline stepped forward. "I would like to see Hector Rodriguez, if he's in."

"I believe he is. Can you find his office? It's in the Records Department."

Caroline nodded.

"Go ahead and go on back. If he isn't there, come back and I'll see if I can find him."

Caroline turned to us. "I'll meet up with you two later." She headed down one of the two hallways leading off the foyer.

"Now, Maxston," Cindy said in a helpful manner, "you know where you're going, don't you?"

"Bet I do. Been there many a time."

Cindy bowed dramatically and swept her arm out in a graceful arc. "You may proceed, Sir." She giggled. She seemed so happy with her life that she couldn't stand it.

As Maxston took off, he called out, "Meet up with ya later, Gavin." Then he was gone.

"And you!" Cindy said harshly as she turned to me, now that we were alone. Her demeanor had changed drastically. Her brow furrowed. No longer was she the glowing, giggling girl I'd just observed. She'd transformed herself into the Wicked Witch of the West, glowering at me as if I'd just killed her pet monkey. "So you want to talk to Howard, do you? I'll bet I know what that's all about. You got sucked into this hell-hole and you think he can get you back home, right?"

Still nervous about my upcoming meeting and intimidated by this woman's abrupt attack, I swallowed hard and squeaked out, "Yes."

She cackled. "Not gonna happen, Dude. Believe me, if there was a way back, I would have been gone a long time ago. Why do you think I work here?" Before I could answer, she exclaimed, "It sure as hell isn't for the money or the perks. I work here because this puts me in the perfect place to hear about all the advancements that Howard and his cronies make. *If*, and it's a big *if*, they find a way to get anyone home, you can bet your last dollar, I'll be the first one in line, even if I have to do it at gunpoint."

Uneasy and confused, I stared at her. "I...I thought you liked it here. You're getting married to what's-his-name and everything."

"Ha, that's a joke. The only reason I'm marrying Jerry is because his dad is single, very rich, and very sick. As soon as the old man croaks, Jerry gets it all. As his new wife, half is automatically mine."

"So, you'll retire and use him to keep tabs on Howard, right?"

"*Wrong*. I'll stash enough goodies away so that if things go wrong and Jerry figures out what I'm up to, he'll never be able to find the cache. Next, I'll slowly poison him to death. After he's dead, *then* I'll retire and still keep an eye on Howard. By then, I'll be able to afford to pay someone to work here and keep me abreast of the latest developments."

This girl was a piece of work. I'd hate to have her on my bad side. "Well, in the meantime, I'd still like to talk-"

"Yeah, yeah, yeah," she spewed. "Down the hall, third door on the left." She plopped back into her chair, tipped her head back, and closed her eyes.

I turned to go, then realized I didn't know which of the two hallways I was supposed to go down. "Uh...which hall?"

"Right," she snapped.

I didn't respond. I was too nervous to answer.

An electrical light, every ten feet or so, lit the hallway. Even so, it was dark. I wondered if the light-bulb makers were having trouble making light bulbs that would put out enough wattage. One one-hundred-watt bulb back in my world would light up this hallway like the sun at noontime. These bulbs couldn't have been more than twenty-five watts, maybe less.

At the third door on the left, I paused and read the name plate.

Howard Blackman
Convergence of Time Anomalies

Layne Walker

Interesting title: Convergence of Time. I wonder what it means? Taking a deep breath to quiet my nerves, I knocked on the door.

A deep bass voice yelled, "Enter."

About to confront the man who held my fate in his hands, I opened the door and stepped into the room.

Chapter 25

Howard Blackman, young, robust, and energetic, wasn't at all what I'd expected. He sprang up from behind his desk and sprinted across the room to welcome me. "Hello, and welcome. I'm Howard. And you are?"

"Gavin Clark."

"Have a seat, Gavin." He ushered me to one of two padded chairs in front of his desk. "Can I get you something to drink? Coffee, water, lemonade?"

My throat was dry from my nervousness. "A lemonade would be great."

He picked up the headpiece of an old-fashioned wooden phone that was sitting on the corner of his desk. He cranked the handle to get the operator. For this world, that was probably a pretty advanced phone system.

While Howard waited, he drummed the fingers of one hand on the oak wood. Tall and stocky, with short blond hair, a small nose, and slanted eyes behind thick glasses, he looked like a cross between a Chinaman and a Swede. He wore a simple homespun shirt and pants with leather moccasins for shoes. I estimated his age at about thirty.

Seeing the phone made me think of my cell in the pack on my back. I wished I could pick it up, call Erica, and tell her I'd be home in a little while. A wave of homesickness washed over me. For a moment, I feared I would have to leave the room to contain myself. I hung my head, bit my lip, and took a few deep breaths. The feeling passed.

I looked around the room at what appeared to be a kind of lab. A number of antiquated machines sat around on scarred tables. There was an old hunt-and-peck typewriter, a homemade microscope of some sort, a large metal box with buttons and unlit lights than might have been an early computer or something the scientists here had put together.

"Yes, Cindy," Howard said when she finally answered. "Could you bring a pitcher of lemonade and two glasses to my office as soon as possible."

While he listened, I could almost hear what Cindy was thinking. It wasn't pretty. Apparently, she didn't say anything negative to Howard because he said, "Thank you. You're a sweetheart," then hung up.

It passed through my mind to tell him just who she really was and what she really thought of him and this place, but I decided it wasn't my job. I didn't want to waste the time.

"So, Gavin, welcome to South Town. I hope you had a good trip. Now, what can I do for you?" He sat up straight in his chair, his hands laced in front of him on the desk. His eager grey eyes looked at me as though he were expecting some exciting news.

I wondered how he knew I'd just gotten to South Town. Cindy might have called him and told him I was on my way. But no, she wouldn't have had time to tell him anything about me. He had to have gotten his information from another source.

I took in a deep breath and spelled out my story from the beginning. My nerves were a little on edge as I told him how I came into the web, some of the trips I'd taken, the things I'd seen, the things I'd been told about how this world worked.

He sat there stoically, staring at me with his hands together, as though he didn't want to interrupt. Only on a rare occasion did he nod, almost like to make sure I knew that he was still paying attention.

I'd decided to hold nothing back, not even my suspicions about needing to die to get home. When I got to that point, his odd grey-colored eyes shifted slightly a few times behind his glasses. It was subtle, but contrasted starkly with his otherwise stoic demeanor. I couldn't help but wonder why the shift. Maybe he knew something. His discomfort distracted me a bit from my own tension.

At one point, Cindy brought in our drinks. I paused while she passed out the glasses and set the tray on the desk. I didn't feel comfortable revealing information with her in the room. I feared if I said something she could use against me, she would. After she left, I finished my story.

Howard took a moment to refill his glass. He sipped the lemonade and said, "I can see how you would think I could help you, but you've got to understand my position. I can't just let you in on everything we've learned over the last-"

I stopped him with an upraised hand. "I don't really care about your *position*, Howard. All I care about is finding a way home." Maybe I was just growing tired of all the runaround I'd been getting from everyone, but I found myself already annoyed with this guy. He was the head scientist, the one who ran South Town. He should know the most. I kept my tone pleasant. "Now, what can you tell me that will help? And don't say you can't discuss it with me because I'm not cleared or any crap like that. I promise, whatever you tell me won't go any further than this room."

He sat back against his high-back chair, placed his right hand under his left elbow, and drummed his left fingers on his cheek. His eyes darted back and forth as his mind seemed to ponder the situation. "Okay," he said cheerfully, "I tell you what. I'll reveal to you everything you want to know, and in return, you will fill out this paper." He reached into a drawer and pulled out a folder. Removing a page, he handed it to me.

A quick glance told me it was a standard nondisclosure agreement, a typical consent form for someone from my timeline. I briefly looked it over. Hell, I wasn't planning on keeping it a secret if I found out the truth. I was going to tell everyone who would listen. Anyway, what could he do to me if I broke the agreement? Sue me? By the time he found out I talked, I'd either be back home or in North Town. Elated that I'd finally get some answers, I took the quill pen he offered, dipped it in the ink pot, and signed. "Done. Now talk." I threw the paper on his desk.

Over the next half-hour, he told me some of the stupidest stuff I'd heard yet. He rambled on about studies they'd done. "We measured the resistance of the web, trying to figure out how much force it would take to break through it. That got us nowhere. We placed dynamite against the web, thinking we could blast our way through, but that didn't work...."

I watched the guy closely. As he spoke, he was much more animated than when he'd listened. With his gestures and eager tone, he came across like a politician trying to convince an audience that he was the right man for the job. I sensed that Howard was trying to get me to buy his clout in this world by being friendly, helpful, and informative, but it all seemed like bullshit to me. I could see why Maxston didn't like him.

"....We tried to capture some of the web in tubes to bring back to the lab. That didn't work either. Some people thought we could dig our way out, so we spent years digging a ten-foot-wide hole in the ground. We got down three hundred feet before we gave up...."

Something wasn't right about this man, just like something wasn't right about many other things in this strange world. I couldn't put a finger on why I felt Howard was some kind of sham or figurehead, but his bogus enthusiasm to win my confidence began to aggravate me no end. I'd been under the impression the scientists here in South Town were smart men who were doing everything in their power to find a way to get out of this world. This stuff I was getting was nothing more than something eighth-graders could figure out. From what Howard was telling me, it almost seemed like we'd be better off holding hands and praying. Nothing he'd told me so far, seemed all that confidential, something that would require me signing off the agreement.

He started listing off numerous theories that people had come up with as to the purpose of the web, including the ideas about us being captured by aliens. Now, he seemed remote, distant, and noncommittal about what he was saying. "....Some seem to think we are an ant farm—entertainment for juvenile aliens."

I stopped him at this point. "Tell me, Howard, what do you think about that? Do you believe we could really be a part of an alien ant-farm experiment?"

He smirked a little, as though it took an effort to form the movement with his lips. "I have to admit, that one is a stretch. But certain people claim to have proof. We have copies of their photos that show aliens looking in at us. Come on. I'll show you." He led me out of his office and down the hall.

We entered a dimly lit room filled with desks, storage cabinets, and equipment. He opened a drawer in a cabinet, took out a folder, and pulled out a bundle of photographs. Spreading them out on a nearby desk, he sat down and said, "I know the clarity isn't all that great, because they were working with primitive cameras, but these guys claim *that*," he said, putting his finger on one spot in a picture, "is an alien, looking inside at us."

I picked up the picture and looked at it more closely in the dull light. If I stretched my imagination, I might have been able to see an alien in the picture, but really, it was just a vague shape that looked like it had been taken through a thin veil of cotton or silk. It reminded me of the blur I'd seen in the sky over the beach. I'm sure these were the photos that Hector had told Caroline about. I wondered if the group of scientists that had been killed by the Indian raid had found more obvious evidence than this. "I'm not convinced," I said to Howard, playing along with him, tossing the picture down and picking up another one. Each picture had the same whitish veil, blurring the details. Whatever it was, something about these photos gave me the willies.

"I'm not either," Howard said with a slight tone of disgust, the first emotion he had expressed, other than cheerfulness. He went on more bitingly. "I wish these amateurs would leave the scientific stuff to me and my professionals. They come up with these outrageous claims. It takes my office months to get control again."

As we walked back into his office, I observed how he took long, graceful glides, more like floating than walking. His arms hung loosely at his sides, but they didn't stay in sync with his body movements, like with normal people. He was maybe six feet tall, the only person I'd talked to in this world who'd come close to my height.

Layne Walker

As I sat down across from him at his desk, his earlier reaction to my talk about disappearing bodies and going home leaped to the front of my mind. I decided to get a little more aggressive. I leaned forward and glared at him with my most threatening look. "So, what about the theory that if you die and your body disappears, you go back to the world you came from? I've heard people mention it."

He squirmed a little, seeming to grow agitated under my scrutiny. He clamped his lips together, like he didn't want to talk about this. "Not hardly," he choked out. "That's one of the wilder claims. It's not even verifiable."

Pressing him further, I demanded, "What do you know about it? Have you tried to figure out what happens to the bodies?"

"Of course not," he stated. "How could we when they disappear?" He seemed to be fighting with himself, like he was trying to get a grip and stay calm.

"You're the scientist. You must have done some kind of studies on this." I couldn't figure out what was going on with him, why he seemed so disturbed. I sat back in my chair and changed the subject. "What about other countries like England, Australia, Japan, and China? Are they out there on the other side of the ocean? Have you tried to find them?"

Almost instantly, the man's demeanor changed. His nervousness fell away. He resumed his original composure and stopped shifting around.

Weird. The disappearing thing seems to really bother him.

A knock came at the door.

Howard jumped up quickly to answer it, like it was a relief for him to find a distraction from me.

I sat back in my chair and ran through the conversation, growing more agitated at myself that I'd been here for well over an hour and nothing of value had come from it. *Is this why everyone else gave up on trying to get answers?*

Chapter 26

A few minutes later, Howard floated back to his desk and sat down. He'd completely regained his composure. "I think I've answered all your questions as best as I can. Now, if-"

"I haven't gotten anything," I blared. "I'm not leaving until I'm ready."

Folding his fingers together on the desk, he nodded reluctantly for me to go on.

I decided to continue with the ocean topic. "I saw a ship one day when I was out fishing with the Indians on the ocean. I was told you are in charge of the ships and that only the scientists use them. You must know more about how far the ocean extends and whether or not there are other countries."

"There are no other countries," he said in his politician's voice. "In fact, you can never sail far enough away from land to be out of sight of it."

I scrunched my nose in puzzlement. "That seems strange. What do you mean?"

"Let me ask you a question first." Now, he spoke and acted as though he had total control of himself and the situation. "When you got transferred to this world, you got caught in an invisible web, right?"

I nodded.

"And if you were like the rest of us, you tried to get back through it to get back home. Is that not right?"

I nodded again, wondering where he was going with this.

"The same thing happens with ships. Once you get out on the ocean just so far, it's like you run into the web. It won't let you go any farther."

I thought about how the horizon had looked almost fake to me the one day as Maxston and I had ridden along the beach. "Does the horizon change at all? Does it look different when someone is up close?"

"No, it stays the same, you just can't go any farther. It's like you just stop."

"If this is a square landmass, does the ocean go all the way around it? I mean, can your ships go all the way north, then travel by sea across to the other side?"

"Yes, my ships can potentially go across to the opposite ocean, but the dangers are so great with the icebergs under the waters in the far northern sections. We've lost a few ships that way. The southern ocean contains fewer threats. We've had some luck getting to the other side, but it hasn't added any benefits to figuring how to get out of this world."

The photos with the *white veil* had me intrigued. "Tell me more about this web thing. When I ran into it, I couldn't see it, is that normal? It shows up in those photos as kind of a veil on the horizon."

"No one can see the web with the naked eye. Even if you stand on the beach, everything looks normal. As you saw, the web veil only shows up on photos."

I sensed he knew a lot more than he was telling me. I felt like he was talking to a child. He answered in only the most basic of terms. It was getting me nowhere. "What is the web?" I said more forcefully. "How does it work?"

His lips moved on his face to say, "All we know is that it's there. And there's no way past it."

"How about the sun, moon, and stars? How do you explain them?"

"We can't." His lips formed the words as though mechanically moving his mouth. "As far as we can tell, they are real. We've tracked the movement of the stars and have found them to appear to move at the same rate they did in the real world."

"What about the tides and the ocean waves. To me, they looked fake, man-made. Is someone or something controlling them?"

"Yes, but we don't know who or how."

I had to hold myself back from exploding at his ignorance and condescending attitude. It wasn't that he was lording it over me so much, but making his statements in such a way as to say everyone should cow-tow to his final word and be satisfied.

"You must understand, Gavin, we don't have the greatest equipment. We have managed to make a decent telescope that works okay for studying the patterns of the sky." He lifted his arm and swept it in an arc, taking in the room. "As you can see, we don't have the most sophisticated equipment to work with, but we get by." He sighed. "What I wouldn't give for a computer, even an early one with limited memory. It would still be better than this."

As I glanced around at the shoddy equipment, I could only imagine what it would be like for someone with highly specialized training from an advanced age of electronic gadgetry to come into a world where the light bulb was a miraculous invention. Still, in my aggravation at him, I couldn't muster up any sympathy. "Tell me your theory about the bodies disappearing when they die," I said, trying to hold back my temper.

"That again?" he said in a tone of disapproval.

I slammed my hand down on the table. "You know something," I shouted. "Tell me."

His grey eyes widened. His face redden to the color of bright-red lipstick. He couldn't seem to get any words out of his mouth as his nostrils flared and perspiration dripped form his forehead.

This is one weird dude. I'd never seen anything like it. Was he having a heart attack? It was like he couldn't control his reactions at times. I wondered if he was like this in the real world, or if coming into this world had screwed up his mind.

He made a great effort to get himself together. The color came back into his face. He said in a shaky voice, "I already told you. We can't explain that either. Some people believe that dying and disappearing is the only way to get back to the real world. If that is true, why doesn't everyone who dies disappear? We've had people kill themselves to get home, but their bodies remained in evidence that they didn't go home. No, the official position is just the opposite of what these people are saying. No one can go home. The disappearing bodies are a phenomena we cannot explain." He fidgeted like a kid caught with his hand in the cookie jar claiming he wasn't stealing cookies. There was something wrong here. Very wrong. He was lying through his teeth.

I kept pushing. "That doesn't make sense. How do you know the disappearing bodies don't go home? What happens to them then?"

"Gavin, we simply don't know. Some people, the ones who believe in the alien theory, the ant-farm theory, think the alien's remove them."

"So the aliens just choose them at random? Throw out some and not others? What purpose would that serve?"

"To keep things neat and orderly."

Why would the deaths and disappearance of some people keep the world neat and orderly, while other bodies would stink it up? It just didn't make sense. I studied Howard a little closer.

He seemed to still be on edge, but holding control of himself.

Frustrated with the whole conversation, I asked, "Who do you personally think is responsible for us being here? Aliens? God? Some other mysterious force we know nothing about?"

"It could only be aliens," he stated quickly. "God wouldn't have any reason to do this to you."

To you? That seemed like a strange choice of words. Didn't he mean *to us*? After all, he was a part of this, too.

"I'm curious," I said. "How did you come to be in charge of this town?" I wondered how this guy ever made his way to the top.

He seemed to relax with the new topic. "When I arrived, the town was in chaos. People were frantic and scared. It took me a while to get my bearings, but when I did, I searched out other like minds, other scientists, and people who'd had authority positions in the real world. I brought them together and we formed a structure to create a more organized society. The structure helped to calm the people and give them a stronger sense of security. As time went on, the others looked at me as their leader. I fell naturally into the role. No one has questioned that authority since."

That seemed like another lie. "What about the renegade scientists who lived in North Town? I got the idea they questioned what's been going on here in your town and in your government offices."

Still a little on edge, he frowned. "There are always those in a society who will not abide by the given rules and regulations. We control the situation the best we can. We ousted those scientists from our community and banished them to North Town. We've had less troubles here since."

A connection suddenly linked in my mind. I leaned forward and narrowed my eyes on him. "And did you have them killed? When they were returning from the east coast with incriminating information, did you send someone out to impersonate Indian warriors and have them killed?"

His eyes shot open. He began fidgeting again.

"All their bodies disappeared," I said more loudly as I scowled at him. "What was that about? Why all those men and not the family who was killed at the ferry crossing? Why did it just so happen that those men disappeared?"

He trembled, his thick glasses steaming up with perspiration. He didn't seem able to open his mouth.

Strange, strange, strange. It's almost like he's scared to death of me.

As I waited and watched, he again pulled himself together. He took a few deep breaths, took off his glasses, wiped his forehead with his sleeve, and put the glasses back on. He looked at me a long moment. Then, he put his hands on the desk and stood up slowly. "Gavin, I think our meeting is over. I don't have anything else to offer you. I don't want to take any more of your time."

"What the hell?" I said, jumping out of my seat. "You haven't told me anything of any value that I didn't already know. What's going on here?" I slapped my hand on the table again. "I'm not leaving until I get some answers."

The man cowered under my anger. Shakily, he sat back down, as though he were a beaten-down dog. He visibly struggled to try to compose himself. He took off his glasses and ran a hand over his face, as if he were trying to rub off dirt. He put his glasses back on and nodded for me to sit down.

I was about ready to strangle the guy I was so annoyed. I remained standing. "What about these disappearing people?" I demanded. "You know something about them you aren't telling me. It has something to do with the scientists you killed."

He opened his mouth but words wouldn't come out. He seemed too frightened to speak.

My mind raced with all kinds of things: the dead scientists, the alien ant farm, the people fighting the government, and the people giving up and just accepting that they were stuck in this world. "When did you come into this world?" I barked at Howard.

"1874," he got out quickly. His eyes widened, like he'd said the wrong thing.

"1874? Are you kidding me? Computers didn't even exist back then. What was all this talk about wishing you had a primitive computer and being a scientist?"

"I…I meant 1974," he blubbered.

I sensed he'd told me the truth the first time: 1874. But he didn't talk like the people of those times, not the ones I'd met. I leaned over the desk and said in an accusing tone, "You're lying, aren't you?"

He started shaking even more, pushing himself back into his chair as far away from me as he could get.

I screamed at him, "Why did you aliens put us in this world to begin with?"

"Because we wanted to see if…" He stopped mid-sentence. His hands covered his mouth as he realized what he'd said.

"I knew it," I shouted, pounding on the desk. "I knew you aliens wouldn't leave us here to struggle on our own. You couldn't take the chance on us figuring out what was going on. They put you here to mislead us if we got too close to solving the mystery of how to get home."

Sweat ran down his face. "You're…You're completely wrong." Totally flustered, he cried out in a high-pitched voice, "I'm trying to solve one of the greatest mysteries of all time…with the most basic of equipment…and a very limited supply of people with the knowledge who can help me. It's a losing battle. You've got to believe me."

"Cut the crap," I yelled. "I've had enough." In the momentum of my fury, I pulled my pistol out of the waistband of my jeans. I leaned across his desk and shoved the pistol into his face.

His mouth froze open. His eyes turned into big, black pools with no center—alien eyes—eyes filled with terror. They quickly receded back into the original grey spheres.

If I hadn't been so angry, I would have been scared myself.

"You know too many things," I shouted at him. "That I'd just gotten into town. No one told you that. You didn't deny killing the rebel scientists. You claim to be doing all kinds of research on how to get everybody back home, but you discount the work of everyone who discovers anything that might be close to the truth. You do everything to keep control over what the people are told. The research you are doing is stupid stuff. It has no bearing on anything, but to keep us here. If you came here in 1874 from my world, you wouldn't know what a computer is, and you wouldn't talk like someone from the Twenty-first Century." I waved the gun in his face. "On top of that, I just saw your eyes. You're an *alien*. Don't try to deny it."

He held his trembling hands high in the air. His body shook so hard, I thought he would make the room vibrate.

I wondered why no one else had been able to figure this guy out. Maybe he seemed so strange and obtuse, everyone just gave up or avoided him…except maybe Cindy.

Sweat poured off Howard's face and around his armpits. His mouth remained frozen, preventing him from speaking. The sweat running down his cheeks looked like tears. Maybe they were.

I felt sorry for him. He had his problems, being in charge of this world, which was some kind of concoction of the alien mind. Maybe he was stuck here like I was. But I had my problems, too. I still wanted to go home.

I lowered my pistol. "Howard," I said softly so I wouldn't agitate him more, "tell me the truth. How can I get back home to my wife and kids? I promise, I won't tell anyone else." Well, I didn't think that would be true, but I wanted him to believe it. I picked up the nondisclosure agreement. "Legally, I can't."

He stared at me for a long moment with a blank look on his face. He closed his mouth. Slowly he lowered his hands to his side. "There…There's nothing more I can tell you," he stammered.

I calmly raised my pistol again. "Not so fast. I've been through a lot in the last seven weeks, I'm not giving up now."

Howard nervously raised his hands again. "I can't tell you anything more."

I put the muzzle of my pistol to his forehead.

He turned green. His black eyes bulged out of their sockets behind the grey façade. "No. No more," he screamed, waving his hands in the air. "Please. We hate violence."

I pressed the muzzle a little harder. "Go on."

"Violence…It's the main reason we're doing this experiment," he spewed nervously. "We wanted to figure out why your race is always fighting each other. We thought if we put you in a controlled environment with a limited number of resources and only brought in non-violent people, you would all get along. We were wrong." He swallowed hard while I waited for more. "There is something wrong with your race. You can't leave well enough alone. You have to always be changing things, making things go your own way. You're always trying to control everything and-"

"Yeah, yeah," I said, tired of his whining and excuses. "I don't care *why* you did it. I just want to know how to get out of this crazy world and back to my family."

I removed the pistol from his head.

He sighed and relaxed, as if the air had been let out of him. His shoulders slumped. He hunched over, defeated. He kept his eyes downcast. "I can't tell you," he said weakly, but it was another lie. From his body language, I knew he was going to reveal to me whatever I wanted to know.

"I already know, don't I?" I said, sitting down on the chair. "It's the dying thing. It gets a person out of this world. I just can't figure out why some people are taken and some aren't. Care to explain that to me?"

He adjusted his glasses. His grey eyes had returned to their normal size and color to resume the physical image he was using to fool the humans brought into this world. "I'll tell you," he squeaked out. He glanced at my gun, still tense about its presence. "People like you don't fit in here. You're too strong-willed. You don't just accept what we tell you. You have to keep digging until you get what you want. There's no place for your kind in this world."

"That's it?" I blurted. I had imagined something more dramatic, like being a hero or earning Boy Scout points or dying a certain way.

"We do not want to keep humans here whose strong desire to go home keeps them connected to their original world and disrupts the basis of our experimentation, which is to integrate humans into this habitat." He blinked a couple of times. "In our observation of you and people like you, we have come to admire your courage and your persistence, something we do not see in our own society. For this reason, we choose to reward you by sending you back home when you die in this world."

"And those are the people who disappear?"

He nodded.

I stared at him a long time. "So…how does that get *me* back home?"

"Now that you know the truth, as others have before you, you will be set free…but not by your own hand."

I'd been right. The rogue scientists had found out the truth. They knew the aliens had created this world. That's why they were killed. That's why they were rewarded, why their bodies disappeared. Swept away, nice and tidy from this world. The aliens cleaned up the mess.

Howard stood up. His legs were unsteady as he supported himself against the desk. He seemed really scared. "Now, you must go."

So that was it. I stared at him as my mind buzzed with thoughts and observations. The people who'd kept pushing, probing, and picking at the problem of getting home, the ones who wouldn't give up or accept this world—they were the ones who eventually made it back home. People like Caroline, Maxston, and Harry were too complacent. They believed what Howard had told them. They accepted that this was their new world.

That made me wonder about Benjamin. Was he an alien, too, like Howard? When I'd slammed my fist down on his table, he hadn't responded like Howard. No, I was pretty sure he wasn't an alien, just someone Howard had appointed to be in charge of the remote town of North Town. Maybe Benjamin preferred that position to having to deal directly with Howard all the time.

Looking at Howard, I wondered how many other aliens were masquerading as normal people. I wondered if the fake Indian warriors who'd killed the scientists were aliens, too. At this point, I really didn't care to know.

If you know the truth, you will be set free.

Yes, now I understood why some people were taken and some weren't. I was going home. This wasn't going to be my world. I put the muzzle of my pistol to my head and started to pull the trigger.

Howard's eyes widened.

Something clicked in my brain. *But not by your own hand.* I couldn't take my own life. As much as I wanted to go home right now, I knew I had to die some other way. *How long will that take?* I wondered. I couldn't shoot myself and I couldn't take reckless chances, trying to get killed. The aliens were watching.

Well, whatever else happened, I was stuck here until fate decided to return me to my world. It might take hours or days. Maybe months or years. *I finally get the answer I've been looking for and I still can't go home. But I'll be back Erica. I'll be back. Just wait for me.*

Howard waited patiently at his desk for me to leave. He still remained nervous.

I stuck the gun in my waist band and walked out the door.

* * *

I walked down the hallway from Howard's office with a bounce in my step. On my way past Cindy, I said merrily, "Hang in there, Kid. The answer is out there. You just have to ask the right questions."

She jumped out of the chair. "What do you mean? Did Howard tell you something? Are you going home?"

I smiled and kept walking.

She screamed for Howard as I walked out the door

Chapter 27

Sitting at a table in the back of Harry's Halfway House, Maxston shook his shaggy head. One of the bird feathers on the string hanging from his hair broke loose and fell on the table. "Don't care what ya say," he said, picking up the feather and sticking it in his belt. "Don't believe a word of it. You be never provin' it ta me."

Caroline, Harry, and Suzy sat with us. I'd just told them what I'd learned from Howard, but my excitement about returning home didn't seem to spark their interest.

"It's just too wild to believe," Caroline said, pushing back a long black lock that had fallen over her face. "Not only that, I'm happy here. It's been twelve years. My fiancé in the other world has surely moved on by now. He's probably married to someone else. It seems so long ago, like a dream. I don't know if I'd like what I'd find if I went back. I'm content to stay here and live this life to its fullest." She squeezed Maxston's shoulder affectionately.

"Harry, Suzy," I said, "what about the two of you? You both wanted to go home, didn't you?"

They looked at each other. Harry said, "Sounds like an option…but…well, I'm not sure either one of us has what it takes to be as persistent as you've been. Sounds like the people who disappear have some kind of determination to get out of this world. We'll try our damndest though." He glanced at Suzy. "We'll go talk to Howard tomorrow, won't we, Honey?"

Suzy nodded with a sad smile. She seemed shocked and torn. She had children in the other world. I suspected she wanted to see them badly, but maybe feared that she might mess up their lives if she suddenly appeared in their grown-up worlds. Or, maybe she feared getting caught between worlds. It was hard to imagine what was going on in her mind.

I set my beer down. "Lean on him hard, Harry, and he'll crack. They hate violence. He won't be able to function with a gun stuck in his face."

Suzy winced. I took it she didn't like violence herself. "It's getting late," she said, rising from the table. "We've got an early morning tomorrow."

Harry stood up. He held out his hand. "Gavin, it's been great seeing you. If you're ever in this neck of the woods again, stop by. We may still be here. From what you said, it might take years to get killed before we can go home. We're going to give it hell."

After Harry and Suzy left, Maxston looked at me with his piercing blue eyes. "Now, Gavin, I know ya ain't gonna go and do anythin' stupid. And I know ya ain't gonna sit around on yer butt and do nothin' neither. Got a proposition for ya."

Deep down, I was hoping he'd arrange for us to go trap dinosaurs or saber-tooth tigers, or maybe something as equally dangerous. What better way to increase the odds of me getting killed "accidentally."

Maxston continued. "Always been my style ta be kind of a loner, ya see. But lately, you and me…well, we…aw damn. I ain't good at this mushy kinda stuff. Am just gonna say it. I need a good partner and we get along mighty good. What do ya think a workin' fer me when we get back ta North Town?"

"I don't know," I said, shaking my head and winking slyly at Caroline. "Could be kind of dangerous. I could get killed."

"Yeah, ya could," Maxston said in all seriousness. "If'n that happens, so be it. I can see ya be bound and determined ta do somethin' other than cleanin' out barns. With me, I can keep an eye out fer ya until the unavoidable happens."

I held out my hand and shook his. "You got a deal, Partner." I couldn't have asked for anything better than to spend my last days in this world with this grizzled old man. It would be an adventure, for sure.

"Wagon train be leavin' fer North Town in three days."

"Wow, that's fast."

"Big train...been making plans fer a might. Got us a passage with 'em. You be ready ta go."

"I'll be there."

* * *

The trip back to North Town went smoothly. The wagons were smaller and lighter than the ones we'd brought south, so we made better time going north. Caroline traveled with us. She planned to return to her home with the Indians.

The new family at the ferry crossing greeted us with joy. They seemed to be happy with their new job, even though they were quite isolated most of the time. Maxston had arranged for several cows and a few sheep to be dropped off to them so they could raise their own livestock.

As we moved through the northern jungle area, I made sure I didn't do anything stupid, like wander off from the train or bring dinosaurs into camp. Luckily, we didn't see any dinosaurs this time. Maybe they were getting more scarce. I wondered if the aliens would replenish them if that happened.

Along the way, I thought often about Erica and my girls. My hopes ran high that I would get back to them before too much time had passed. From my talk with Howard, I got the feeling that the aliens abhorred people like me living in their little experimental world. It wouldn't surprise me that they would fear I'd tell too many people how to get out. I hoped that meant the aliens would take me out sooner than later.

One question that arose in my mind was the time element. Did time move the same here as it did in my own world as Howard had said? Would I go back to the time I had left Lake Havasu City, the same point I'd started this crazy ride, or would I end up at a time comparable to the time I'd spent here? The thought passed through my mind that the aliens could place me ten or twenty years in the future, or even in another era. Wow, that was scary. I decided not to think about it. Whatever happened, I would just have to deal with it when it came, just like I had to deal with arriving in this world. My gut feeling told me that I would be back with Erica and the girls. I kept that thought in front of me. That's all I really wanted.

It took only twenty days to reach the outskirts of North Town. As I rode through the bewildered derelicts, living in the shacks and lean-tos, I knew I didn't want to lay around depressed and desperate like these poor souls. No, I was going to throw myself into my new life one-hundred-percent. I was going to enjoy the adventure with Maxston to the fullest while I had the chance.

That brought up the thought of Hannah. What should I do about her? Should I avoid her? Should I enjoy her company as a friend? Or should I marry her as she desires. Now, knowing that I would be going home, I intended to remain loyal to Erica. I would just have to get around Hannah and her family by simply being a friend.

It turned out that Hannah and her family hadn't been too happy that I wasn't willing to jump into a marriage with her. She remained convinced that I was *the one*. I might have been, if I hadn't set my heart on going home. I tried to tell Hannah that my new job was dangerous, that I could be killed, but she retorted by saying that we should spend as much time as we could together, not knowing when either one of us would die. It made me sad that I could never have the kind of relationship with her that she wanted.

To resolve the problem with Hannah and her family, I found a room at the fort and spent as much time as possible with Maxston on the trail. We made the journey to take Caroline home. When I returned, Master Benjamin had me officially assigned to work for the government as a scout alongside Maxston.

* * *

Two months after talking with Howard, I was out on the trail with Maxston and ten other men trying to find a band of Mogul warriors who'd been transferred into this world somewhere in the desert hills some fifty miles out of North Town. The warriors had started raising all kinds of hell, killing the poor men on the outskirts of town and grabbing the women and children. Rumors came back about the atrocities, raping and killing, that were being perpetrated on the hostages. It sounded to me as brutal as the Mayans. I thought Howard had told me the aliens only brought non-violent people into this world. What the hell were they doing bringing in aggressive Mogul warriors from centuries past?

On this particular day, we traveled southwest of North Town, moving in the same general area where I'd come into this world. This was the first time I'd returned to the area since I'd met Maxston, almost four months before. It felt a little strange being back in the desert area. I kept thinking I should see my truck, still parked in the wash where I'd left it. As always, I carried my backpack on my back with all my valuables from the other world.

The nostalgia of being close to my real home washed over me. I couldn't help but think about Erica and the kids. As my mind got lost in the memories, it took me a moment to refocus when the silence of the desert was broken by shouts of valor by the Moguls. They seemed to appear out of nowhere.

Even Maxston had been caught off guard by the ambush.

Screams of fear by our own men rose up as the sharp crack of arrows hit flesh. More than half of our men went down in the first volley.

I turned on my horse to get a shot with my rifle. An arrow buried itself into my right thigh, locking my leg to the saddle. My rifle fell. I yanked my horse's head around and pounded my heels into its ribs in an attempt to outrun the enemy.

Another arrow found its way into my left shoulder. I glanced at the bloody arrowhead sticking out of my buckskin shirt. My stomach lurched and I grabbed the saddle horn to stay upright.

The hooves of at least two horses pounded the hard-packed desert floor after me.

I briefly wondered what happened to Maxston, if he was already dead or if he would survive.

A whishing noise flew past my ear. I ducked my head lower.

My horse grunted and stumbled.

Oh, God, if my horse goes down, I'm in deep trouble.

The hoof beats behind me got closer and closer as my horse slowed. Breathing hard, a bloody froth leaked from the horse's mouth and nose.

Turning to my right, I saw two Mogul warriors not ten feet behind me.

They grinned from ear to ear, as if they were out for a joy ride instead of a murderous rampage. As my hand reached to grip my pistol, one of them lifted a short bow.

Before I could pull the gun out of the holster, an arrow slammed into my right arm, just above the elbow. My horse tripped and fell, ripping my leg from the arrow in the saddle and vaulting me head over heels. I landed on an outcropping of rocks. I came to a stop on my stomach, bruised, bloody, and broken.

The two warriors stopped next to me.

I tried to remain perfectly still, playing dead, but my lungs gasped for breath.

One of them got off his horse and said something to his partner.

I reached for my pistol again. I struggled to push myself over and pull it from the holster, but my fingers were numb from the arrow.

The warrior stood over me and smiled. He raised his bow.

I closed my eyes as the arrow drove deep into my chest. My body fell backward by the impact. My head slammed into a rock.

A sense of peace descended over me as visions of Hannah, Erica, and my children flashed before my mind.

Chapter 28

I came back to my senses slowly.

The first thing I noticed was the heat. It felt like an oven. Sweat ran freely down my face. Lifting my head, I opened my eyes. All around was desert, like I was in the middle of nowhere.

I sat up and looked for the warriors. After a 360-degree scan, I saw no one, not even my fallen horse. That seemed strange. I was sure it had been killed. There was no reason for the warriors to carry it off.

Remembering the arrow in my chest, I looked down and reached for the shaft. Nothing. I rubbed my hand over my buckskins. Not even a drop of blood.

My pistol was still in the holster. I quickly felt for my backpack. I pulled it off my back and opened it. My wallet, keys, and cell phone were still there. Because these things remained precious to me, I'd continued to keep them with me everywhere I went, especially on the trail. I wasn't about to leave this world without them. I felt a great relief that the Moguls hadn't taken them.

I suddenly realized I'd been moving my arms pretty freely for someone who'd taken arrows in them. I checked them out. Like my chest, they showed no signs of being shot. I did find, however, big purple bruises in the places I'd been shot.

I stood up and took a better look around. Not a hundred yards away sat a familiar-looking outcropping of greenish rock, the interesting outcropping I'd been headed for the day I'd been trapped by the web and transferred into this new world. Chills ran down my spine. This had to be the same area.

I heard a roar in the sky and looked up. "I can't believe it," I muttered. Contrails flowed east and west, evidence of jets carrying passengers through the air. Sunlight glinted off the airplane passing right over my head.

Lightheaded, I sat back down. I had to get my bearings. This was the Havasu desert. I knew it. I knew I was home. I had been right all along. Dying was the way out.

I looked around for Maxston, but I knew I wouldn't see him. He was still in the other world. Dead or alive, I'd never know. I preferred to think of him as alive, going on with his life as usual. He'd become a true friend. I was going to miss him.

It was too bad, really, that I couldn't let Maxston or anybody else know that I'd made it back to my world okay. I was pretty sure they'd know though, if no one could find my body. Poor Hannah, she had waited for me for years. I'm glad I didn't get involved with her. It would have been all the more difficult for her to let me go.

As the thought of Hannah passed out of my mind, Erica came in. I pulled out my cell phone to see if it was working again. Regrettably, the battery remained dead.

I jumped up and took off in the direction of the wash where I'd parked my truck that day so long ago. Coming up to the top of the last ridge where I'd be able to see the town and my truck, I stopped. What was I going to see on the other side this time? Was I really back in my original world? Was I in a completely different world? I stood there a long time, fearing what I would see. Finally, slowly, inch-by-inch, I crept forward.

The first thing I saw were the mountains in the distance, then the flat, slightly sloped foothills leading down to the river. More than a river—a lake! I moved up a little farther. Sprawling out before me was the town of Lake Havasu City. It looked pretty much like I'd left it. Joy flooded through me.

Unfortunately, my truck wasn't where I'd left it. At least I'd come back to where I'd started. I'd just have to find out what year and month it was.

I hurried down into the wash hoping to find signs of some kind telling me I'd really been there before. No such luck. There were tracks—plenty of tracks—but none of them were from my truck.

Well, that left only one thing to do: walk home. *Home.* As much as I thought of home when I was in the other world, the word sounded strange, like it was just out of my reach. Now, I was traipsing toward *home*, but what would I find there? Would Erica still be in the house? Would someone else be living in it? What if she'd moved on? Remarried? What then? Would she come back to me or stay with her new husband?

I was anxious to find out, but I also dreaded what I'd learn.

*   *   *

The downhill trek didn't take me more than an hour to reach the front door of my house, which sat on the southern outskirts of town. Everything looked the same: the swing on the front porch, the yard decorations, the rock garden. I still had no idea about how much time had passed.

I tried the knob. The door was locked. I knocked a few times, my head sweating from the heat and the worry about what I would say or what Erica would do if she answered the door.

No one responded.

I knocked again.

Still no reply.

I pulled out my key ring and stuck the house key in the lock. It turned. My heart raced, knowing Erica was still living here. I just hoped she hadn't moved on without me.

I opened the door and walked in. All the familiar odors and sights assailed me at once. My knees felt weak with relief. "Hello," I called out, "anybody home?"

No answer.

A newspaper sat on the kitchen table. I hurried to pick it up. *Friday, the first day of August.* I'd been gone just over four months, the same length of time I'd been in the other world. This was the time the kids would be at summer camp.

I opened the door to the garage. There sat my truck in its normal spot. Erica's car was gone. I checked the tools on my work bench and toolbox. All my tools were there, pretty much where I'd left them. I sighed with relief. Erica hadn't gotten rid of my stuff.

What about my clothes?

I rushed to the bedroom and opened the closet. *Yes!* Everything was there. I jumped around for joy.

I heard a familiar sound. The garage door was going up.

My heart froze in my chest. *Oh, my God, Erica must be home.* Excited and scared at the same time, I ran into the kitchen. My palms perspired as I waited. My mind tried to grabble with the possibilities of the face-to-face reunion. *How will she react when she sees me? Will she be happy? Will she be angry? I've been gone so long.*

She pulled the car inside. The overhead door was shutting. The car door slammed. Shoes clicked across the cement.

My heart pounded.

Just as I heard her get to the door, I opened it.

She froze in place. Shock registered on her face, soon replaced with tears. She dropped her purse and rushed into my arms. "Oh, my God, Gavin, you're home. You're home. Where have you been? We looked everywhere for you and-"

I put my fingers gently across her lips. "Slow down, Honey. I'll explain everything later. I just want to hold you for a minute. I've missed you so much." I buried my face in her hair and drank in her familiar fragrance. A sob racked my body. I let myself go. I'd been holding everything back for so long.

Five minutes later, I let her go and held her at arm's length, studying her face, her eyes, her hair. I loved everything about her. My eyes roamed up and down her body. I couldn't get enough of her. She looked much the same, but for having gained a little weight in the stomach area. She looked beautiful.

"Where have you been, Gavin?" she asked angrily, her voice rising as she stepped back. "Where in the hell have you been? Why did you desert us like that? Why are you wearing buckskins?" She pounded her fists on my chest. "Why, why, why? I've been so terrified that something horrible happened to you. I thought I'd never see you again."

"It's a long, strange story," I said, pulling her to me again. "I promise I'll tell you all about it later, but for now I just want to be with you and hold you. I've missed you and the kids so much. They're in summer camp, aren't they?"

She looked up at me with tears in her eyes. Her manner seemed to relax. "Well, yes. Three of them, anyway."

I wondered if she was trying to get back at me for being gone so long. "What are you talking about? We only have three."

She took my hand and placed it on her belly. "Number four is in here."

Someone could have knocked me over with a feather. "You're pregnant?" My eyes got big. "Really?"

"Really." She pinched my chin like she always did. "I just got back from the doctor's office. That's where I've been all morning. The doc even told me what it's going to be. You want to know?"

"Well, yeah, of course."

"A boy."

I wanted to jump around like I did in the bedroom. *A boy. Our first. Wow.* I'd always wanted a boy. I loved my girls, but a man needed a son, someone to play ball with, to take fishing, and to carry on the family name. I couldn't wait.

"I'm so glad you're home," she said, laying her head against my chest and crying softly. "What a wonderful surprise to have you home to share this good news. I thought I'd be raising this child alone, but here you are, just where I want you to be."

My eyes welled up again.

"And Gavin," Erica said, pushing herself back enough to look up at me, "I have something I'd like to ask you…about the baby." She bit her lip and looked worried. "When the doctor told me I was going to have a boy, a name flashed into my mind. Well, it's sort of been hanging around in my mind for awhile. Would you mind if we name him Maxston?"

I took her in my arms and held her tight. "He would be honored," I whispered.

They said it wouldn't
happen in his lifetime,
but it did.

On December 21, 2012, the Yellowstone super-volcano erupts.

Everything within 50 miles is instantly vaporized.

150 miles to the East in Buffalo, Wyoming, Sam Jones is watching the evening news when he's suddenly thrown across the room by a violent earthquake that quickly reduces the surrounding countryside to something resembling a war zone.

Sam flees, intent on getting his wife and two teenage kids to safety, but things go horribly wrong when his wife is shot in Casper, Wyoming.

A feisty Wyoming woman, a country in turmoil, and bad luck all conspire against Sam as he's

Escaping Yellowstone.
Look for this and other books
by Layne Walker at amazon.com

An action-packed novel by the author of
Escaping Yellowstone

LAYNE WALKER

TAINTED

GOLD

An alternate world offers Donny unimaginable wealth,
but will he survive long enough to get it home?

Unimaginable Wealth,
Unimaginable Beauty,
Unimaginable Danger.

When Donny Jamison discovers a portal to an alternate world, he quickly realizes the financial possibilities and enlists the help of his brother, Eric. They put together a team of ten other people and, with the aid of the other-world natives, set off on a quest to gather all the gold they can find. But problems soon arise. Donny has to contend with an angry native who thinks the portal and everyone who comes through it is evil. Donny finds a world that's more dangerous and unforgiving than he'd ever imagined. One of the members of his group gets drunk and is accused of killing a young native girl. Will Donny and his group die violent, horrible deaths at the hands of bloodthirsty natives? Or will they make it through the portal and back to their world and safety?

Look for this and other books
by Layne Walker at amazon.com

Layne Walker lives in Lake Havasu City, AZ, where he enjoys exploring the desert, dancing, and writing. He began his writing career in the summer of 2010 when he was challenged to write his own novel after years of being an avid novel reader. Once the writing fever got hold of him, he found himself on the adventure of his own life, constantly filled with new ideas for more novels, more action, more fun, and more surprises yet to come. To find out more, visit his website at www.laynewalkerbooks.com.